My Field
Of Roses

Aubrey Hancock

AUTHOR'S DEDICATION

My Field of Roses is dedicated to the three roses in my life, my sister, Brenda, who has served as my mother since I was fifteen years old, my wife, Tonya, who has been my great encourager, and my mother, who was the most loving and compassionate person I have ever known.

INTRODUCTION

Steven and Sarah have lost their mother, Anne. She was only fifty-five years old and she was the most important person in their lives. Two weeks before her death, Anne gave Sarah a small box filled with family photos and other memorabilia. While going through the items, Steven and Sarah discover an unusual mystery from the past that must be solved.

The two travel to rural Mississippi searching for answers but find more questions about their mother's heritage. Their search eventually leads to the discovery of an incredible family secret that Anne had kept hidden for decades. When the truth is revealed, Steven and Sarah are amazed at their mother's courage and strength. Welcome to *My Field of Roses*.

CONTENTS

Part 1

Part 2

My Field of Roses
Part 1

1 *Farewell Roses*

"Thank you. Thank you so much for coming. Thank you. Thank you, pastor." One by one they all left. Steven and Sarah sat there in the cold and rain knowing that it was time to go. But they just couldn't leave. The service at the funeral home was difficult but walking away from the cemetery was more than they could handle. It made everything seem so final. They had just buried their mother. She was only fifty-five.

Hundreds of friends came to pay their respects. At times, there wasn't enough room in the chapel for all the guests. And the roses... Well, everyone said that they had never seen so many beautiful roses. The entire chapel was filled with their soothing aromas. The family asked that friends make donations to the children's home and many did. But everyone wanted to remember Anne with their roses.

It was truly a sight to see, roses in December. The weather had been unusually mild. It was the first time, however, that anyone had seen roses still blooming that late in the year. Some friends in the community said that it was God's way of welcoming Anne into Heaven.

Steven didn't know most of the older guests at the visitation. He came along rather late in his mother's life. She was forty when he was born. Sarah was twelve years older than Steven. At the visitation, Steven tried to learn more about his mother when she was younger. Anne never talked about her childhood or her parents. Steven couldn't remember even one time when she shared memories or stories about those early years. He never saw pictures of his mother when she was a child.

As Steven visited with friends, each one told a story of how Anne had helped them in some way. Dee Manning told Steven about the time when she broke her foot in a car accident. "I wasn't able to drive for six weeks. Your mother delivered my groceries to the house herself. She would make a pot of coffee and catch me up on what was going on in town." Steven interpreted that as catching Mrs. Manning up on the local gossip. "I'll never forget how your mother helped me through those days."

Some of the stories about Anne were more humorous in nature. Elsie Jenkins told Steven of a time when she and Anne were at the cannery. The cannery was a food processing plant owned by the county. Anyone could use it. People cooked and packed their preserves there. Steven's mother loved to can figs from the large tree in their back yard. Mrs. Jenkins started laughing even before she began the story. "It was a Saturday morning. Belle and her son, Billy, were the only ones there when we came in. Anne was canning some figs and I had brought some strawberries and peaches. Well, as Anne was putting the sugar in her figs, she noticed that the sugar was actually salt. Someone had switched the two containers. Anne glanced over at Belle's boy and saw that he had an odd grin on his face.

Well, Anne whispered to me and said, "Call Belle over here. I want to ask her something." I did and Anne asked her if Billy could have put the salt in the sugar canister. Belle knew her son well. She said, "I bet you he did it." Anne said, "Well why don't we make a special batch of figs for Billy." Belle winked at your mother and we fixed Billy a real treat. Belle told us that three weeks later when Billy bit into one of those salted figs he made the most horrible face. She made him eat the whole jar and told him that if he did something like that again, he'd get a lot worse than having to eat some salted figs." Steven laughed and Elsie said, "Yes son, your mother was something else. I sure loved her. Everyone did."

Steven was grateful for the stories. When you're a child, it's hard to know what your parents are really like. To you, they are just your parents. To others, they are neighbors and friends. It seemed as if everyone had the same opinion of Anne. She was kind, considerate, and helpful. Steven was proud to be her son.

Sarah and Steven finally left the cemetery and went to the hospital where their father, Jim, was recovering from a heart attack. He was not able to attend the funeral. Jim was sixty-two. He was a sharp business man who had worked hard most of his life. His father died when he was a teenager and he quit school to support the family. Jim owned several rental properties and he and Anne owned a small grocery store. Anne operated the store and Jim managed the real estate. Unfortunately, their health issues led to the closure of the store which had a devastating effect on the family's finances.

Steven and Sarah sat with their dad for a while. They

told him about the funeral and conveyed the condolences of friends and family. Jim was still struggling with his loss. It was the first time that Steven and Sarah had seen their father cry. He and Anne had been married for thirty-five years. They had their ups and downs but Jim loved Anne and didn't know how he was going to continue without her. Of course, he hoped that Anne could have won her battle, but that did not happened. Now he was overwhelmed with grief at the loss of his wife.

When they left the hospital, Steven and Sarah went home. Richard, Sarah's husband, was at the house. He had gone to meet church members who had prepared food for the family. Richard was a great guy. He and Sarah had been high school sweethearts. They married not long after Sarah graduated.

Richard had been drafted during the early years of the Vietnam War. Steven remembered the day when Richard took the bus to New Orleans for his physical. Sarah was pregnant with their first child, Dawn. Everyone was crying. If Richard passed the physical, he would not even come back home to tell the family goodbye. He would be shipped to the nearest base to start his training.

Sarah and Anne were so upset about the possibility of Richard going to Vietnam. Every night they saw the news reports of casualties. One family in Pine Hills had already lost their son. When Steven got in from school that afternoon, they still had not heard from Richard. Even Jim was concerned. It was five o'clock and Richard had not called. The family didn't have a number that they could call to check on what was happening. All they could do was wait and pray.

At six thirty, the phone rang. Sarah picked it up. It was Richard. "Hey, dear. What's going on? Yes, I remember. Oh, Richard!" Sarah burst into tears. Anne went over to her for support. "Yes, honey. Right now." When Sarah hung up the phone she said, "Richard is at the bus station. He didn't pass the physical because of a football injury to his ankle. He's coming home." Steven remembered that they all cried again, even more than when Richard left for New Orleans.

Later, everyone knew at least one reason that God allowed Richard to stay home. He had been a great help to the Carpenter's during Anne's illness. He used all of his vacation and sick time to take Anne for radiation treatments in New Orleans. After Jim became ill, Richard helped around the house and took Steven to his ball games. Everyone was grateful for Richard.

After supper, Sarah asked Steven if he wanted to spend the night at their house. "No. I'll be OK", he said. They shared a few more tears and hugs and Sarah and Richard left. Steven sat in his father's recliner, numb with grief. He was fifteen. It was the week before Christmas. His mother was gone. He cried himself to sleep.

The next morning, Sarah came to the house early to fix breakfast for Steven. When she walked in, he was on the sofa looking at the family photo albums. Steven's father loved to take pictures. He owned several cameras. Some were very old. The albums were filled with pictures of vacations, special events, and more. Steven was going through the photos and remembering special times with his mother.

Sarah brought Steven's breakfast to him and sat down to look at the pictures. "I remember that", she said. "You were about four years old. It was the first time that we took you to

the circus. You were afraid of everything." Steven could barely remember the trip but smiled, knowing that it must have been a good time for the family.

As they continued to browse through the albums both recalled fond memories of their mother. "This was your fifth birthday. Do you remember what happened at the party?" Steven did remember. It was hot as usual. August in the South is almost unbearable. Steven and his friend Albert always had their parties together. Albert was born the day before Steven. Twenty-five to thirty of their friends came for the celebration.

Everything was going fine until Jake, one of Steven's little friends, opened the gate on the dog pen. Max and Lizzy, Steven's Cocker Spaniels, bolted out into the yard. At first, everyone was amused. The dogs knocked over a few kids and licked a few to death but that was it. What happened next was unbelievable. Max was the first to spy the cake, the big beautiful birthday cake. Max got that crazy look on his face and starting running for the table. Lizzie followed close behind.

Jim and Anne both tried to get to the table before the dogs, but the canines were just too fast. Max jumped up on the table and dug into the cake. Lizzy went for the punch. Efforts to get them away from the food were futile. Everyone started laughing, not realizing that they were not going to get any cake. Finally, Jim got the dogs off the table and back into the pen. Anne spoke up and said, "Well, at least we still have the ice cream."

Steven smiled and said, "Momma was always looking on the bright side of things." He was right. Anne had the uncanny ability of making lemonade out of lemons. Even during her illness she maintained a positive attitude.

As they finished looking at the last album, Steven said, "Sister, I want to ask you something about mother." Steven, by the way, never called his sister by her name. She had always been Sister to him and Sarah loved it. It was, for her, a term of endearment because she knew that her little brother loved her with all his heart.

Steven asked, "Sister, did mother ever tell you about her childhood and her parents? Have you ever seen pictures of her with her family when she was growing up?" Sarah didn't answer immediately and Steven noticed that she had a strange look on her face; almost like a nervous frown. Steven said, "What's wrong?" Sarah finally spoke up, "Well, mother didn't talk a lot about her life. She was sort of private about certain things." Steven agreed. "I know. I have wondered if there was something wrong with her." Sarah sat up straight and said forcefully, "No. There was nothing wrong with mother. She was a wonderful person." Steven could see that he had hit a nerve.

Sarah looked at her watch and said, "I have to pick up the kids from the Howards. Are you doing anything today?" "No. I'll go and check on dad at lunch and then just come home." Sarah responded, "OK. We'll have supper at our house tonight. Come about six or before if you want to. Love you." "Love you." They hugged and Sarah left.

Steven got dressed and went to the hospital to see his dad. When he arrived, his father was still in therapy. Steven found some magazines to read and waited for Jim to return. That's when he started thinking again about his mother and Sarah's odd reaction when he asked about her life. What was it? What was the secret that no one would talk about? What

had his mother faced when she was young?

When Jim came back to the room, Steven helped him into bed and sat down to stay for a while. Steven's dad wasn't much of a talker. That was true of all the Carpenter men. At family reunions the women never stopped talking and the men watched football games with little or no conversation. If it had not been for the women, the Carpenter children would never have learned to speak.

As Steven sat with his dad, all he could think about was Sarah's strange response. He considered the possibility that everyone was keeping something from him. He didn't want to ask his dad about it because he was still recovering from the heart attack. But he decided then that he would press Sarah for some answers at dinner. Steven finished the visit with Jim and headed back home.

When he arrived at the house, Jake, the mailman, was in the driveway. He had delivered their mail for the past fifteen years and knew Steven and his mom very well. Jake told Steven how sorry he was about Anne's death. "Your mother was a real special lady, Steven. She made everybody feel like family. She was a good listener too. I know a lot of people who felt that she was like a counselor who knew exactly how to help them." Steven thanked Jake for his kind words and asked him about the box that was on the porch. Jake said, "Oh, that's a box full of cards and letters from friends. I told you, your mother was more than special."

Steven thanked Jake again and took the box inside. As he started reading the cards and letters he realized that most of them were from people he knew. They were customers who came to his mother's grocery store. The store was just down the road from their house next to Ellen's Restaurant.

Steven loved having a family grocery store. Aside from the obvious benefits of free candy and soda, Steven thought it was cool to have his name on the side of the building – Carpenter's Grocery. Most days, after school, he would help his mother in the store for an hour or two. He stocked the shelves, took bags of groceries to customer's cars, and sat behind the counter with his mom.

As Steven made his way through the letters, he noticed something strange. Several of them included money. Steven thought at first that friends were helping his family with funeral costs. But as he read the letters he discovered something very special. It seems that over the years when people were having a hard time paying their bills that Anne and Jim helped them out.

In one of the letters, the lady talked about how her husband had been laid off at the paper mill. He went without work for several months and they didn't have the money they needed to feed their three children. Jim and Anne gave them the groceries they needed during that time. Another friend told of how the Carpenters paid her electricity bill because she was ill and unable to work. Steven had no idea that his parents had helped so many people.

One of the last letters that Steven read was rather puzzling. There was no return address on the envelope. The postmark was from Nashville. The letter was written by someone named Abigail. Like the others, she conveyed her condolences and let them know of her prayers. But the odd thing about the letter was that Abigail referred to Anne as aunt Anne. Steven didn't know of a cousin named Abigail. None of the girls in his dad's family were named Abigail and none of Anne's close friends had daughters named Abigail.

As a matter of fact, Steven couldn't think of anyone he knew named Abigail.

It was obvious from the content of the letter that the person knew Anne. She mentioned Anne's work at the church and talked about the roses. She seemed to know Sarah and mentioned the grocery store. But who was Abigail and why did she think of Anne as her aunt? Steven put the letter in his pocket and decided to ask Sarah about it later.

As Steven placed the rest of the cards and letters back in the box, someone knocked on the back door. It was Lea Keller, Albert's mother. Lea was one of Anne's closest friends. She had also been Steven's den mother when he was a cub scout. Can I help you Mrs. Keller?" Lea said, "Oh no, I 'm just here to pick some roses. I hope it's okay. I am so sorry about your mother. She was a good friend. I'm praying for you and Sarah every day. By the way, how's your dad?" "He's stable. Thanks for asking." "Please let him know of our prayers. We love you all. Let us know if we can help in any way."

Lea went out to the field and Steven went back to reading the cards and letters. He was simply fascinated at some of the comments. Evidently, Jake was right. Anne was like a counselor for so many of her customers. Steven knew that his mother had just the right words to say when he needed comfort or advise but he had no idea how many people she had helped in that same way.

That night, Steven went to Sarah's for supper. When he came in the house, Dawn and Allen, his niece and nephew, ran to him as they always did, giving him the biggest hugs they could. Dawn was six years old. She was Anne's heart. Allen was two years younger and everyone knows how grandmothers are with their little grandsons. Both of them knew that Maw Maw was gone but they were too young to realize the finality of it all.

Steven played with the kids until supper was ready. After the meal, Dawn and Allen went to their rooms. Richard went out to clean the grill while Steven and Sarah washed the dishes. Steven was ready to ask Sarah about his mother. "Sister, I want to know about mother's life. This morning when I asked about pictures of mother as a child, you acted strange like you knew something you weren't telling me." Sarah asked, "Why are you so interested in mother's childhood? She grew up in Foxboro. She and dad got married and moved to New Orleans during the war and then they came here to Pine Hills." "I know all that," Steven said. "But what are you not telling me?" Sarah didn't respond.

Then Steven asked, "Do you know someone named Abigail who would think of mother as her aunt? Steven showed Sarah the letter. Sarah said, "I don't know. Maybe she called mother aunt the way you and I call Letha aunt." Steven responded, "Well, do you know her? She seems to know you." Sarah stared at the correspondence. "Look, it's postmarked Nashville. Do you know anyone in Nashville who is related to us?"

Richard came in and Steven asked him, "Richard do you know someone named Abigail who would call mother aunt Anne?" Richard said, "No, I don't think so." Steven turned to Sarah and said, "Well, do you know who she is?" Sarah shook her head and said, "No. I've never heard mother or anyone in the family mention an Abigail or an Abby."

Steven returned to his original question. "Do you have pictures of mother as a child?" It was then that Sarah asked

Steven to sit on the couch. She turned to Richard and said, "Go get the box please. Richard went to their bedroom and came back with a large, cardboard dress box. It had a faded red ribbon around the middle and was well worn on all four corners. Sarah put the box in her lap and rubbed it with her hands as if it was something that was very precious to her. She slowly removed the ribbon and opened the box. Inside were all sorts of old papers, report cards, certificates, and pictures. Sarah looked at Steven and said, "Mother gave me this about a week before she died."

Steven picked up each piece as if it was a rare and delicate treasure. He was particularly amazed with the pictures. There were school pictures and family pictures, birthday pictures, and more. For the first time he was able to see his mother as a little girl with freckles and wavy auburn hair that looked just like his. Sarah helped Steven identify several family members in the pictures. He saw his mother's grandparents for the first time. There were pictures of his mother with aunts and uncles he had never met.

At one point Steven was simply overwhelmed with emotion. He wept uncontrollably. But his tears were not the tears of grief that filled his days during his mother's illness and death. These were tears of joy as he realized that each item in the box represented a special chapter in her life.

As they continued to look through the items, Steven found a long, thin jewelry box. He thought, perhaps, that it was one of his mother's necklaces. Jim bought Anne jewelry on a regular basis. He loved buying it and Anne loved wearing it. When Steven opened the box, he was surprised to find a single, pink rose bud. The flower was small and looked as if it had been cut when it was very young. It was amazingly well preserved. Steven looked for a note, something that would tell them why the little rose was so important but nothing was found. Evidently, it was special to his mother.

The little rose reminded Steven of the flowers that filled the chapel at his mother's funeral. They reminded him of so many good times with his mother. Someone called them Anne's farewell roses. Steven was having a hard time saying farewell to his most valued rose.

2   *Rose Treasures*

Steven woke up to the smell of freshly brewed coffee and skillet fried bacon. Sarah had come again to fix breakfast for him. One of Steven's fondest childhood memories was family time at breakfast. They started every day at the table with grits, bacon, eggs, and biscuits. Anne would normally say a prayer, asking God to bless each member of the family for the day. That's just who she was. She was a wonderful Christian woman. When Steven and Sarah were younger, Anne would read Bible stories to them at bedtime. The last words she shared with Steven before she died were about the comfort and peace of God.

Sarah actually became that comfort and peace for Steven during Anne's illness. She was going to take care of her little brother. Sarah was just like Anne. She knew what to say and how to help someone who was struggling. She was that rock Steven needed as he tried to cope with his mother's illness and death. They had grown closer in the last few months than they had ever been before. Steven was grateful to have a sister who loved him so much.

As they ate breakfast, Steven noticed that someone was

in the garden. It was his aunt Letha. She was watering the roses close to the house. Letha wasn't Steven and Sarah's biological aunt. She was one of Anne's best friends. They met at church when the Carpenters first moved to Pine Hills. Letha and Anne started their friendship at church when they served in the nursery together. In the midst of changing diapers and chasing toddlers, they forged a friendship that became more than special to both of them. Anne helped Letha through the loss of her husband a few years earlier and now she was helping Steven and Sarah.

Steven went outside on the back porch and gave Letha a big hug. "Why are you out here so early aunt Letha?" "Well, I just wanted to come and water Anne's roses." Steven could see that Letha was working hard to hold back her tears. She loved Anne with all her heart and was having a hard time herself, having lost one of her best friends. Steven invited Letha to come in for breakfast but she said that she was keeping her grandson for the day and had to pick him up soon. She finished watering the roses and left.

Steven went back in and found Sarah on the couch with the box of Anne's papers and photos. She was staring at it just as she had the night before. It was hard for Steven to interpret what Sarah was feeling. When she looked up at him, he saw that she had been crying. He sat down next to her, put his arm around her, and just waited. He had learned from his mother that love doesn't always need words to convey its care.

After a few minutes, Sarah took a deep breath and opened the box. For a good while they both just looked at the pictures. When Steven found one that he wanted to know more about, he would put it on the coffee table. Soon, there

were more pictures on the table than there were in the box. While Steven looked through the remaining pictures, he saw what looked like an old, document. When he picked it up, he knew immediately that he was looking at his mother's birth certificate. His heart swelled with emotion. His eyes filled with tears.

First, he saw the date of birth. Steven loved celebrating his mother's birthday. He and Sarah would often hide her presents around the house and give her clues as to where she could find them. He remembered one special time when his father bought his mother a new wedding ring. Steven and Sarah wrapped the ring in seven boxes and placed them one inside the other. He would never forget his mother's face when she opened that last small box. Their father had made her so happy.

As Steven continued to scan the birth certificate, he noticed that the box for the father's name was blank. Steven thought the name had not been recorded because his grandfather had died in World War I before his mother was born.

The more confusing item was the record of his mother's last name. Anne's family name was listed as Hill. Steven had seen his mother's Social Security card when they were handling the arrangements at the funeral home. It showed her maiden name as Gray. Steven was confused. He asked, "Sister, why is mother's name wrong on her birth certificate?" Sarah responded, "What do you mean, wrong?" "Look. It's right here. Her name is listed as Hill, not Gray."

Sarah looked at Anne's birth certificate. She saw the same thing that Steven had noticed. Their mother's name was listed as Hill. Sarah quickly looked at the space that included the mother's name. It was listed as Marie Hill. Sarah said, "Well, that's strange isn't it? Who knows?" Sarah returned to her search through the pictures in the box.

Soon she found the photo of an older couple with a young woman and a baby. They were sitting on the steps of a porch that surrounded a simple but beautiful farm house. The home actually looked very similar to their own. The board and batten styled shutters were almost identical. The porch rails were supported by beautiful white balusters just like the Carpenter's home. In front of the porch, there were several large rose bushes. The flowers were in full bloom. Sarah recognized several of the varieties as ones that her mother had planted in their yard.

The man in the picture was dressed in denim overalls. He had a dark completion and seemed to be quite tall. He looked a little like the farmer in that famous painting with his wire rim glasses, thinning hair, and stoic look. The woman, who appeared to be his wife, was wearing a day dress that most housewives of that era would have worn while cooking and cleaning. She was much shorter than her husband and looked to be a few years younger.

The young woman with the baby must have been the couple's daughter. The family resemblance was easy to see. She was wearing a dress that was much too large for her. Evidently, the newborn child was hers. The baby, who was sleeping at the time, was wrapped in a crocheted blanket. She didn't have much hair which is probably why she was wearing a pretty little bow on her head.

Sarah pointed to the infant in the picture and said, "I believe that's mother." Steven smiled and took the picture from her hand. He stared at it for a while and said to himself,

"I knew that she hadn't just fallen down from Heaven. She had a childhood just like everyone else. She had parents and grandparents. She went to school. She was a teenager. She probably had boyfriends and went out on dates. She had a real life."

Steven then asked Sarah about the photo. "Are these mother's grandparents?" "Yes. That is our great grandfather George and his wife Eliza." "Did you ever meet them?" "No. They both died when mother was young." "Who is the woman holding mother?" "I guess it's our grandmother." Sarah and Steven had never met Anne's mother. Anne never talked about her.

Sarah continued. "Mother was actually born in that house. She lived there with her grandparents and aunt Macy. Aunt Macy married a man named Ben Thompson. They had a little girl who was still born. Ben and Macy just didn't get along after that and aunt Macy moved back to Foxboro to live with the family."

Steven picked up another picture and asked, "Is this aunt Macy?" "Yes that's her." The picture was taken out front just off the porch of the family home. Macy and Anne were standing in front of a bed of roses, showing off their new Easter dresses. Aunt Macy was wearing a low waist dress with a floral print on top and a solid white lacy bottom. She donned a white cloche hat and had shoes and a purse that matched. Anne's dress was a long jumper with a round collar and a wide sash at the waist. She had a ribbon in her hair that was as big as her head. Anne looked to be about four years old.

Steven loved the picture but went back to his question. "Where was mother's father? Do we have any pictures of him?" "No. I've never seen any." Steven started looking through the pictures again. He seemed to be focused on finding something specific. One by one he quickly went through at least twenty or thirty photos before he looked at Sarah and asked, "Are there any other pictures of our grandmother?" Sarah looked through the box but couldn't find any other pictures of the woman. "I don't know Steven. Maybe the rest of the family has her pictures. Remember, she died when mother was very young."

About that time a truck came up the driveway. Steven went out to see who it was. It was Kirk Walker from Walker's Nursery. "Hi Steven. I'm so sorry to hear about your mom. She sure was a special lady." "Thank you Kirk. What do you have?" "It's a load of compost. Everybody uses it to protect their plants during the winter. I know where it goes."

Steven followed Kirk around back. "Your mother really knew a lot about roses." "Yes she did." "I remember many times when my dad called her for advice. He referred to her as Pine Hills' Rose Queen. No one even came close to growing roses that looked as beautiful as your mom's."

They both turned and looked out over the field. Steven remembered when there were just a few dozen bushes in the back yard. Anne had Jim make a path around the trees with beds on both sides. Steven had even helped his mother plant a few of the roses himself.

Somehow over the years the garden had spilled out into the field behind their house. Steven remembered his mother's friends bringing rose bushes that she would plant for them. Steven didn't really know why. He thought that maybe the soil was good for growing roses. There was a small stream that ran through the middle of the field. It was a rock

bottom creek with the clearest water you've ever seen. His dad told him that the creek was fed by an artesian well that was on top of Indian Hill. He remembered the day that his dad took him up to see the well. The water was ice cold and tasted like pure spring water.

When Kirk left, Steven went back inside. Sarah had made some coffee for them. "Who was that?" she asked. "It was Kirk Walker. He delivered a load of compost for the roses." It was time for lunch and Sarah called in their order at Ellen's. Steven went down to pick it up. Ellen met Steven at the pickup window. "Hi honey. Here's your order. I am so sorry about your mother. She was an angel. I can't tell you how many times I poured my heart out to her at the store. She was a real good friend. How's your dad?" Steven gave her a brief update on his father and thanked Ellen for her concern.

Steven and Sarah continued to look at the pictures and documents as they ate lunch. One of the items was Anne's baptismal certificate. Anne was nine years old when she was baptized. The certificate was signed by her pastor, Reverend Samuel Smith. On the back Steven found a long list of names. He wasn't sure but thought that the names might have been the others who were baptized at the same time. Once again, Steven noted Anne's name. Her baptismal certificate showed her last name as Hill.

Some of the more interesting items in the box were Anne's school report cards. Anne's grades were excellent. Her conduct grades were perfect and she had very few absences. The thing that was most intriguing to Steven and Sarah was that the report cards included things they had never seen before. Marks were given for cooperation, dependability, citizenship, initiative, and more. Again, Anne had high scores in all areas.

As they were looking at the report cards, Steven noticed what he had seen before. His mother's name was Elizabeth Anne Hill. It just didn't make sense. Why did her social security card have her maiden name as Gray? As he continued to look at the report cards, Steven had an ah-ha moment. Parents had to sign report cards. He turned to the back of one of the cards and looked for the signature. There was no signature. He looked at all the others. No signature. All he found were two initials in the signature line – M.H. Who was M.H.? Certainly the H was for Hill. But who was M. Hill? Steven showed the initials to Sarah. "Do you know who M.H. might be?" "No. I can't think of anyone." Steven asked, "Who would know?" "I'm not sure." Steven and Sarah were now faced with more questions that had no answers.

Sarah reminded Steven that they had to leave soon for the hospital. The doctors were meeting with Jim to lay out a rehab plan for his recovery. They needed to be there for the meeting. After visiting with their dad and talking to the doctors, Sarah went to pick up the kids. Steven went back home. He spent the rest of the night looking through more of the papers and photos. But the item that thrilled him the most was the picture of Anne as a newborn in front of her grandparent's home, the place where a rose was born.

3   *Three Special Roses*

The next morning, Steven woke up late. It was Wednesday. Three days before Christmas. His father was coming home on Friday. Sarah would be over soon to help get his dad's room ready. A special bed was being delivered that day along with a portable oxygen machine. Sarah and the kids came in just as the bed arrived. Mr. Thomas, who owned the medical supply company in Pine Hills for years, came along with the delivery crew. His son Randy was one of Steven's best friends.

As the men set up the bed, Mr. Thomas talked with Sarah and Steven about Anne. "I was so sorry to hear that your mother passed. I know that she had been in quite a battle these past couple of years. You know, your folks have been so good to everybody in town. When they had the store, people would come in just to visit. They made every single customer feel like family."

"Thank you, Mr. Thomas. Your family has also been a blessing to so many when they were in need." "Well, the Lord has taken care of us and we need to do the same for others." Mr. Thomas gave Sarah and Steven a few instructions on how to adjust the bed. As he was leaving, Sarah asked about the bill. Mr. Thomas smiled and said, "I'll send it later." Of course, the bill never came.

Dawn and Allen went upstairs to play while Sarah and Steven talked about how they were going to take care of their father. Jim was going to need constant care for at least a few weeks. Sarah could help some but had to take care of her own family. Steven was still in school. They decided to hire a sitter for the mornings. Sarah would help in the early afternoon hours and Steven would take care of his dad after school. They would try that for a while and make changes if needed.

Sarah and Steven sat down again to look at the pictures and papers in the cardboard box. Steven found several pictures of his mother with three friends. They were all young, about five to eight years old. In one photo they were playing on the porch of a house. Steven asked Sarah if she knew who the girls were. "Yes. Those are mother's cousins. That's Aunt Willie. She is a year older than mother. The tall one is Aunt Jennie. She's about three years younger than mother." "Is that Aunt Ellie?" "Yes. Aunt Ellie and mother were the same age."

Steven asked, "Is that the girl's house in the picture?" "Yes. They lived in Norman. It was about six miles down the road from Foxboro. Mother was like the fourth sister." "You know, I can see that. Every time we have a family reunion they just talk and talk about the good old days."

Looking again at the picture, Sarah said, "I remember mother and aunt Ellie talking about how they loved playing on that porch. Aunt Ellie said that her father would tie old sheets together and make a playhouse for the girls. They would play out there for hours with their dolls. Sometimes at night, they would stay on the porch and watch the fireflies

dance. Her dad would run out in the yard and catch a few in a jar for the girls."

"They told me that every once in a while, they would spend the night out on the porch. Aunt Macy would tell her famous ghost stories and the girls would talk about boys. They told me about the time when a skunk came up on the porch. They were all sleeping. The skunk laid down next to Jennie. When she saw the skunk, she screamed and got sprayed. Her mother had to give her a bath in tomato sauce to get rid of the smell."

Steven was certainly enjoying the stories and wanted to hear more but it was time for lunch. They ordered from Ellen's. Steven took Allen and Dawn with him to pick up the food. They ate out on the back porch. The kids gobbled down their burgers and went back in to play. Sarah and Steven stayed out on the porch, and shared memories of good times with their mother in the garden.

As Sarah looked out over the field, she asked Steven, "Did mother ever tell you that roses don't actually have thorns?" "Yes. She did. She said that roses have prickles." "That's right. Thorns grow much deeper into a plant's stem. If you pull the thorns out, the plant dies. Prickles are not so deep. They can be removed without killing the plant." Steven said, "All I know is that whatever they are, they hurt when you grab one of them." Sarah laughed. "Yes they do."

About that time they heard someone singing. It was Mrs. Minnie Wascom. She was another one of Anne's best friends. Steven and Minnie's son, Craig, played baseball and football together. Mrs. Minnie was a saint. She lost her husband just a few years after adopting her two children. Unlike most women at that time, she had to work to support her family.

Minnie and Anne were a lot alike. They both had such gentle spirits and they loved helping people.

Steven invited Mrs. Minnie to join them on the porch. "I came by to pick some roses. I hope you don't mind. How are you all doing? I just can't believe that Anne is gone." They talked for a while about the funeral and how helpful everyone had been. Sarah asked, "What are the roses for?" "Well, we're going to Rest Haven tomorrow for the annual Christmas party. We're trying to find enough flowers to give all the ladies a small bouquet."

Sarah said, "Please, take all you need." Minnie hesitated, "Well, I couldn't take everybody else's roses. I'm just going to take some of mine." Sarah insisted, "Take some of mother's that are here close to the porch." "Well, OK. Thank you Sarah. We're still praying for you all. Please let us know if we can do more." Steven helped Mrs. Minnie pick some of his mother's roses and loaded them into her car.

After Minnie left, Steven and Sarah started going through the pictures again. Soon Steven came across the photo of an old building that looked like a school. He asked Sarah if she knew where it was. "No. Let's see." There at the bottom of the picture were the words, "Taylor County Elementary School." "This must be where mother went to school. You know. I think that there is a picture of her class in here somewhere. There it is."

Steven couldn't believe his eyes. He was looking at a picture of his mother's first grade class. They were standing outside in front of the school. Most of the boys were wearing overalls and the girls were wearing plain, everyday dresses. A few of the boys were not wearing shoes, which was probably quite common in rural Mississippi at that time.

Steven immediately looked for his mother. There she was, front row, third from the right. He just stared at her for a while and wondered what life was like for her then. Was she happy? Did she have a lot of friends? Steven turned the picture over and was surprised to find a list of the student's names. He immediately looked for his mother's name. That's when he saw the same name that was on her birth certificate, Elizabeth Anne Hill. He still didn't understand. It should have been Gray, Anne Gray not Anne Hill.

As they continued to go through the pictures, they found at least twenty photos of Anne with her cousins. Evidently, they were inseparable. The photos ranged from elementary school through their teenage years. Steven looked at Sarah and said, "I bet you there are a thousand stories behind these pictures. Do you think that we could talk with aunt Ellie or aunt Jennie about mother?" "I don't know. We could try. Aunt Ellie lives in Atlanta with her daughter Pat. Aunt Jennie and Uncle James live in Beaumont." "Do you think we could call them?" "Sure. I have to go home and cook supper for Richard and the kids but I'll try to call Pat tonight. Do you want to come home with us?" "No. I think I'll go and spend some time with dad at the hospital. Will you call me tonight after you talk with Pat?" "Sure." They all shared a hug and Steven left for the hospital.

That night Sarah called Steven with some good news. Pat told her that their families were getting together after Christmas. They were going to meet at Ray's house in Hampton. Ray was Jennie's oldest son. Hampton was just an hour drive from Pine Hills. They were staying for three or four days and Steven would still be out of school on Christmas break. Sarah told Pat that Steven wanted to learn more about their mother from the aunts. Pat thought that her mother and aunt Jennie would be glad to spend some time with Steven. They set the meeting for Monday afternoon. Steven couldn't wait.

The next day, Sarah and Richard took Allen and Dawn to exchange presents with Richard's family. Steven had the whole day to himself, at least that's what he thought. About ten o'clock people started coming to the house. They were gathering the last roses out of the field. Steven sat out on the porch. One by one they came to talk with him about his mother. He spent the entire morning and half the afternoon listening as friends shared their stories about Anne.

The thing that fascinated Steven most was the fact that everyone saw his mother as one of their best friends. Steven thought, "How can a person be best friends with so many people?" But it was true. Anne made everyone feel like they were her best friend. She knew all the names of their children and grandchildren. She knew about their hobbies and interests. She always had an encouraging word and she always helped when someone was in need. It was amazing. She was amazing.

That night, Steven went to see his dad at the hospital. The next morning Jim would be coming home for the first time since Anne's death. Steven knew that it would probably be an emotional time for his dad. They watched television until Jim fell asleep and Steven went home.

Christmas for the family was not the same without Anne. She was the fun one who made it all special for the kids. Jim spent most of the day in bed resting. Sarah and Richard tried to enjoy some time with the kids and Steven was focused on his visit to Hampton.

Monday morning, Steven met Jim's new home care worker Alice. He gave her a tour of the house, talked with her about his dad's medications, and gave her Sarah's phone number. After lunch, Steven told his dad goodbye and headed for Hampton. He brought the box of pictures with him, hoping that the photos would help his aunts remember stories about his mother.

On the way, Steven stopped by Dunham's Bakery to pick up some donut holes. His aunts both had a sweet tooth just like his mother. Anne loved donuts, particularly chocolate dipped donut holes. Dunham's was the only one in town that had them. Every Sunday morning Jim would pick up donuts for breakfast. Steven and Sarah often left for church with the sugar on their faces.

When Steven arrived at Ray's, Ellie and Jennie were in the sunroom that overlooked a large pond behind the house. They loved the view and enjoyed watching the squirrels try to steal the birdseeds from Ray's feeders. Steven gave them both a big hug and put the three bags of donut holes on the table. Ellie asked, "Are those for us?" Steven laughed. "Well, sure they are." They both dug into the bags as if they hadn't had donuts in years.

Steven asked where his aunt Willie was. "Oh, honey, she is so sorry that she couldn't come. Ralph is having some tests run and Willie had to drive him to the clinic. She said to tell you that she loved you and would have to see you some other time."

Willie was the oldest of the three sisters. She lived over in Justice which was just a few miles outside of Pearl Valley. Willie was a quiet soul who loved her family. Her first husband died in his forties. Many years later she married

Ralph Fornet who managed a local supermarket. Steven remembered going to aunt Willie's house on Sunday afternoons when he was a little boy. She lived on a farm and he loved being around the horses and cows.

Aunt Willie's son, Fred, who was Sarah's age, rode horses in rodeo competitions. He was a good barrel racer. Fred would let Steven ride Old Mack when he came up for visits. Old Mack didn't compete in the rodeos anymore and Fred didn't ride him much. Steven rode him every chance he had and thought of Old Mack as his own horse.

Aunt Jennie was the boisterous one in the bunch. She talked fast and loud. Steven always thought of her as one of those windup toys with the cymbals. Jennie also had the most southern accent of the girls. When she said, "Jesus", it became a four syllable word. Jennie was also the biggest hugger of the three. Steven remembered that when he was little, he would actually brace himself for an aunt Jennie earthshaking hug.

Aunt Ellie was Steven's favorite, probably because she was most like his mother. She and her husband, Gene, lived in central Louisiana most of their married life. Anne and Ellie actually married in a double wedding ceremony. They were very close. During Anne's illness, Ellie called to talk with her every week. At the funeral, everyone could tell that Ellie's grief was deep because she loved Anne with all her heart.

As Ellie and Jennie finished off the treats, Steven opened the box of pictures. "I know that Pat told you why I wanted to talk with you." Jennie spoke up and said, "Honey, your momma was as good as gold. There was nobody sweeter." Steven smiled and thanked Jennie for the kind

words. Steven asked, "Can you tell me about mother's childhood? I have these pictures of her with you and aunt Willie. Do you remember what she was like? Can you tell me some stories about her?" Ellie and Jennie took the box and laid all the pictures out on the table. One by one they held each photo as if it was a family heirloom. "Oh, Ellie look. There's our house. That's the porch. We used to have so much fun out there."

Ellie smiled. "Yes. Do you remember? Daddy built us a big dollhouse and put it out on the porch. Steven said, "Mother did tell sister about you all playing on the porch. Aunt Jennie, do you remember something about a skunk?" Jennie cackled. "I sure do. I couldn't breathe the smell was so bad. It took days for momma to get that off my body and my clothes."

Steven could tell that Ellie and Jennie were loving their walk down memory lane. Each picture prompted another story. "That's papa's store. Jennie, do you remember how we used to play hide and seek in the store?" "I sure do." Ellie explained that sometimes, when they had to help their father in the store, they would ride the school bus into town and work until closing time.

"Steven, I remember one time when we were playing hide and seek that we just could not find Anne. We looked everywhere. Do you remember Ellie? We looked upstairs, back in the warehouse, and even on the roof. But we just couldn't find her. Do you know where she was? She jumped into a pair of overalls on the clothes rack and put a pair of rubber boots on her feet. Papa saw her hide but he didn't tell us where she was. He let us think that he was going to close the store and go home without her. We started screaming.

"Anne, we're going to leave you. Papa's locking up the store. Come out." But she wouldn't. Just when papa was about to turn the lights out, he said, "Okay Anne. You can get out of those overalls. You win." Anne jumped out of the clothes with the biggest grin on her face. She had fooled us all."

Steven enjoyed hearing the stories about his mother. It seemed to help with his loss. Even though Anne was gone, she was still alive in the memories of everyone who loved her. That was special to him. As they continued looking at the pictures, Steven pulled out Anne's birth certificate. He showed them the space where her father's name should have been. Ellie said, "That's odd. We never did know much about Anne's dad."

Steven then asked about Anne's name on the birth certificate. "Was mother's name Hill?" Ellie and Jennie looked a bit puzzled. "Well, sure. Yes." "Then why is her maiden name Gray on her Social Security card?" Jennie said, "I don't know. Are you sure?" "Yes, I have it right here." Steven pulled the card out of his wallet and showed it to them. Neither one of them could guess as to why her name on the card was different.

About that time, Judy, Ray's wife, came in the sunroom with some freshly brewed coffee. "You all have been in here gossiping for over two hours. I thought you might like to take a break." Judy was right. It was four o'clock. Steven only had a few more hours to spend with his aunts. He had to get back home to take care of his dad.

As they enjoyed Judy's coffee, Ellie said, "Steven, I don't know about your mother's last name but I can tell you a good one about her first name." Anne's first name was Elizabeth. Her family had a rather unusual tradition for naming their

children. They chose the name of a deceased relative for the child's first name. Then they chose a middle name which became what they called the child's "familiar" name. So the child had a first name, a familiar name, and a family name. Often times, the children did not even know their first name.

Steven's parents did the same to him. His first name was Asa which was Jim's grandfather's name. Sarah's first name was Victoria. She was named after Anne's great aunt. Sarah followed the tradition with her children. Allen's first name was Benjamin and Dawn's was Elizabeth. Steven vowed to break the curse if he ever had children and call them by their first names.

Ellie told her story. "Anne and I went to our first day at school. We were both in Mrs. Fanny's class. We didn't know it, but Mrs. Fanny was very strict. She would give you a spanking in a minute. We found out later that the children called her Mrs. Fanny Wacker." Jennie laughed. "I remember getting my fanny wacked many times by that mean old teacher." Steven was amused. He never thought of his aunts as little girls in elementary school.

Ellie continued. "Well, it was our first day and Mrs. Fanny was calling the role. When she called your name, you were supposed to stand and say, "Present." When she got to the Hs, Mrs. Fanny called out the next name. 'Elizabeth Hill.' Your mother didn't stand or answer. Mrs. Fanny called the name again. 'Elizabeth Hill.' Again, Anne didn't move. She actually looked around the room thinking that one of her relatives was in the class. Mrs. Fanny said, "Are there any Hills in this room?" One of the boys spoke up and said, "No ma'am there ain't no hills in here. All the hills are outside."

"Everyone just burst out laughing! Well, everyone except Mrs. Fanny. We could tell that she was really mad. That's when Anne stood up and said, "Mrs. Fanny, my last name is Hill. I'm Anne Hill." Anne truly did not know that her first name was Elizabeth."

"Mrs. Fanny looked down at some papers on her desk. When she looked up, we could tell that she was furious. She yelled, "Child, don't you know that your name is Elizabeth Anne Hill.?" Anne could tell that she was in trouble. She started shaking. I thought that she was going to panic and run out of the room. Mrs. Fanny said, "Well, answer me. Don't you know that your name is Elizabeth? Elizabeth Hill. Elizabeth Hill. Say it child. Elizabeth Hill.""

"About that time the classroom door opened. It was Mr. Finch the principal. Mr. Finch was one of papa's best friends. They were both deacons at the church. His wife was our Sunday school teacher. Mr. Finch asked, "Mrs. Fanny, what's wrong?" She responded, "Well, sir, one of my students doesn't even know her name.""

"Mr. Finch could see that Anne was standing and surmised that Mrs. Fanny was talking about her. What happened next was so funny. Mr. Finch looked at your mother and asked Mrs. Fanny, "Are you talking about Anne?" Mrs. Fanny leaned over her desk, opened her eyes as wide as she could and said, "Her name is Elizabeth! Elizabeth Hill!""

"What happened next was the funniest thing of all. Mr. Finch walked over to Anne's desk, turned back to look at Mrs. Fanny, opened his eyes real big and said, "Her name is Anne! Anne Hill!" We all wanted to laugh so badly but we knew that we had better not. Mr. Finch looked at your

mother and said, "Hello, ANNE. Good to have you in school today." He looked at Mrs. Fanny with a raised eyebrow and then casually walked out of the room. We all took a deep breath and looked at Mrs. Fanny to see what was coming next. She just looked down at the role and called the rest of the names."

"After school we all laughed and laughed about Mrs. Fanny. Mr. Finch had put her in her place. The next day when Mrs. Fanny called the role and got to your mother's name, she gritted her teeth and said, "Anne Hill." Your mother stood and said, "Present." Every single day when Mrs. Fanny called Anne's name, we all thought about that first day when Mr. Finch said, "Hello ANNE. Good to have you in school today."

Ellie and Jennie had Steven rolling on the floor with laughter. He loved hearing the stories about his mother. As they continued to browse through the photos and other memorabilia, Jennie found an old postcard. The picture on the card showed a small canyon with a very deep ravine. For some reason the place looked familiar to Steven. Jennie asked, "Steven, do you know where this is?" Steven looked at the card and read the caption. "Indian Cliff, Mississippi."

From a short paragraph on the card, Steven learned that the canyon had been formed by erosion. It was over one hundred and fifty feet deep and was half a mile wide. The most striking feature was the variety of colors in the soils which ranged from brilliant purples to deep reds. Evidently, the large trees at the bottom of the canyon did not actually grow there but slid down from the top as the canyon walls eroded.

Ellie spoke up. "Steven, I think that you all went to

Indian Cliff when you were little. Do you remember?" Steven had a vague memory of the trip but couldn't recall much. Jennie said, "I was always afraid to go there because of that couple." Ellie laughed. "Jennie, do you still believe that old tale?" Steven asked about the story.

Jennie continued. "I guess you know that there are several old cars at the bottom of the canyon. Every once in a while people would park too close to the edge. The ground would give way and their cars would fall down to the bottom. Well, when we were little, a young couple went out to Indian Cliff one night. They parked over there on the bad side where most of the cave-ins were.

That night they didn't come home. Their parents called the sheriff and the next morning they found them at the bottom of the ravine. Their car had fallen over the edge. The police report said that they parked too close to the edge and the ground gave way, sending them to their deaths. But a lot of people think that someone pushed the car over with them in it."

Ellie said, "Now Jennie, you don't believe that, do you?" "I don't know but that's why so many people say that if you go out there at night, you can hear that couple crying out, 'Help us. Help us.'" They all laughed. Steven smiled and winked at Ellie.

Judy came in about that time and told them that supper was ready. Ray met them in the dining room and once again shared his condolences with Steven. As they enjoyed the great meal that Judy cooked, Jennie started telling another Anne story. "Ellie, do you remember when we used to borrow some of old Mr. Toney's plums?" "Jennie, you don't have to tell everything you know." Judy laughed and said, "Well, she

always does."

Jennie continued. "Anyway, Mr. Toney had about forty trees in his orchard and they were the best tasting plums you've ever eaten. Anne never wanted to take the plums. She would preach a sermon to us and tell us that we were going to get sick from eating stolen plums. She still went with us though and would look out for Mr. Toney while we picked a few of the plums. If she saw Mr. Toney, she would whistle like a bird and we would run.

Well, one day we had just started picking the plums when all of a sudden we looked up and saw Anne sitting on the fence talking with Mr. Toney. She had not whistled to warn us. Evidently, Mr. Toney had not seen us. So we got down on our hands and knees and crawled out of the orchard. Then we went to where Anne and Mr. Toney were talking like we had just walked up.

That's when we heard Mr. Toney ask Anne real loud, "Anne, would you like some of my plums?" Anne shouted, "Yes sir, I sure would." Mr. Toney said, "Well, maybe Ellie and Jennie will give you some of those in their pockets." We almost died! Mr. Toney and Anne both started laughing. Later, Anne told us that that was the only way she could figure to stop us from stealing. That was the last time we borrowed Mr. Toney's plums."

Steven was so grateful to his aunts for sharing the stories about his mother. It seemed that she was as special as he had known her to be. After supper, they all went to the den and looked at some more of the pictures. "Ellie, do you remember this?" "Well, I do. That's the day we were all baptized." Steven looked at the picture and saw his mother and the three aunts all dressed in white baptismal robes.

"You were all baptized at the same time?" he asked. Aunt Ellie said, "Yes. You see, our little community church only baptized twice a year; once after the annual fall revival and once in the spring for everyone else who joined the rest of the year."

Back then, we went to the river to be baptized. There was a big sandbar in the bend of the river over at Mr. Adam's place. The water was shallow there and you didn't have to worry about snakes. A baptism in those days was a community-wide event. It was something to see. Everybody came out for it. We would have dinner on the ground and sing hymns. Sometimes there would be twenty or thirty of us baptized at one time.

We were baptized after the fall revival. The water was pretty cold by then. I remember Anne saying, "It's going to be cold Ellie. It's going to be cold." She was always cold natured. It could be ninety degrees and Anne would still be wearing socks to keep her feet warm."

"Well, some of the ladies helped us get those robes on and we waited in line for our turn. Brother Smith was our pastor then. He was a wonderful, kind man. He wasn't a screamer. I heard papa tell someone that Brother Smith was the best picture of Jesus he had ever seen. Well, we all walked down to the river. Anne pushed me ahead of her so I was baptized first. She was right. That water was cold. Brother Smith put me under and I came up shivering.

Anne was next, then Willie, and then Jennie. When Jennie was..." That's when Aunt Jennie spoke up and said, "Now Ellie, Steven doesn't want to hear any more about that." Ellie said, "Oh, I think Steven would love to hear the rest of this story. When Brother Smith put Jennie under, her

feet popped straight up in the air. Brother Smith lost his grip on her and she started floating downstream. Her arms and legs were swinging all over the place. She was shouting, "Help me! I'm drowning! Help me!" That's when Anne shouted, "Stand up Jennie! Stand up!" The water was only about three feet deep but Jennie thought that she was about to die. We laughed until we cried. On our way home we started throwing our arms and legs and shouted, "I'm drowning! I'm drowning!"

Steven was doubled over laughing along with everybody else in the room, even Aunt Jennie. She said, "Well, I knew that I was going to Heaven but I just didn't want to go right then."

After everyone finally composed themselves, Steven asked for some more church stories. Ellie said, "Well, we only had church on the first and third Sundays of the month. Our preacher was a circuit rider. He preached at our church in Norman and at the church in Justice. He preached over there on the second and fourth Sundays.

On the Sundays that we didn't have church, papa would read from the Bible and mother would lead us in a few hymns. At church, we had Sunday School and then the worship service. Sunday School was fun but when we got to the service we had to be quiet and everything was real serious."

Jennie interrupted. "But I remember a couple of times when the serious went out the window. One year, we had this evangelist for our revival who was a shouter. He even shouted when he read the Scripture. I remember Anne asking me if he was deaf. Well, he had this odd thing that he would do. He would grab the pulpit, lean way over, open his eyes real wide, and shout, "If you don't repent, you're going to fall down into the pit of Hell!" He did that every night."

"Well, the last night of the revival when he did that, he leaned over too far and the whole pulpit came loose. He tried to pull it back but it was too late. The pulpit fell down on the communion table and slid off on to the floor. The evangelist fell backward into the choir, right on top of Mrs. Wilson. She screamed and we all started laughing. Momma slapped my hand but I couldn't help it. Anne whispered to me, 'Well, he kept telling us that we were going to fall. I guess he wanted to show us how.'"

"Needless to say, for all practical purposes, the service was over after that. I don't think anybody heard another word that was said. You could see people all over the church looking at each other. As we were leaving, papa stopped to talk to Brother Smith. Both of them had big grins on their faces. They thought it was funny too."

Steven was in stitches. He just could not stop laughing. When he finally caught his breath he said, "I could listen to your stories all night, but I have to get back home." Ellie asked, "Well, would you like to come back tomorrow?" "I couldn't take another day of your time with the family." "Ray and Judy don't mind. Besides, we like looking at the pictures." "Well, tomorrow I have to take dad to his appointment at the hospital but I could come back Friday." "That will be great. I think that Willie could join us then. Would you mind if we kept the pictures until Friday? They might help us remember more stories." "Sure. Thank you all so much." They shared hugs and kisses and Steven made his way back home.

The next morning, Steven helped Jim get ready for his

first physical therapy session. Jim bought some jogging shoes and sweats which were required for the therapy. Steven never saw his dad dressed like that before. They both laughed about the new look. Before they left, Jim asked Steven to pick a few roses from the garden. He wanted some of the large ruby red ones that were close to the back porch. Those seemed to be his mother's favorites. She used them only for special occasions.

While Steven was waiting at the hospital, several nurses and others stopped to share their condolences. "Hi, Steven." "Hi, Dr. Walden." "I was so sorry to hear of Anne's death. Your mother was an incredible woman." Dr. Walden had been Anne's gynecologist. He had seen her through the difficult pregnancy with Steven. "Thank you Dr. Walden." "If there is anything I can do to help, just let me know."

As Steven continued to wait for Jim, Mr. Leon Simon stopped to talk. Mr. Simon was in charge of maintenance for the hospital. Steven actually worked for him during the summer. Steven's sole job was changing lightbulbs. "Hey, Steven. Are you here with your dad?" "Yes sir. He has therapy three days a week." "I was sure sorry to hear about your mother. She was one fine lady. My wife, Laura has some roses out at your place. Your momma sure knew how to take care of those flowers. If you need anything we can help you with just let us know. Okay?" "Yes sir. Thanks."

After Steven had a few more visits with friends, Jim finished his therapy and was ready to go. When they left the hospital, Jim told Steven that he wanted to visit the cemetery. Steven wasn't sure if that was a good idea, but he knew that his dad probably needed to go. When they arrived, Steven got the flowers from the back seat and walked his dad to the gravesite. They shared a few tearful moments together. After several minutes, Jim asked Steven to wait for him in the car. Steven left his dad alone hoping that he would be okay. Jim placed the roses on Anne's grave and sat for a while on a bench nearby. Steven waited patiently.

On the way home, Jim started talking about Anne. "Steven, your mother was one of the most special women I've ever known. I didn't always treat her right but I did love her. She was the closest thing to perfect that there ever was. She loved you and Sarah. She loved my family. She was just wonderful." Steven held back the tears as he listened.

"She taught Sunday School. She fixed food for families when they lost loved ones. She gave people groceries when they were out of work. And the roses, well, she helped everybody in town with their roses. She was amazing. I know that she's in a better place but I just miss her so much" Steven patted his dad on the shoulder but couldn't speak. They both missed her beyond measure.

That night Sarah prepared supper for the whole family. It was the first time that they had all been together since the funeral. Jim enjoyed having the grandchildren in the house again. Richard made a comment about Jim's new therapy wardrobe. "Pop, it looks like you're training for the Olympics." Jim said, "I thought I'd try boxing. You want to go a few rounds?" Everyone chuckled.

After the meal, they all went out on the back porch. Richard made a fire in the pit so the kids could roast marshmallows. Sarah and Steven sat near their dad. They knew that he was thinking about Anne. "Did your mother ever tell you why we built out here? It was because of that creek and the soil. She knew that it would be good for her

roses." Steven asked, "Dad, do you know why mother loved roses so much?" "No, not really. I know that back home her aunt Macy had a lot of roses in her yard. I guess they just liked giving them to people. Your mother gave people roses all the time. She took them to the hospital and the nursing home. When people had anniversaries she would make a bouquet for the couple."

"Daddy, when did other people start planting roses in the field?" "I don't know, son. I guess about twenty years ago. Your mother planted a bush way out there and then several of the ladies just started planting around it. After a while it started looking like a field of roses. Anne helped several of the ladies plant theirs. She sure loved her roses."

After a while Sarah, Richard, and the kids said their goodnights and left. Steven put out the fire in the pit and sat for a while on the porch with his dad. When it got dark, Steven went inside. Jim stayed on the porch. It was where he and Anne spent many evenings together.

The next morning, Steven fixed Jim's breakfast and then headed back to visit with his aunts. Once again, he stopped by the bakery for those chocolate covered donut holes. When he arrived, Aunt Willie met him at the door with a big hug. She was able to leave her husband for a few hours to visit with Steven. Jennie and Ellie were in the sunroom. "You didn't bring more donut holes, did you?" "Yes, Aunt Jennie. Here." "Bless you. Bless you. Bless you." "Hi, Aunt Ellie." "Hi, honey. How's your daddy?" "He's doing well. We went to his first therapy session yesterday and he did fine." "You tell him that we asked about him." "Yes, mam."

After his aunts inhaled the donut holes, Ellie said, "Steven, thank you for leaving the pictures. We stayed up half the night looking at them. Sure brought back a lot of good memories." Jennie said, "They sure did. Here, look at this postcard. This is a picture of the train station in Hampton. It was one of the first passenger trains in Mississippi. Do you know why your momma kept this?" Steven had no clue.

"You see, when we were about ten or twelve, papa bought us tickets and we rode the train all the way to Mapleton. It was in June, right after we got out of school. Papa said that it was a reward for all of our good grades." Willie, spoke up and said, "Well, some of us made good grades." Jennie rolled her eyes and continued. "We all wanted a window seat so we could see. We had never been anywhere but Hampton."

"Well, anyway, when we got on the train, pretty soon the engineer blew that horn real loud and we all jumped like we had been shot. When the train started moving, we held on to our seats real tight. Ellie was..." "Ellie was what?" his aunt asked. "You better not say that I was scared to death because I remember when we went over the big bridge at Middleton you started screaming, "We're going to die. We're going to die." Steven and Willie looked at each other and started laughing.

"Well, what I was trying to tell Steven was that Anne looked out the window the whole trip. Every once in a while she would say, "Isn't that beautiful. Isn't that beautiful." I looked out one time and there was just a field of old weed flowers but Anne thought it was beautiful. When we got close to Mapleton you could almost touch the leaves of the trees. It was like we were going through the woods on a narrow path. Anne said, "Isn't that beautiful. Isn't that beautiful. She really loved nature."

That's when Willie spoke up and said, "Ellie, do you remember this?" Willie found a very small picture of the girls that looked as if it was taken in a studio. There was a drape of cloth behind them. They were all very close together in the picture. Ellie said, "That was at the circus. It was the first time that anyone of us had seen one of those photo booths. Papa gave us a dime and we all squeezed in the booth to take our picture."

Steven asked, "What was the circus like?" Jennie spoke up. "Oh it was fun. You know, we had never seen elephants and wild animals in person before. They brought the animals in on the train and then they had a big parade down Main Street in Hampton. People came from as far away as Gulfport to see the show. They put up this huge tent down by the stockyard. The circus was only Friday and Saturday. We were so excited. When we got there, the band was playing real loud. We heard one of the tigers roar and one of the elephants made that loud trumpet sound. We were just mesmerized by the whole thing."

Willie said, "The thing I remember about the circus was that Anne and I bought a cotton candy together. It was the first time that we have ever seen it and, well, we really didn't know how to eat it." Steven said, "I can't picture mother eating cotton candy. She couldn't stand to get anything sticky on her fingers." Willie laughed. "Well, maybe that's why because by the time we finished eating it, there was cotton candy in our hair, cotton candy on our clothes, and cotton candy stuck to our faces. Momma was not happy with us."

As Steven continued to enjoy the stories, he thought of asking Willie about Anne's birth certificate. "Aunt Willie, I have a question about mother's birth certificate and her social security card. Do you think you could take a look?" "Sure. What is it?" Steven showed her the blank box marked for the father's name on the birth certificate and then showed her the social security card. Willie looked at the documents for a minute or two and then said the strangest thing. "I don't know but maybe it has something to do with why Anne lived with us."

Steven was shocked. "Lived with you? What do you mean?" All three of the aunts looked puzzled. Ellie said, "Well, honey, we thought you knew that Anne stayed with us." Steven didn't know what to say. The aunts could see that he was struggling with the situation. Steven asked, "So mother and her mother lived at your house?" Willie spoke up. "No, your mother and Aunt Macy." Steven was speechless. All these years and he didn't know that his mother was raised by the Henrys. Now he had even more questions with no answers.

Then Steven thought about Anne's report cards and the initials – M. H. He showed one of them to the aunts. Ellie spoke up. "Well, that's momma's initials. She signed all our report cards like that." "Steven asked, "What was your mother's name?" Jennie said, "Mabel. Her name was Mabel, Mabel Henry." Steven couldn't believe what he was hearing. He thought that the H was for Hill. But his mother's report cards were signed by his aunt Mabel.

Steven just shook his head. He had some more information but it still didn't answer the question about his mother's name. After a while, Ellie said, "Steven, maybe aunt Macy knows some details about this. She and Anne were real close. You know, she lives over in Pearl Valley at the nursing home. Maybe you could go over and ask her about it." Steven

didn't even know that Macy was still alive. He had not seen her since he was a little boy. Ellie said, "I tell you what, after lunch, I'll go over there with you and we'll ask her about Anne." "Would you do that aunt Ellie? Oh, thank you so much."

The family had a wonderful lunch together. The aunts told a few more stories on each other and Steven shared some of his memories of them when he was a young child. He hugged Willie and Jennie and said his goodbyes. Steven was excited about the possibilities with aunt Macy but he was also grateful for the love of Ellie, Willie, and Jennie, three special roses.

4   *A Fragile Rose*

After lunch, Ellie and Steven headed for Pearl Valley. On the way, Steven asked his aunt, "What was mother really like, you know, her personality?" Ellie responded, "Well, when we were little we were all just a bunch of giggly girls. I guess when we got to be teenagers you could see our differences more. Anne was like me, somewhere between Jennie's loud and Willie's quiet. But Anne could talk with people. I mean, she could talk with adults just like she talked with us. I remember that papa would come home and Anne would ask, "Did you have a good day Uncle Robert?" When church was over sometimes she would walk up to Brother Smith and say, "Thank you for the sermon pastor. It really spoke to my heart." She just seemed confident and maybe a little more independent than the rest of us."

Ellie continued. "Anne was also real nice to everybody. It didn't matter who you were. You could be as poor as dirt and Anne would try to be your friend. She was always helping people too. I remember one day when she came into the store and asked papa if she could have a pair of shoes. He asked her why she needed shoes when hers looked just fine. Anne

told him about a little girl she saw on the road who had holes in her shoes. I thought papa was going to cry. He gave Anne the shoes and some socks for the little girl. But that's just how Anne was. She couldn't stand seeing somebody going without."

Steven held back his tears of joy. "Tell me more." "Well, your mama was real religious. I mean, she read her Bible a lot. She prayed real prayers, not the "Now I lay me down to sleep" kind. She prayed for all of us. She prayed for the missionaries. She prayed for people who were sick. She prayed for families when somebody died. And then every once in a while, it was sort of funny, she would get a little preachy with us." "What do you mean?" "Well, one of us would do something wrong and she would say, "Jesus is not happy with you." or "Jesus is frowning at you." I remember one time when Jennie said, "Well, Jesus will just have to get over it." I heard mama say one time that if Baptist had women preachers that Anne would make a good one."

Steven was enjoying every story that Ellie shared. He was finally putting together the picture of his mother that he had longed to see. "What else can you remember, Aunt Ellie?" "Well, you're not going to believe this, but your mother was quite an athlete." "Really?" "Yes she was. She could run just as fast as any of the boys and she was the best shooter on our basketball team.

I remember one time when we were watching the boys play baseball. One of the guys on the other team hit a foul ball and Billy Johnson, our catcher, started running to get it. Billy stumbled and fell on the ground. Anne reached over the stands and caught the ball with her bare hand. Then she stood up and threw it all the way back to the pitcher.

Everybody said that if the coach would let Anne play, they could win more games." Steven was amazed. He always enjoyed sports but didn't know that his mother was such a good athlete.

Ellie said, "I guess by now you're thinking that your mother was just about perfect. Well, she was close to it but I can remember at least one time when she showed us that she was human. "What happened?" "Well, Anne was impatient. She could do just about anything. But when you couldn't do it as fast as she wanted you to, or if you were lazy, she got frustrated with you. You see, Anne was always in fifth gear. She woke up like that and stayed like that all day long. If you were walking with her, you almost had to run to keep up. She'd say, "Time's a wasting. Time's a wasting."

"Well, one day it caught up with her. We were picking corn in the field. It was hot as blue blazes. Willie and I were doing the best we could. Anne was going a hundred miles an hour. But Jennie was just messing around like she always did. Well, Anne got tired of it. She went over to Jennie and started fussing her out. "You must be the slowest person in the world. Old Betsy the mule moves faster than you. We're going to be out here 'til midnight. Now get busy!" Ellie hesitated. Steven asked, "What did she say?" "Well, she said a bad word." "Mother?" "Yes, your mother. We were shocked. Actually, Anne was too. She put her hand over her mouth. Her eyes got real big. Jennie started laughing and said, "Anne! Jesus is not happy with you."

Willie and I started laughing. Anne's face turned as red as a beet. She didn't know what to do. After a few seconds, she started laughing too. I know that she was afraid that we were going to tell momma and papa but we never did. Every

once in a while when Willie or Jennie or I would let out a word or two, Anne wouldn't say a thing. We'd all smile because we never forgot that day in the field when Anne the angel fell from grace." Steven was amused. He was thankful even for the story about his mother's slip of the tongue.

After a few more stories, Ellie and Steven arrived in Pearl Valley. Steven had visited his father's family there many times when he was younger. It was a quiet little county seat town with a population around 5,000. The town was built just east of the Pearl Valley River which ran from northern Mississippi to the Gulf of Mexico.

The town actually had a rather rich history. When cotton was king, the town had a flourishing port where the white gold was loaded on barges and taken downriver to New Orleans. In the early 1800s, it served as the temporary capital of the state. Pearl Valley was also known as the home of the Mississippi Rodeo.

The thing that Steven remembered most about Pearl Valley was its white squirrels. In the late 1930s the governor of Mississippi, a Pearl Valley native, had the squirrels imported from North Carolina. Steven remembered going to the park with his dad and watching the rare critters. He even thought about trying to catch one and bring it back to Pine Hills. He asked his dad about it and was told that the squirrels were protected by a city ordinance. Anyone trapping one of the squirrels could be arrested. Steven abandoned his plan.

When they made it to the nursing home, Ellie and Steven went to Aunt Macy's room and found her sound asleep. They hated to wake her but Ellie rubbed her shoulder and Macy roused up. "It is time for supper?" "No, aunt Macy.

It's Ellie." "Ellie?" "Your niece, Ellie. Robert and Mabel's daughter." "Oh, hi Ellie." Steven chimed in, "Hey, Aunt Macy. I'm Steven, Anne's son." "Steven? Oh, hi Steven. It's good to see you. How's Anne?" Ellie spoke up, "Anne's fine." The family decided not to tell Macy about Anne's death. She had always been rather fragile emotionally and was now suffering from Alzheimer's. Steven understood.

"Aunt Macy, Steven has been over at the house and we've been talking about when you and Anne lived with us in Norman. Do you remember?" "Yes." "We told Steven about how you played games with us when we were little. Do you remember?" "Yes." Ellie and Steven really couldn't tell if Macy understood the conversation. Macy said, "I remember when it snowed and we went outside and played with your little dog." Ellie couldn't remember Macy playing with them in the snow but Steven did. He was about five or six. His Aunt Cheryl gave him a red dachshund puppy for his birthday. She had it delivered on a large truck all the way from Texas. Steven remembered Macy coming over to the house and playing with him outside in the snow. The puppy would jump up on top of the snow and then disappear. Aunt Macy nicknamed him Shorty.

"What was your puppy's name?" "His name was Corky." "That's right. He was a cute little thing. I remember how he would try to bury his food in the carpet." Macy was right. Sometimes when they gave Corky a treat, he would go behind a chair and paw the carpet as if he was digging a hole. He would place the food in the imaginary hole and then push his nose in the carpet as if he was covering the treat with dirt. Of course, the food was just lying on top of the carpet. It was a funny thing to see.

Unfortunately, Macy was remembering more recent events. Ellie and Steven hoped that she could recall the earlier days when she and Anne lived with the Henrys. "Aunt Macy, do you remember when Anne was a little girl?" "Yes. I remember her red hair and all those curls. You know, she didn't like her hair but we all thought it was beautiful." Steven was smiling. He had inherited his mother's auburn red hair and curls. He didn't like it either but the older ladies at church would always say how they wish they had hair like his.

"Anne was a real loving child. The first thing she did when she saw you was give you a big hug. Then she would say, "I love you bigger than big." She was a loving child. And she was full of energy. Sometimes I thought that she was just going to jump out of her own skin. She always wanted to play or go somewhere or do something. She couldn't sit still very long. I used to call her Little Rabbit because she reminded me of a fast little bunny hopping from one thing to another."

"And she loved roses." Steven's ears perked up. He had always wondered why his mother loved roses. "Why did mother love roses, aunt Macy?" "Well, silly, because they keep blooming." Steven wasn't sure what Macy meant. "Because they keep blooming?" "Sure. You know, sometimes Anne would go in the garden and just smell the roses. She would visit every bush and breathe in its aroma. I came out one time and Anne was actually talking to the roses. She was saying things like, "You sure look pretty today. I see you have some new buds coming out." "That child was something."

"I remember one time when she was out there just talking away and I snuck up behind her and said in a deep voice, "Anne, this is God." She jumped like she was shot. I said, 'What's the matter Little Rabbit? Did God scare you?' Ellie and Steven laughed. "You probably don't know this but every Sunday, she would go out and cut three or four roses and take them to church. Some of the other ladies would bring their roses and make a bouquet to put on the altar. You could smell the roses all over the church. It made everything real peaceful. Yes, that girl loved roses."

Steven wanted to know more about the roses but his other questions were more pressing. "Aunt Macy, do you remember mother's father?" "Sure. He was a good man. Poor thing. He died in the war just before Anne was born."

"Steven, do you remember when we used to go down in the cellar and play?" The cellar that Macy referred to was actually a storm shelter. Jim built if for Anne soon after they bought their house because she was terribly afraid of bad weather. When that first clap of thunder sounded, Anne would go into a panic mode. "Oh lordy. Get in the shelter. Get in the shelter." Steven remembered her praying, "Lord, please keep us safe and save our house."

"We had a lot of fun in the cellar, didn't we?" "We sure did." "Do you remember that time when I told you that I saw a ghost?" Macy was always trying to scare Steven and his cousins with ghost stories. It was one of the ways that her childlike personality came out. Macy laughed. "You know, I never told you but there was really no ghost down there. I just loved to scare you." "And you did a good job of it too." They both chuckled.

Steven was enjoying Aunt Macy's recollections but he wanted to know why his mother's name on her Social Security card was different than the name on her birth certificate. "Aunt Macy, did you know any Gray families back

in Norman?" "Gray? I don't know. Seems like there may have been a Gray family from over at Hicks. Yes. I think they had three girls. One of them was my age. Is it time for supper?"

Steven could tell that his aunt was getting tired. Ellie said, "Yes mam, it sure is." Ellie let Steven know that they needed to finish their visit with Macy. Steven agreed. He certainly didn't want to upset her with more questions. They escorted Macy to the dining room and said their goodbyes. Though he learned nothing new about Anne, Steven was grateful for the love of another rose, aunt Macy, a fragile but precious rose.

On the way back home, Steven asked Ellie if she could remember anything about a Gray family from the Hicks community. She said, "Well, if the children were aunt Macy's age, I would not have known them." Steven asked, "Well, how can I find out about them?" Ellie thought for a moment and said, "Well, I guess you could go and look at the cemetery." Steven hadn't thought about that. "Which cemetery would they be in?" "I guess they would be in the Pleasant Hill cemetery. That's where most people were buried back then.

Steven thanked his aunt for going with him. Ellie was actually happy to see Macy again. It had been a long time since she had seen her. Ellie had many fond memories of her aunt. Macy had often been the glue that held the Henry family together. Steven dropped Ellie off at Ray's and made his way home. All he had gained from the visit was a faint lead that would most likely be a dead end. Nevertheless, he would pursue it. He would do anything to solve the mystery of his mother's name.

5   *No Name For The Rose*

The next morning, Steven got up and fixed breakfast for his dad. Jim was on a restricted diet but he fudged every once in a while and Saturday was a good day to fudge. Steven shared some of his aunt's stories with his dad. Jim enjoyed them as much as Steven had. Sarah came in while they were eating. "Hey, daddy. How are you doing?" "I'm good. What do you have in the bag?" "Oh, just some little treats." Sarah had stopped by the bakery and picked up a few of those chocolate covered donut holes. "Now, two or three are all you can have." Jim said, "Sure", as he grabbed the bag from her hand.

"Hey, little brother." "Hey sister. What are you doing over here so early?" "Well, I came to see my daddy and to hear how your visit with the aunts went." Sarah sat down close to Jim and gave him a big hug. She was glad that he looked better. "How was your trip to Hampton? Is everyone doing okay?" "Yes. They told me all kinds of stories about mother. You are not going to believe some of them."

Then Steven said, "Did you know that mother was

raised by the Henrys?" Sarah looked surprised. "No. What do you mean?" "Mother grew up with the aunts. She lived in their house with Aunt Macy." "Aunt Macy?" "Yes." Sarah turned to Jim and asked, "Daddy, did you know this?" "No honey, your mother never told me anything about her childhood. That does explain why they were all so close." Sarah asked Steven, "Did you show them the social security card?" "Yes." "And?" "They had no idea why her name was different. I asked aunt Macy if she knew of a Gray family. She told me that there were some Grays from Hicks. Aunt Ellie told me that we should check out the Pleasant Hill cemetery. That's all I know to do." Sarah agreed.

About that time, there was a knock on the back door. Steven went to see who it was. "Well, hey Mrs. Herring." "Hey, Steven. I just wanted to let you know that I was here. I hope it's okay to work on my roses." "Sure." Dell Herring was another one of Anne's friends. Steven went to school with her daughter, Caroline. The Herrings owned a tire business in Pine Hills. Mr. Herring was a great guy. He went out to the prison every week and taught a Bible study. Steven really admired him.

"I am just so heartbroken about Anne. I can't imagine what you all are going through. She was so young." "Yes, mam." "I tell you, nobody was better. When my mother was ill, Anne brought food to the house for them. And she was such a comfort to me when my father died." "Yes, mam." "And the garden, what a blessing. I'm sure you know how much it means to us all. Well, I'm just going to do a little pruning and composting so my roses will be safe for the winter. Praying for you all. God bless." "Thank you, Mrs. Herring."

Steven and Sarah greeted several people who came to the garden. They were all preparing the roses for the cold weather. One of the ladies was Mrs. Evelyn Rush. She actually worked for Anne when they had the grocery store. They were best friends. Every Saturday night before Anne and Evelyn closed the store, Mr. Rush would meet Jim at the Carpenter's house. After closing, the couples would enjoy watching a Saturday night variety show on television.

One of the funniest memories Steven had of his mother happened when Anne and Evelyn came running in the house after closing the store. They were both screaming at the top of their lungs. "He was trying to rob us! He was trying to rob us!" Jim said, "Who are you talking about?" Anne shouted, "Delaney! He was lying down in the car. He was waiting for us. Call the police. Go get the car. Bring your gun. He may still be there waiting for us. Hurry!" Steven remembered the hysteria. He never saw the ladies that upset before.

Delaney was the town hobo. He traveled all through the South thumbing rides with whoever would stop to give him a lift. He rode boxcars and sometimes had a bicycle. He was part of the local flavor of Pine Hills. Stories swirled about him. Some said that he was everything but a bum, that he had a fortune and just acted like he was poor. He lived in an old shack close to the railroad track. Steven saw him from time to time. He would bring soda bottles to the grocery store for money. One time he scared Steven and his friends when they were camping in the back yard.

Jim and Mr. Rush got in the car and went down to the store. When they arrived, Delaney was long gone. They found an empty whiskey bottle on the back floorboard. Jim and Mr. Rush surmised that Delaney was just looking for a place to

sleep. They both chuckled and then drove the car home. When they went back in the house, Steven remembered his father telling a big one. "Well, he was still there. Bob and I pulled him out of the car and he started fighting with us. We'd get in a few good punches and he would come back with his own. Bob picked up a big rock and hit him over the head. But he just kept coming. So I shot him." The ladies were horrified. That was when Jim and Bob both started laughing. The ladies knew that they had been had. Anne said, "Well, if he was in your car you would start screaming too." Steven smiled. Somehow, he couldn't see his dad and Mr. Rush screaming like a couple of little girls.

"Hello, Mrs. Rush. How are you today?" "I'm fine. The question is, how are you all doing?" Sarah spoke up, "We're making it with everyone's prayers and support." "I know it's hard. But in times like these you discover what the Lord can bring you through. You know I lost Mr. Rush last year." "Yes mam." "I am praying for you all every day." "Thank you so much."

"I hope it's okay to work in the garden today." "Yes, mam." "You know, Anne is the one who got me started with the roses. She used to bring some in the store every day. They smelled so good and she would tell me stories about her roses. That's when I started raising them myself." Once again, Steven just didn't understand how roses could have such an effect on people. He was simply glad that his mother had helped someone else enjoy them.

It was almost ten o'clock before Sarah and Steven were able to leave for the Pleasant Hill cemetery. On the way, Steven shared more details of what the aunts told him about Anne. When they arrived at the cemetery, they reviewed what they were looking for. Sarah said, "We are looking for Grays and Hills. Is that right?" Steven concurred and they started their search.

Pleasant Hill was a rather large rural cemetery. The population of the area had been much greater years before. Now there were only a few cattle farms and the Pleasant Hill Baptist Church. The cemetery was located on the hill that gave the area its name. A large double gate served as the entrance. As cemeteries go, it was a beautiful and peaceful place. The temperature that day was mild and a gentle breeze filled the air. Steven and Sarah split up with Steven going to the east end and Sarah to the west end. Both hoped to find a grave that would give them a clue to their mother's past.

As they searched, Steven and Sarah discovered that the graves were not very old. They did, however, find some rather unusual tombstones. Steven spied an interesting marker that looked like a tree log. The inscription read, "Woodmen of the World." Sarah found a marker that looked like a church with a steeple. It was the grave of a pastor who died in the 1950s.

After about an hour of searching, Sarah and Steven had not found one grave for Hill or Gray families. As they made their way to the car, two women entered the cemetery gate. The couple appeared to be a daughter and mother. They had some flowers and were obviously there to visit a loved one's grave. Steven thought that they would know someone from the two families but he was hesitant to approach them.

Sarah, who was normally the timid one, walked over to talk with the ladies. "Hello. My name is Sarah Howard and this is my brother Steven. I'm sorry to bother you but we are looking for someone who might know about any Gray or Hill

families." "I'm Ruby Reynolds and this is my mother Adelaide Fisher." "Mother, do you know any Gray or Hill families?" "Well, there were a lot of Hills who lived here at one time. But that was years ago." "Do you remember any of their names?" "Well, let me think. I believe that one of mother's friends was named Liza or something like that." Steven spoke up, "Could it have been Eliza?" "That's it, Eliza, Mrs. Eliza Hill. She and mother sang in the choir together. Did you know her? Oh, I'm sorry. You're way too young. That's what happens when you get my age."

Sarah and Steven were both intrigued that Mrs. Fisher may have known their great grandmother. But then they wondered. Could their mother have had the same last name as her grandparents? Mrs. Fisher said that the area was filled with Hill families. Perhaps many of them were not related to each other. Sarah asked, "Mrs. Fisher, do you remember the name of Eliza's husband?" "Well, you know, I was just a little girl. No, I can't remember his name." Steven asked, "Did they have any children?" "I believe they did. Yes. They had two girls. Both of them were a little younger than me." "Do you recall their names?" "Let me think. I think that the younger one was named Macy."

Sarah and Steven were beside themselves. "What about the other daughter? Do you remember her name?" They were hoping that she knew their grandmother. "She was a few years older than me. No, I can't remember her name" Sarah and Steven knew that Mrs. Fisher was talking about their grandmother. Steven asked, "Mrs. Fisher, did you know any of their children?" "No." "Did you know their husbands?" "No. I'm sorry."

As Steven listened to Mrs. Fisher, he realized something.

Mrs. Reynolds, her daughter, may have gone to school with his mother. He interrupted the conversation. "Mrs. Reynolds did you attend school here? "Yes. I was born and raised in Taylor County." Steven asked, "Do you remember going to school with any Hills or Grays?" "Well, let me think. I'm sure I did. Well, I guess I'm getting old too. I just can't recall." Steven said, "Do you remember a girl named Anne? She was a short red-haired girl." "Anne? You know, I think I do remember her." Sarah and Steven were ecstatic. "Anne. She was a few years older than me. I think she played basketball. She was a nice girl. Friendly. Loved people. Yes. Anne. Do you know her?" Sarah spoke up. "She was our mother."

Steven asked, "Do you remember mother's last name?" Mrs. Reynolds looked a bit puzzled. Steven explained. "You see, there is some question about mother's name. Her birth certificate has Hill as her last name but her marriage license and social security card have Gray." Mrs. Reynolds was still perplexed. Steven asked once again. "Do you remember if mother's name was Hill or Gray?" "No. I just can't remember. I'm sorry. That was two lifetimes ago. Have you gone to the school to look at her records?"

Sarah and Steven had never thought about Anne's school records. That's probably where they could find the answer. Mrs. Reynolds spoke up, "The school is closed for the Christmas holidays but it opens the day after New Year's." "Thank you so much Mrs. Reynolds. You've given us the best lead we have so far."

Before they left, Sarah asked Mrs. Reynolds if there were any other cemeteries in the area. "Your family members are most likely buried at the Old Pleasant Hill Cemetery." Steven and Sarah didn't know about the old cemetery. "Can you tell

us how to get there?" "Sure. You get back on the highway toward Pearl Valley. Go down about four of five miles and turn left on Cemetery Road. You can't miss it."

Steven and Sarah headed out for the old cemetery. They were so excited that they found someone who knew Anne's family. Maybe they could find the answers to their questions at the other cemetery or the school. Before going to the cemetery, Sarah and Steven stopped at a little diner for lunch. Jim had told them about the place. It was called The Southern Fried Squirrel. What a name. Sarah tried the gumbo and Steven ordered a shrimp poboy. The food was great!

While they were eating, Steven asked Sarah, "Do you think that we're ever going to know the truth about mother?" "I don't know, Steven. I just wish that there was someone else we could talk with. Aunt Macy is the only one who could know." "Well, let's think of the possibilities." Sarah said, "We don't even know what mother's father's name was for sure. Maybe it was Hill. Well, where did Gray come from? If his name was Gray, why is mother's last name on her birth certificate Hill? It's all too confusing." Steven agreed.

When they arrived at the cemetery, they split up just like they had before. They could quickly see that this was a much older cemetery. They found the graves of a few Civil War veterans and several who died in World War I. Sarah found the first Hill family grave. "Steven, over here." The names were not familiar. Jacob and Catherine. They looked at the adjacent tombs. In just a few moments, Steven yelled, "Here they are! Here they are!" Sarah ran over. They had found the graves of their great grandparents, George and Eliza Hill. The funny thing was that there were fresh cut roses on each of the graves.

The two just stared at the headstones. Both of them considered the heritage of life that was before them. They felt a sense of connection with the past that neither one of them had experienced before. The moment was surreal but very special.

After a while, Sarah's eyes moved to the next grave. It was also adorned with a bouquet of fresh roses. Sarah was puzzled. It was a little girl. Her name was Eva Mae Thompson. There were no other graves next to her. Steven saw the confusion on Sarah's face. "Do you know who that is, Sister?" "Yes I do. That's Aunt Macy's daughter." Steven fixed his eyes on the marker. Sarah said, "Look. There is one space next to her. I bet you that's for Aunt Macy." Steven nodded in agreement. Once again the power of the moment captured their souls.

After several moments, they continued their search, Steven found a section of the cemetery where the Grays were buried. He called Sarah over to look with him. All together, they had found five different families. Sarah suggested that they write down the names and see if they could find out anything about them.

As they drove back through Pearl Valley, Sarah and Steven enjoyed the old time charm of the county seat town. First Baptist Church had a nativity out front. Almost every store had a Christmas wreath on the door and two blocks of the downtown area were covered with lights. Halfway down Main Street, Steven noticed a sign for Pearl Valley High School. He turned off Main and headed toward the school. Sarah asked, "Where are you going?" Steven smiled and said, "You'll see."

Neither of them had ever been to the school. When they drove up, they were amazed. The building was incredible. Rather than the typical, old style architecture, the facility was built in an early art deco design. Steven and Sarah walked to the front entrance and saw that the date on the cornerstone was the year that Anne would have started high school. The two had another special moment. Their mother had stood on these grounds and walked down these halls as a teenager. They were overwhelmed by the thought.

The school was closed for the holidays just as Mrs. Reynolds said. Steven and Sarah would have to wait a few weeks before they could inquire about Anne's records. They were both hopeful that it would help them solve the mystery. For now, however, there was still no name for the rose.

6   *The Roses Sleep*

The new year came and went without much excitement for the Carpenter family. Things just weren't the same without Anne. She had always been the one who made the holidays special. Jim was recovering physically but everyone would see that Anne's death was taking its toll on him emotionally. Sarah was worried about him.

Steven went back to school. His teachers and friends were very supportive but Steven was struggling. He missed his mother more than anyone could ever imagine. She was his anchor. He relied on her for everything. Now he was practically on his own.

The school counselor met with Steven and suggested that he see a therapist but Steven told her that he would be

okay. Sarah was concerned about him also and asked their pastor to give Steven a visit. Steven welcomed the pastor's efforts and did find some comfort from their time together but, to Steven, no one knew what it was like to lose his mother, not even Sarah or Jim.

The mild weather finally surrendered to the cold of winter. It was the time of year when no one came by the house unless a deep freeze was on the way. That's the only time they would need to protect the plants. Sarah and Steven had watched as their mother covered the ground around the rose bushes with mulch in preparation for a freeze. At times, Anne would even wrap the plants in newspaper and put a small amount of soil inside to protect the bushes from the cold.

When Steven and Sarah were young, Anne told them that the roses were sleeping because they needed to rest. She likened it to the hibernation of bears. Sarah and Steven also learned from their mother that sometimes the roses didn't want to go to sleep and needed a little help. They had seen her and others strip the leaves away to promote the dormant stage. When the limbs turned purple, they knew that the roses were asleep.

The cold seemed to magnify the pain of Steven's aching heart. He missed his mother more each day. Some said that things would get better with time. That time had not come for Anne's son. He spent hours in his room alone. He had trouble concentrating at school. He stayed home on the weekends instead of going out with his friends. For a while he experienced a crisis of faith. How could God allow his mother to die? She was a good person, a devoted Christian, and she helped other people with their problems. Why was there no miracle for her?

Sarah was coping somewhat better than Steven, perhaps, because she had spent long hours with her mother before her death. Anne, in some ways, had prepared Sarah for her loss. That may have made the difference in how she and Steven were processing their grief. Anne had communicated a sense of peace and acceptance in her conversations with Sarah. Steven did not have those times with his mother. Jim and Anne chose not to tell Steven how serious the illness was.

Sarah became so concerned about Steven that one day she went to the house to talk with her little brother. "Steven, let's go and sit on the back porch. I have something to share with you." They went outside and sat down on the old rocking swing that Jim had made for Anne. Steven had no idea what Sarah wanted to talk about. "Steven, I know that you're having a hard time coping with mother's death. I want to share some things with you that mother told me before she died." Steven listened.

"A few weeks before mother died, she could see my struggle and knew that I wasn't doing well. She started talking about the roses. I didn't understand at first. But she read some passages of scripture that talk about falling asleep in the Lord. It was so beautiful and comforting. Steven, mother has fallen asleep like the roses in the winter. But just like the roses, she woke up in the spring." Steven began to weep. "I know. I believe that too. But it's just so hard living without her."

Sarah continued. "Then mother talked to me about how satisfied she was with her life. She was so grateful for the blessings of God. She felt as if God fulfilled his purpose

through her and that now it was time for her to rest." Steven was grateful for Sarah sharing his mother's words.

But then Sarah looked at Steven and said, "But mother spent most of our time together talking about you." Steven was shocked. "What do you mean?" "Mother loved you Steven. She loved you so much. You were an answer to her prayers." "What do you mean?" "Mother never told you this but about six years after I was born, she became pregnant again. Things were going fine for the first couple of months but then she had a miscarriage. She lost the baby. Doctor Walden told her that she shouldn't try to have any more children. It was too dangerous for her. Mother was in her late thirties by then."

"Well, mother waited a few years but she really felt God leading her to have another child. She talked with the doctor and, again, he advised against it. But mother didn't listen. She wanted a little red-haired boy and God answered her prayers."

Steven was overwhelmed. He had never heard that story before. He thought that, perhaps, he was one of those oops babies that come from time to time. Years earlier he actually thought that he was adopted. He believed that little boys were supposed to look like their dads and he didn't look anything like Jim. Steven never knew the story surrounding his birth. "I can't believe it. She risked her own health, her own life to have me." "That's right, Steven. Mother wanted you so much. She loved you Steven." Tears started to flow. Steven hugged Sarah and thanked her for sharing the story. The two stayed out on the porch until dark, reminding each other of the good times they had shared with their mother.

In the midst of all the adjustments that everyone was

making, Steven had not forgotten about his mother's school records and the possibility that they might shed some light on the mystery of Anne's name. When he came home from school one day, he called Pearl Valley High School. He spoke with a records clerk and told her what he needed. "Hi. My name is Steven Carpenter. I'm trying to find my mother's school records. She went to Pearl Valley High School in the early 1930s. Can you help me?" The clerk was very polite and told Steven that they did indeed have school records and annuals from the 1930s. She informed Steven that he would have to send a notarized letter with identification before she could release any information. Steven assured her that he would secure the necessary documentation and send it to her as soon as possible.

Steven immediately called Sarah to let her know the good news. Sarah was thrilled. "Do you think that they can send us photos of mother? I'd give anything to see her high school pictures." They talked for a long time about the possibilities. Steven said, "If she graduated as Anne Gray, we will know that her named was changed before she finished school. Then, we could go to the courthouse and find adoption papers." Sarah chimed in, "But what if her name was Hill? Then we won't know any more than we do now?" "We'll just have to wait and find out. I'm going to ask dad how we can get the papers we need to send to the school. Love you. Talk with you later."

That night, Steven told Jim about his call to the school. "Dad, I talked with the folks at Pearl Valley High School today. They told me that they do have mother's school records but that we would have to send a notarized letter and identification to secure the documents. Who can we get to do

the work?

"What are you doing that for, Steven?" "Dad, I want to find out why mother's name is different on her birth certificate and her social security card." "Son, that's not important. You might find out things that you don't want to know." Steven was surprised. It sounded as if his dad knew more than he had shared. "Do you know something about that dad?" "Look, all I'm saying is that family secrets can sometimes be very hurtful. There is a reason your mother never told us about her childhood and it's probably not good. Why don't you just let it go? Your mother was the best Christian woman I have ever known. She raised you and Sarah and even me to have faith in God. Isn't that enough?" Steven was undeterred. "No, dad, it isn't. I have to know the truth." Jim just shook his head and agreed to get the papers together.

Steven's renewed focus on Anne's identity seemed to help with his grief. At least he didn't appear to be as depressed as he had for the past several weeks. He also went back to church, participated in some youth ministry events, and even went out to see a movie with his friends. Getting back in the land of the living was helping Steven move forward with his life.

One day when Steven came home from school, he saw a large envelope sticking out of the mailbox. The return address showed that the package was from the Taylor County School Board. Steven was ecstatic. He ran inside, ripped the envelope open, and began looking for his mother's name. It was in the cover letter that accompanied the school records. "Dear Mr. Carpenter, enclosed you will find the Taylor County High School records of Elizabeth Anne Hill."

There is was. Hill. Not Gray but Hill. When his mother graduated high school her last name was Hill. Steven was stunned. He really thought that the records would show his mother's name as Gray. But there it was, officially. Elizabeth Anne Hill.

This didn't solve anything. It was another dead end. He had not even considered the possibility that her name was changed after she finished school. Adult women didn't change their names unless they got married. Then it hit him. Had his mother been married before? Did she have other children from a previous marriage? The thought of that possibility was simply overwhelming. Immediately, Steven called his father at the office. "Dad, I received mother's school records in the mail. Her name was Hill not Gray which means that her name was changed after she graduated high school. There's only one reason that her name would be changed as an adult. She was married. Dad was mother married to someone before she married you?"

Jim did not respond immediately. "Dad, are you there?" "I'm here Steven. No, your mother was not married before we met." "Then when was her name changed from Hill to Gray?" "I don't know son." Steven was having a hard time believing that his father didn't know the answer. Then another thought came to Steven's mind. "Dad, was mother in some kind of trouble back then? Did she change her name to hide her identity?" Jim responded as he had before. "I just don't know Steven. Your mother never talked with me about her past."

For a moment, Steven let his mind run wild. He envisioned his mother in some type of witness protection program where she had to change her name. He even considered the possibility that she may have had a criminal

background and needed a new name to start over. After a few moments of crazed speculation, Steven came back down to earth and dismissed his outrageous musings. But the question still remained. Why did Anne change her name?

That night, Sarah and Richard came over with the kids to eat. Steven showed Sarah the school records and told her about his conversation with Jim. Neither of them could think of any other scenarios which would prompt their mother to change her name. Sarah asked Richard what he thought about the situation. Richard said, "Well, I don't know why she would change her name but some of her friends might know." Steven and Sarah both had an ah-ha moment. Anne talked with everyone in town and had a number of close friends. She normally played the role of counselor but perhaps she had shared her story with some of them.

Sarah immediately thought of their aunt Letha. "If anyone would know, it would be Aunt Letha. She and mother were the best of friends. I'll call her in the morning. I bet she has some answers for us." Steven concurred. They made a short list of other possibilities and Sarah promised to make contact with each of them. Someone, somewhere, had to know something about Anne's name.

The next morning Steven was awakened by the sound of voices in the back yard. About a dozen of his neighbors came to protect their roses from a heavy freeze that was predicted to blanket the region in two days. Steven got dressed and went outside. Mr. Walker was delivering a second load of compost to help with the plants. He asked Steven about his father. "Dad's doing much better. Thank you for asking. How much do we owe you for the compost?" Mr. Walker just smiled, patted Steven on the shoulder, and told him to call if more was needed.

Steven spent all morning helping people with their roses. He manned the compost pile, filling one wheelbarrow after another. By noon, more than thirty people had come to the field. One of them was Gayle Overstreet. Gayle and Anne had been friends for years. They sang in the choir together at church. Gayle and her husband owned a local jewelry store. Steven's dad and Mr. Overstreet loved old coins. They would go to coin shows about four times a year. Steven often went with them.

Mrs. Overstreet's roses were fairly close to the house. She was one of the first to plant in the field. Steven helped her with the compost. "Thank you Steven. You know, I can't do what I used to. My arthritis is getting the best of me. How are you and your family doing? I know you must miss your mother." "Yes mam. We're okay. It's just hard you know." "Oh, I know. I lost my mother twenty years ago. She was kind and just loved people. She was a lot like Anne." Steven smiled.

"She also loved roses like Anne did. I remember as a little girl, going to her house. The aroma of her roses filled the air with their fragrant bouquets. Dear Ones. That's what she called her roses. Dear Ones. She sure loved her roses." Steven knew exactly what she meant. Anne seemed to love her roses as if they were people she cherished. Every once in a while he would catch his mother talking to her roses. He couldn't hear what she was saying and he thought that it was a bit odd, but he later read that some scientist said that talking to roses helped them grow. Steven wasn't so sure about that but he knew that his mother's roses were the best in the whole county.

After helping Mrs. Overstreet and others, Steven went inside for lunch. Jim fixed some sandwiches and Sarah and the kids came by to join them. Steven asked, "Where's Richard?" "Oh, he's in the woods on his deer stand." Richard was an avid hunter. If something was in season, Richard was hunting it. Jim didn't enjoy hunting, so Steven's hunting experiences came through trips with Richard. Steven learned a lot about life from Richard through the times they spent together hunting.

While the Carpenters were enjoying lunch, someone started knocking hard on the back door. It was Bill Davis. He was yelling, "Call for the ambulance! Call for the ambulance! Mrs. Rush is having a heart attack." Jim and Steven raced outside while Sarah called the hospital.

When they got to Mrs. Rush she was laying on the ground next to her rose bush. Flow Wilson, a local nurse, was checking her vitals. Jim tried to talk to her, but Mrs. Rush wasn't responding. Soon the ambulance arrived and took her to the hospital. Later that night she died. Everyone was devastated. The chill of winter had taken another rose. First Anne and now Mrs. Rush. Pine Hills was in mourning once again.

The Carpenters attended the visitation for Mrs. Rush a few days later. A flood of emotions filled their minds and hearts. It had been less than three months since they lost Anne. As they mourned the passing of a good friend, the Carpenters dealt once again with their own grief. Sarah spent some time talking with Barbara, Mrs. Rush's daughter. They were good friends in high school and had stayed in touch with each other since then. They both remembered days at the grocery store when Evelyn and Anne worked together. It was the first time that Sarah had the opportunity to help someone else through the loss of their mother. Though she was still grieving herself, Sarah was like Anne. She helped others with their hurts as she dealt with her own.

For the next few weeks, the weather dominated life in Pine Hills. Winter delayed its coming but when it came it hit hard. It rain almost every day. Freezing temperatures. Like most areas in the Deep South, Pine Hills rarely had snow but it did have another menacing foe. Sleet. The freezing rain wreaked havoc on roads, bridges, trees, and power lines.

Steven woke up one Saturday morning to the sound of cracking limbs. Jim had removed most of the trees close to the house but those that remained in the front and back of the property were breaking under the load of the ice. Steven knew that later he and his dad would bundle up, go outside, and inspect the damage.

Steven put some logs in the fireplace, fixed breakfast for himself and sat down close to the warming hearth. As he enjoyed the bacon and eggs, he watched a couple of birds at the feeders on the back porch. Anne loved birds almost as much as she loved roses. She placed feeders and bird baths everywhere. She planted flowers that attract hummingbirds. She had Jim build bluebird houses. She even had squirrel feeders placed in the yard so the furry scoundrels wouldn't eat the bird food.

Steven remembered one time when his mother actually fed a hummingbird from her hand. She filled a small glass cup with the ruby red nectar that she had made. Then she rested her arm on the edge of the Adirondack chair and waited. Soon one of the hummers started flying close to the cup. It was hesitant at first but eventually gave in to the

temptation. Steven remembered the smile on his mother's face each time she fed the birds by hand. He also remembered once when she told him about the passage in the Bible that tells how God provides the birds with everything they need. Steven knew that his mother felt God was using her to meet those needs.

Soon Jim got up and joined Steven by the fire. "Good morning Dad." "Good morning son. Thanks for the coffee." "Did you hear the limbs popping this morning Dad?" "Yes, I did. Happens every winter. Those darned pine trees. This afternoon we can go out and survey the damage." "Yes sir. Hey Dad, have you had any other thoughts on mother's name?" "No. I still can't understand why it's so important to you. But I do have to admit that it is odd."

It was the first time Steven felt that his dad didn't know the story behind Anne's name change. Jim said, "You know, son, I worked with a man named Irvin Gray before we moved to Pine Hills. He was from a small town outside of Pearl Valley. I don't know if he's still living. He was ten years older than me. Have you thought about trying to locate family members who are still living in the area?"

That idea never crossed Steven's mind. Maybe there were still Gray family members in the Pearl Valley area who knew his mother. The possibility renewed Steven's enthusiasm once again. "But how can we contact them, dad?" "The library has phonebooks for all the towns within a fifty mile radius of Pine Hills. You could start there."

The library was open all day on Saturday. Steven asked if he could go. Jim laughed, "Sure son. I don't think I could stop you if I tried. Go ahead. We'll check on those broken limbs this afternoon." Steven got dressed and headed for the library. If he could find just one person who knew his mother, maybe the mystery could be solved.

When he arrived at the library, Steven immediately went to the reference section where the phonebooks were located. His dad was correct. There were directories for every town large and small. The Mississippi section had no less than twenty different volumes. Steven found books for towns he never knew existed. Towns like Pickwood, Seeker Springs, and Rolling Hills. Some had fewer than one hundred listings.

He gathered all the directories of towns that were within twenty miles of Pearl Valley. It didn't take Steven long to see that the Grays were not a very prolific family. In Pearl Valley he found only four listings. When he finished going through all the books, he found eight families total. Steven was both excited and concerned. He was excited because the list was manageable. He was concerned because the opportunity to find someone who knew his mother was small.

Steven hurried back home hoping to contact the eight families that afternoon. When he arrived, Sarah and the kids were there. Sarah had made a pot of venison stew. Richard had harvested a small buck the week before and the processor made some pork and deer sausage with a large portion of the meat.

"Hello little brother." "Hi sister. Did dad tell you where I've been?" "He did. What did you find?" Well, I found that the Grays are few and far between in Taylor County. I only found eight families." "Well, that narrows the field. Maybe you can find someone who knew mother." "That's what I'm hoping for. I'm going to call them this afternoon."

The family enjoyed their meal together. Allen and Dawn finished and went upstairs to play while Steven, Sarah, and

Jim sat down by the fire. Sarah asked, "Dad, do you think we have a chance at finding someone who knew mother?" "I don't know dear. They would have to be around my age or older." "Steven said that you knew a man named Gray who was from the area." "That's right. Irvin Gray. He worked with me in the shipyard at New Orleans during the war." "Steven, is there an Irvin Gray on your list?"

Steven had totally forgotten about Jim's friend. He grabbed the list, looked and said, "No. No Irvin Gray." Jim asked to see the list. After a moment he said, "Well, there is an Alfred I. Gray, Jr. Maybe the I is for Irvin. Steven took the list from his father and saw the name. There it was. Alfred I. Gray, Jr. Maybe Irvin was his middle name.

Steven looked at Jim and asked, "Can I call the number? Can I dad?" "Sure son. Go ahead." Steven reached for the phone and dialed the number. A woman answered, "Hello." "Hello mam. This is Steven Carpenter. I'm calling for Mr. Irvin Gray. Is he in?" "Irvin Gray? This is Alfred Gray's residence. Irvin was his father's name." "Is Mr. Irvin there?" "No. I'm sorry to say that Mr. Irvin died a few months ago. Heart attack."

Steven conveyed his condolences and then told Mrs. Gray why he called. "You see Mrs. Gray, my mother, Anne, was from the Pearl Valley area. She went to high school there and my family and I are trying to learn more about her life. She also died a few months ago. Do you know of anyone in your family who would be willing to talk with us?"

Mrs. Gray spoke up and said, "Well, my father-in-law had three brothers. His younger brother Ed is the only one left. He lives in Sandy Creek." Sandy Creek was just over the river from Pine Hills. Steven was excited. "Do you think that you could give me his phone number?" "Sure. I have it here somewhere." Steven jotted down the number and thanked Mrs. Gray for her help.

When he got off the phone, Steven told Jim and Sarah what he found. Sarah said, "Well call him. Call him now." Steven dialed the number and waited for someone to answer. "Hello. Hello. Who is it?" "Mr. Gray, my name is Steven Carpenter. Your nephew Alfred gave me your number." "Is everybody ok?" "Yes sir. I'm trying to find someone who knew my mother, Anne Gray. Alfred's wife thought that you might have known her."

"Anne Gray. Did she live in Taylor County?" "Yes sir. She was from Norman." "I can't remember an Anne in the family. You know there are two sets of Grays from up there. They are not related to each other. Our family came from Tennessee. Those other Grays came from South Carolina."

Steven tried another approach. "Well, did you know any Hills from that area?" "Sure. There were a lot of Hills. I went to school with several." "Do you remember a girl named Anne? Anne Hill. She was rather short and had red hair. She played on the basketball team for Pearl Valley." "Sure I knew her. She was one fine ball player."

Steven was beside himself. "So you knew her?" "Yes. I was two years ahead of her in school but everybody knew Anne. She's your mother?" "Yes sir." "Where do you all live?" "I live in Pine Hills. Mother died a few months ago." "Oh, son, I'm so sorry." "Thank you. Mr. Gray, my family and I are trying to solve a mystery about my mother's name and we thought that maybe you could help us with it." "What's it about?"

Steven told Ed about Anne's name change. "No. I don't

know anything about that. In school she was always known as Anne Hill. That sure is strange though. You sure about that?" "Yes sir. Do you know of anyone who might have some information about this?" Mr. Gray thought for a moment and said, "Well, like I told you, there was another set of Grays. They were from up around Norman. We never had much to do with them but I remember one of them was named Jess. He had three or four brothers and a sister. Their daddy was a barber." Steven remembered that name. Jess Gray. It was on his phone list.

By this time, Jim had retired to his room for an early afternoon nap and Sarah went upstairs to check on the kids. Steven found the number for Jess Gray and made the call. A lady picked up. "Hello. Gray residence." "Mrs. Gray?" "Yes." "This is Steven Carpenter. Is Mr. Jess in?" "Steven Carpenter?" "Yes mam. My mother was Anne Carpenter. Well, I mean Anne Gray. We're trying to find some information about her that your husband might be able to help us with." "Well, my husband's not here right now." "Do you know when he'll be back?" "No. I'm not sure. He's in town buying some things." "Well, can I call back tonight?" "No. We're visiting our daughter tonight."

Steven felt that he detected an uneasiness in her voice. Then he thought that, perhaps, Mrs. Gray might have known his mother. "Mrs. Gray, did you know my mother? You may have known her as Anne Hill." "No. No. I don't think so. I don't remember that name." Again, the lady seemed a bit nervous. Steven asked, "Well, mam, could you ask your husband to call me when he gets back?" "Yes. I sure will." Before Steven could give her the number, Mrs. Gray hung up.

Steven sat there for a moment and thought back through

the brief conversation. Something was wrong. He couldn't put his finger on it but Mrs. Gray wasn't comfortable talking about his mother. She certainly didn't want her husband talking with him.

Steven spent the next hour trying to contact the other six families on his list. Several were not at home and the others knew nothing about his mother. It seemed as if Steven had hit another dead end. Still, he was perplexed about the call with Jess Gray's wife. Did she know more than she was willing to say? Steven felt that she did.

About mid-afternoon the sun peeked through the clouds and Jim woke up from his nap. Steven and his dad bundled up and went outside to check the damage from the ice. Most of the trees had faired pretty well. There were only a few large limbs down. While they were driving, Steven provided his dad with an update on the calls he made. "Dad, do you know Jess Gray from Seeker Springs?" "No son, I don't believe I know him." Steven told Jim about the unusual conversation he had with Mrs. Gray. "Well, that does seem a bit peculiar. But most of us are a little peculiar, wouldn't you say?"

Steven smiled at his dad's attempt at a little humor. "Dad, I thought that maybe you could call her back and get some answers from her." "Oh no, son. I'm not going to call her. She could get mad at all of us and that wouldn't be good." Steven was not happy with his father's response but he understood.

Sunday after church, the family had lunch at Sarah's. After lunch everyone took a bit of a siesta. Richard fell asleep in his recliner, Jim stretched out on the couch, and the kids went to their rooms. Steven and Sarah washed the dishes and

sat down at the kitchen table to finish off the apricot nectar cake Sarah made. Apricot nectar was their favorite because it was their mother's favorite. She baked one almost every Saturday. Steven asked Sarah if she had talked with any of their mother's friends about Anne's name. "I did. I talked to Mrs. Keller, Mrs. Wascom, and Mrs. Overstreet. None of them knew anything about mother's name. I even called aunt Letha again and asked her. She said that mother never talked to her about her childhood." Steven asked, "Did any of them seem as if they weren't telling you the truth?" "No. Of course not. I just don't think that we're going to find out what happened."

Steven had run out of options. He couldn't think of any other way to solve the mystery. They talked with family members. They tried to find graves in cemeteries. Anne's school records didn't provide any answers. Sarah had talked with her mother's closest friends. All of that for nothing. A bit of resignation set in for the pair. It seemed that they might never discovery the truth about Anne's name.

Along with all the dead ends of their search, a second round of grief visited the Carpenter family. The finality of Anne's death was sinking deep into their hearts. Steven walked quietly through his days depressed. Sarah missed the long talks she had with her mother. Jim remained stoic, pushing through the pain. It was early March. Winter was outstaying its welcome. The days were rainy and cold. The roses continued to sleep.

7   *An Unexpected Rose*

Two weeks before Easter, the awful weather finally ended. The dark clouds of winter faded away and a hint of spring was in the air. Life in the Carpenter family was improving to some degree. Jim completed his physical therapy and returned to work. Sarah's days were filled with school and church activities for the kids. Steven was facing a bit of a challenge. With the loss of the family store, he had to work after school to help pay the bills.

Steven was working at the hospital. He was in charge of changing lightbulbs. For three hours, he walked throughout the facility looking for lights that needed replacing. When he was caught up on the lightbulbs, he helped Mr. Simon with other maintenance projects. Steven didn't realize it at the time, but being with people every afternoon was good for him. His short visits with patients and others kept him in the land of the living.

Steven didn't mind working but he missed playing sports. It had been an important part of his life. He had even dreamed of playing college football. His new reality, however,

was a serious threat to that dream. It would be years before he could see how all things work together for good as his mother had taught him from the Bible.

The coming of spring was an exciting time at the Carpenters' farm. People came almost every day to work on their roses. They removed the mulch that had been used to protect the plants in the winter and pruned the stems to promote new growth. In addition, most people put down a little fertilizer to help their plants get a good start. Steven remembered that Anne always added a little Epsom salt to her fertilizer. She swore that it helped the roses grow faster.

The Saturday morning before Palm Sunday, Steven saw Mrs. Audrey Case in the field. Mrs. Case lived just up the road from the grocery store. She had been a long-time friend of Anne's. They were both members of the Eastern Star group. Once a month Mrs. Case would pick Anne up and take her to the meetings. Mrs. Case picked Anne up for some reason, Anne didn't drive. Oh, she had a driver's license but she never drove.

Sarah told Steven that before he was born, Jim took Anne out one day for a driving lesson. Sarah said that it was the only time she ever saw her parents fight. Evidently, the lesson didn't go well. Jim and Anne didn't talk to each other for three days. A few months later, Anne walked in and showed Sarah her new driver's license. But neither Sarah nor Steven ever saw their mother drive a car and neither was brave enough to ask her why.

Steven went out to the field to see if he could help Mrs. Case. "Hello, Mrs. Case. How are you today?" "I'm fine. I just wanted to get a jump start on my roses. The weather's been so bad, that I couldn't get in here to start working on them."

Steven gave her a nod of understanding. "How are you all doing Steven? I sure do miss Anne. I know that it must be very difficult for all of you." Steven responded, "Yes mam it is. But things are getting better. Can I help you with your roses?" Audrey said, "Well, that's so nice of you to ask. I could use a little help getting some more fertilizer from the barn." Steven took the wheelbarrow and loaded the fertilizer for Mrs. Case.

"Oh, Steven, I remember so many good times with Anne. You know, we did a lot of charity work together through the Eastern Star. I remember her saying all the time, "God loves the orphans and the widows. We have to help them know that God loves them." I know that she loved them. I remember one time when we went over to Erma Benson's house. It was right after Erma lost her husband. You know, Erma. She's the one who had all those dogs. Lord only knows how many there were. Anyway, everyone except Anne was afraid to go and see Erma because of her dogs.

Well, one day your mother and I were taking Erma some chicken and dumplings. She had a real bad cold and wasn't able to cook for her family. When we got there those dogs starting barking and just wouldn't quit. I was scared to death. I suggested that we leave the food with her neighbor, Madge Cox but Anne would have none of that.

She picked up that big pot of chicken and dumplings and walked along the fence to the back yard. Those dogs smelled that food and followed her all the way. Then she took a scoop of the dumplings and threw it over the fence in the dog pen. Those hounds jumped in after it and Anne slammed the door to the pen shut. She walked back around and we went in the front gate without a dog in sight. Yep, Anne outsmarted

Erma's dogs."

Steven had a big grin on his face. He believed every word of the story. That was his mother. Anne almost always found a way to get things done. She was the most resourceful person he knew. Anne and Jim had grown up during the Great Depression which forced their generation to get the most out of the little that they had. They were the first ones to recycle on a large scale. Steven remembered his mother telling him how they used old tires to re-sole their shoes. The couple learned to recycle during World War II. Jim actually made money by restoring old car batteries.

Steven finished helping Mrs. Case and was headed inside when Kirk Walker drove up. Steven met him at the front gate. "Hey Kirk. What are you doing over here on a Saturday? Kirk responded, "I have a delivery. It's a rose bush." Steven asked, "Who is it for?" "Well, the card says that it's for your family." Steven was puzzled. He knew that he had not ordered a rose and he didn't think that Sarah or Jim had ordered anything.

"Where did it come from?" Kirk looked at the order. "It says here that it came from Legacy Roses, Fremont, California. It came in on a truck late yesterday. It was the only thing they delivered." Steven was puzzled. "How much is it?" "Oh, there's no invoice. It was just addressed to us with instructions to deliver to you." "Well, ok. Maybe somebody had it delivered here to plant in the field. Thanks, Kirk. Tell your folks hello for me." "Sure will. See you soon."

Steven put the rose bush next to the house in the shade and sat on the porch to cool off. Soon, Jim joined him. "Hey, dad. How are you feeling?" "I'm good. Who were you talking with?" "That's was Kirk. He delivered a rose bush." "Who ordered it?" Steven told Jim about the delivery. They both felt that someone would come soon to claim the plant.

"Dad, I'm working on a new angle to try and find out why mother's name was changed. If I could get a copy of her high school annual, I could track down people who went to school with her. Have you ever seen her annual?" Jim said, "No son. I doubt that the school has annuals from the 30s. Even if they did, you would have a hard time finding her classmates. You could spend months on that project and still come up empty handed. I still don't understand why you think it's important." Steven chose not to argue with his dad. He just let the conversation die. But he didn't let his idea die. On Monday, he was going to call the Pearl Valley High School and find out if they had his mother's annual.

Later that morning, several people came to the field to work on their roses. Steven asked each one about the plant that Kirk delivered. No one knew about it. A little after eleven o'clock, Bill Dunham came to the field with his mother, Mrs. Sallie. Bill worked with Richard at the mill. He was in his mid-50s. Bill's dad died two years before. A few months later Mrs. Sallie moved in with Bill and his family. They were nice people.

Steven went out to the field to meet the Dunhams. "Hello, Mr. Bill, Mrs. Sallie. Can I help you with anything?" Hi, Steven. We just came out to get the roses going for another season. How are you all doing?" "We're fine. Getting a little better every day." "That's good to hear." Bill waved at Jim. "Is your dad back to work?" "Yes sir. He's still moving a little slower than he used to but the doctors say that he's coming along just fine."

Steven asked Mrs. Dunham about the rose bush. "Mrs.

Sallie, did you order a plant and have it shipped to us?" "No. I don't think so. What color is it? You know, I could use another bush." "I don't know about the color. There was no tag on it." Mrs. Dunham responded, "Well, if somebody doesn't claim it, I'll be glad to plant it here with mine." Steven agreed.

Bill spoke up and said, "Steven, everyone sure misses your mother. She was a wonderful person." Steven said, "Yes sir. I miss her too." Bill said, "I remember when we were in high school together." Steven was shocked. "You went to school with my mother?" "Yes. You know of lot of us here in Pine Hills came from Mississippi when the paper mill was started. It was where the jobs were."

Steven was beside himself. He couldn't believe what he was hearing. "You mean that there are other people in Pine Hills who went to school with mother?" Bill said, "Well, I know a few. Bobby Baker, the dentist went to school with us. He was a senior when I was a sophomore. Mrs. Mattie Oliver was in our class. Do you know Mr. Byron Harvey who works over at the Gibson's Discount Store? He was a year or two behind us."

Steven didn't really know the other folks but he was more than excited to talk with Bill. "Mr. Bill can you tell me about mother? I mean, can you tell me what she was like, things she did?" "Sure. Let me help mother with her roses and I'll be glad to tell you what I can remember. You know I'm not as young as I used to be. That was forty years ago."

Steven ran back to the house. "Dad! Dad! Mr. Bill Dunham went to high school with mother. Can you believe it?" Jim said, "Well, isn't that something. You know, I was 7 years older than your mother and we all lived in different little towns that were spread out around the county. I guess I just missed knowing Bill." Steven said, "Mr. Bill told me that there are other people in Pine Hills who went to school with mother." "Is that right?" "Yes sir. I bet you somebody knows about mother's name."

Steven waited anxiously for Bill to finish helping his mother with her roses. When the two came to the porch, Bill said, "Steven, I need to get mother home. She's pretty tired from working in the field. Tell you what, I'll come by tomorrow afternoon and we can talk about Anne. Is that okay?" Steven agreed. "Yes sir. That's fine. Is three o'clock good for you?" "Yes. I'll be here then." "Mr. Bill, one more thing. Do you have a copy of your high school annual?" Bill laughed. "Oh I don't know. But I'll look for it tonight."

The Dunhams said their goodbyes and left. Steven went inside to call Sarah. "Sister, you're not going to believe this. Mr. Bill Dunham went to high school with mother. He's coming tomorrow afternoon to tell us what he remembers. Maybe you could come over. He'll be here about three o'clock." Sarah said, "Why don't I fix lunch for all of us and we can just stay at the house until Mr. Dunham comes?" "That'll be great. I'll tell dad. Hey sister, did you order a rose bush from California?" Sarah said, "No." "Well, Kirk delivered a rose that had no name on it and it was already paid for." Sarah responded, "It's probably for someone who has roses in the field. They will pick it up soon." Steven agreed and finished the call with his customary, "Love you sister." Sarah said, "Love you little brother."

It was lunch time. Steven grilled some hamburgers out on the porch. After lunch Jim went inside to take a nap and Steven stayed outside. He greeted everyone who came to

work with their flowers. He asked each of them about the unexpected rose but, no one claimed that it was theirs. Steven also asked anyone who looked his mother's age if they knew her when she was in school. Again, no luck.

Steven did have another encounter that afternoon that was rather puzzling. About four o'clock, three ladies that Steven did not recognize came to the back gate. The older woman looked as if she was in her early fifties. The younger woman appeared to be her daughter, and the young girl looked like a granddaughter. Steven welcomed the ladies. "Hello. Welcome to Carpenter Farms. Can I help you?" The daughter spoke up and said, "We're visiting family in the area and heard about your roses. We just wanted to come by and take a look if that's okay." "Sure. Come on in."

Steven asked, "Where are you from?" "My daughter and I live in Truitt. My mother lives in Mississippi." Addressing the older lady, Steven said, "My mother and dad are from Mississippi. Where do you live?" The daughter spoke up and said, "She lives in Hampton." Steven responded, "My cousin Ray Applewhite lives in Hampton. Do you know him?" The daughter said, "I don't think so." "My mother and father are from Taylor County outside Pearl Valley. I'm sure you know where that is." The older lady responded with a smile and a nod. Steven said, "Well, you can look around all you want. Let me know if I can help you with anything."

The ladies stayed in the field for about fifteen minutes. As they were leaving, Steven said, "It was good meeting you. I'm sorry but I didn't get your names." The older lady smiled and her daughter answered, "I'm Abigail Johnson. This is my mother Florence. The girl spoke up and said, "And my name is Mary." Steven said, "Well, again, it was good to meet you.

Come back anytime. We'll be here. God bless."

The ladies left and Steven went back to the house. Jim joined him on the porch. "Who were those ladies?" "They just wanted to see the roses. They are visiting family in Pine Hills." "I wonder who they're related to." "I don't know dad. The older woman never said a word. Her name is Florence. She lives in Hampton. Her daughter is Abigail Johnson. She and her daughter live in Truitt. Do you know them?" Jim thought for a moment. "No. I don't remember a Florence or an Abigail. That's when it hit him. Steven had not caught it at first. The woman's name was Abigail. He remembered the letter in the mail that referred to his mother as aunt Anne.

"Dad, do you remember the letter I asked you about from someone named, Abigail?" "Yes, son." "Maybe that's her." "Oh, I don't know, Steven. There are a lot of Abigails in this world." Steven felt that it was no coincidence. "Dad, I saw their car. I think I can go into town and find them. Jim said, "Wait a minute, son. You don't want someone to think that you're some kind of stalker." Steven knew that his dad was right but he couldn't help but think that the lady who came to visit was the lady who sent the letter.

Steven spent the rest of the afternoon helping a few others who came to work on their roses. He asked each one if they had ordered the plant that Kirk delivered earlier in the day. No one knew about the roses. About six o'clock Steven closed the barn and went inside. Jim had grilled enough hamburgers for supper and the two enjoyed a special time together.

Steven was still thinking about the unexpected rose and the unexpected visitors. He wondered if there was a connection between the two. Florence's reluctance to talk

with him seemed odd. He also realized that he had not gotten her last name. If her daughter was married, then Florence's name was not Johnson. Steven then took a leap of imagination and considered the possibility that her name was Gray. Maybe she was related to his mother. Perhaps that was why she was distant and silent.

Steven went to bed that night thinking of one thing, his meeting Sunday afternoon with Bill Dunham. He just knew that Bill had some answers about Anne. Steven fell asleep wondering what he would learn. Maybe Bill knew about his mother's name. Maybe he knew more. Steven couldn't wait.

Sunday morning, Jim and Steven went to church. Calvary Baptist was a wonderful congregation. Everyone had been so supportive since Anne's death. The pastor, Dr. Bailey, visited in the Carpenter home several times during and after Anne's illness. Jim and Steven were both still having a hard time being in church without Anne. It had been such an important part of her life. She was proud to have her family in church. The Carpenters sat in the same pew each Sunday – third row from the front on the right. It just wasn't the same without Anne.

After the service, Jim and Steven went home. Sarah cooked lunch along with everyone's favorite, apricot nectar cake, Anne's signature dessert. After lunch, Steven told Sarah about the three ladies who came to visit the farm. Sarah, like Jim, didn't seem too interested in the visitors but she was interested in the rose bush that Kirk delivered. She went outside with Steven to look at it.

Sarah started looking for a label that identified the species of the rose. Steven said, "There is no tag. Jim showed me the invoice. All we know is that it came from a grower in

California." "That's odd. Maybe we could call them tomorrow and see if they can tell us anything about it." "That's a great idea, sister!" "What's the name of the nursery?" "It came from a place called Legacy Roses in Fremont, California. Here's their number."

The two went back inside and waited anxiously for Bill Dunham to arrive. He showed up right at three o'clock. "Come in Mr. Bill. So good to see you." "Thank you, Steven. Hello, Sarah." "Hi, Mr. Dunham. Thank you for coming over." "Oh, no problem. I don't know if I can be of any help but I'll try." The three of them sat down at the dining room table.

Steven noticed immediately that Bill had brought a high school annual with him. He could not contain himself. "Mr. Bill is that your high school yearbook?" "Yes it is Steven. My wife found it in our old chifforobe. It's in pretty bad shape but all the pages are still in it." Bill handed the book to Sarah and Steven. They were both stunned to think that they were holding their mother's high school annual.

The forty year old cover had only a hint of its royal blue color remaining. The once vibrant gold lettering, The Pearl, had faded to a pale yellow. Bill spoke up, "I marked the pages that have pictures of Anne." Steven carefully opened the volume to the first tab. Sarah moved in closer to see. Bill pointed to the photo of a group of girls standing with two women who appeared to be teachers. The caption read, "Future Homemakers." Bill pointed to a girl on the front row. It was Anne.

Neither Steven nor Sarah said a word at first. They both just gazed at their mother's image. There she was. She was on the front row because of her stature. Anne was barely five

feet tall. Her wavy hair was rather long. She was wearing a knee length dress that had a ribbon sash at the waist. Soon Steven turned to the next page. There he saw a picture of the girls' basketball team. Sarah pointed to Anne, again on the front row. She was listed as a guard. It was the first time they saw her name listed as Anne Hill. Steven looked at Sarah. "Do you see her name?" "Yes." Bill asked, "What about her name?" Steven explained. "Mother's name on her social security card is Gray, Anne Gray." Bill looked surprised. Steven continued. "That's one of the questions we had for you. Do you have any idea why her name would be different? Did you know any of your classmates named Gray?"

Bill thought for a moment and said, "Well, let's look through the class photos." They began looking class by class. They first saw Bill's picture. Sarah said, "There you are Mr. Bill. You sure were handsome." Bill laughed. "Well, thank you. I lost my good looks a long time ago." They then saw that there were no Grays in Anne's class. Of course, they stopped to see Anne's senior picture. Sarah and Steven just stared at the photo.

After a moment, they continued looking. There were no Grays in the junior class or the sophomore class. But when they came to the freshman class, they found two girls named Gray. One was Francis and the other one was Florence. "Oh, my goodness." What is it Steven?" "That's her." "Who?" "Florence, Florence Gray. That's the lady who was here yesterday." "Are you sure?" "I'm positive. Oh my goodness. That's why she didn't say anything. And her daughter was named Abigail like the one who wrote that letter. I knew that they were hiding something. That lady is kin to mother. I just know she is."

Steven turned to Bill and asked, "Do you remember these two girls, Francis and Florence Gray?" Bill put his glasses on and looked closely at the pictures. "I don't know. They look like twins. Those names are not ringing a bell. Maybe I could ask my wife, Margie. They were in her class. See that's Margie, Margie Easley." Steven asked, "Can you call her now?" Bill smiled and said, "Sure."

While Bill called Margie, Steven looked through the annual to see if he could find other pictures of Francis and Florence. He thought that if he could find a group that one of the girls was in that it could help Margie remember them. "There she is, Florence. She played on the junior varsity basketball team." Steven ran to the phone. "Tell Mrs. Margie that Florence played on the girl's junior varsity basketball team."

"Florence played on the junior varsity basketball team. Does that help? Ok. Bye." "Well, did she remember them?" "Yes. Margie played on the team with Florence." "What else?" "Well, she remembered that the girls lived in the Rolling Hills community. Margie was from Pickwood. They all rode the same bus to school." "What else?" "Well, that's about it. She didn't remember their parents or any other brothers and sisters."

Steven was convinced that Florence Gray had visited the farm the day before. He looked at Sarah and said, "We have to find Florence Gray. She lives in Hampton." "But didn't you tell me that you don't know her married name?" "I don't know but we have to get in touch with her. I just know that she is the key to solving the mystery of mother's name. We have to find out who Florence was visiting in Pine Hills. Do you think that you could ask around?" "Sure. I'll start

tomorrow." "Great."

Sarah put on some coffee while Steven and Bill regrouped. "So what can you tell us about mother Mr. Bill?" "Well, Steven, your mother was just one of the nicest girls at the school. She never got in trouble. She was kind and considerate. I remember several occasions when teachers would use her as an example. They would be fussing at someone and say, "You need to be more like Anne." "I'm sure it embarrassed your mother and the teachers shouldn't have done that but Anne was a model for us all." Steven was enjoying the praise that Bill gave his mother.

Sarah came to the table with the coffee. "Mr. Bill, did mother go out on dates with the boys?" "Oh she went out some. You know in those days our parents were really strict. Most of the time we all went out on group dates. I think that I actually went out a few times with Anne and her cousins. I actually liked Ellie for a while. She was nice like your mother."

Sarah and Steven had not thought of the aunts being in the school annual. They opened it again and found several pictures of Ellie and Jennie. Both were active in school clubs. Ellie was in the Glee Club and Jennie was in the Thespian Society that produced the school plays. When Steven saw Jennie's club picture he saw Florence Gray again. Then it hit him. Maybe aunt Jennie knew who Florence Gray married. "Sister, call aunt Jennie right now." "What?" "Call aunt Jennie and ask her if she knows who Florence Gray married."

Sarah said, "Well, ok. Let me find her number." As Sarah searched for the number, Steven continued looking through the yearbook with Bill. "That's a picture of our football team. That's me, number fifty six. I was a linebacker. We had a pretty good team. We won a couple of district titles but no state championship. I enjoyed it though. I still stay in touch with some of the guys."

Steven was listening to Bill but frantically searching for some clue that could lead him to Florence Gray. Sarah found Jennie's number and Steven called her. "Aunt Jennie, this is Steven." "Well, hey dear." "Aunt Jennie I need to ask you about a girl who was in your high school class. Her name is Florence Gray. Do you remember her?" "Well, yes I do." "What can you tell me about her? Do you know who she married?" Jennie was silent for a moment and then she said, "Well, when we were seniors she dated a guy named Joseph. I don't know if they got married or not." Steven asked, "What was Joseph's last name?" "Oh, I don't know. Let me think. It was Walton or Walters, something like that. That was a long time ago Steven. Why are you interested in Florence Gray?"

Steven gave Jennie the short version of the story and thanked her for helping. He ran back to the table where Sarah and Bill were still looking through the annual. "Mr. Bill, do you remember a Joseph Walton or Joseph Walters?" "I don't think so. Let's look. Here's a Joseph Walker." "Keep looking." "None in the juniors. Here is, Franklin J. Walton." Steven said that must be him. The J is for Joseph. Do you remember him, Mr. Bill?" "No, I can't say that I do but, again, Margie might know him. I'll ask her when I go home."

Steven and Sarah knew that Bill was ready to leave. He offered to let them keep the annual with them for a few days and they agreed to take good care of it. When Bill left, Steven said, "Sarah, I'm going to call information right now to see if a Frank or Joseph Walton lives in Hampton. Maybe this is the key to finding Florence Gray and maybe it will open the door to find out about mother."

.even went to the phone, Sarah continued to look u.. ↓ the yearbook. She was fascinated at what high school life was like in the 1930s. She reflected on her own high school days and how different things must have been for her mother. Anne didn't have either of her parents to help her through those important years. Sarah thought of the support Anne provided for her. She wondered how her mother had gotten through. Seeing her mother active in sports and other activities did seem to indicate that Anne got through fairly well.

Jim woke up from his afternoon nap and came into the dining room. "Hi, daddy." "Hey, sugar. Where's Steven?" "He's on the phone trying to find someone that may have married the woman who visited yesterday." "That's a long shot, don't you think?" "Yes sir, but you know how obsessed Steven is with this thing about mother's name." "Yes I do."

Steven came running in. "I found him. I found him. Franklin Joseph Walton. He lives just outside Hampton in Petal. I'm going to call him right now." Jim spoke up, "Whoa. Wait a minute. Tell me what's going on." Steven replied, "Well, we found the lady who visited yesterday in mother's high school annual and aunt Jennie told us that she dated this man in high school. And I found him." "Aunt Jennie? High school? Don't you think this is a bit of a stretch?" "It's the only lead we have dad."

Jim didn't want to pour cold water on Steven's enthusiasm but the chances of these people knowing something about Anne's name were slim to none. Jim also didn't want to get people angry with annoying phone calls. "Come sit down for a minute. If you get the man or his wife on the phone, what are you going to say?" "Well, I'll ask the woman if she was the one who came by yesterday and then I'll ask her if she remembers mother." "Then what?" I'll ask her if she knows anything about mother's name."

Jim was very reluctant to let Steven make the call. But he could see that his son was so determined that he would probably call without permission some other time. So he said, "Ok. I'll let you call them. But you have to be very careful not to offend these people. Do you understand?" "Yes sir. I'll be as nice as can be."

Steven brought the phone from the kitchen over to the table and dialed the number. After a few rings a man answered. "Hello. Walton residence." "Mr. Walton, this is Steven Carpenter from Pine Hills. How are you?" "I'm fine. What can I do for you?" "Well Mr. Walton, I'm trying to find some information on my mother Anne Carpenter. I think your wife went to school with her and I need to talk with Mrs. Florence. Is she there?" "No. She's spending the weekend with our daughter Abigail."

That's when Steven knew that he had found Florence Gray. "Mr. Walton, is that your daughter who lives in Truitt?" "Yes. Do you know Abby?" "Yes sir, I met her, Mrs. Florence, and your granddaughter yesterday. They were at our farm in Pine Hills. As I said before, my mother went to school with Mrs. Florence and we're trying to trying to gather some information about her. When will Mrs. Walton be returning?" "She should be back late tonight." "Do you think I could call her tomorrow afternoon?" "I don't see why not. Better yet, I'll have her call you, say about six o'clock. Is that good?" "Yes sir,"

Mr. Walton asked, "By the way, who is your mother?" "Anne Gray. I mean Anne Hill." "Oh, I knew your mother.

Short, athletic ball player. She was something." "Yes sir."
"How is she?" "Mother died in December." "Oh. I am so
sorry. I didn't know. Well, I'll tell Flo to call you tomorrow at
six." "Thank you Mr. Walton."

Sarah said, "Well, that sounded like good news." "Yes.
She'll call tomorrow evening at six o'clock." Sarah said,
"Well, Richard is off from work tomorrow night. I could
come over." "That's good sister." Jim spoke up. "You two are
hopeless. You're not going to stop until you find something
no matter what it is. It's okay. I'm a little curious myself."
They were all hoping that Florence Walton would have some
answers about Anne.

Steven went through his Monday with only one thing on
his mind. Florence Walton was calling at six o'clock. He
arrived home from working at the hospital around five
fifteen. Jim cooked a pot roast and Sarah made an apple pie.
Richard and the kids had come with Sarah and everyone
enjoyed the family time together around the table.

When they finished eating, Allen and Dawn went
upstairs with Richard to do their homework. It was ten
minutes before six. Steven brought the phone from the hall to
the kitchen and the three of them sat down at the breakfast
table to wait for the call. Steven spoke up. "I think that Mrs.
Walton is the key to us finding the truth about mother." "I
sure hope so little brother." "Dad, do you think Mrs. Walton
can help us?" "I don't know, Sarah. I don't remember them.
They are all a little younger than I am. But maybe they
remember something about your mother."

The minute hand on the kitchen clock finally moved to
twelve. It was time. Everyone waited in anticipation for the
phone to ring. It didn't. Five after six and nothing. Steven

said, "Why do you think she hasn't called, dad?" "Give her some time son. Maybe she had something come up." At ten after six, Sarah looked a little concerned. "Steven, are you sure she was calling tonight? It was seven o'clock tonight?" "Yes. Mr. Walton said that she would call tonight at six." It was a quarter after six and nothing. Steven said, "Well, I think I'll just call them." Jim said, "Oh, I don't think that's a good idea, son." "Why dad?" "Well, you don't want to offend Mrs. Walton. Let's give it a few more minutes." Steven was frustrated but agreed with his father's wisdom. The last thing they wanted to do was aggravate someone who might have some information about Anne.

Sarah put a pot of coffee on while they waited for the call. Richard came down downstairs and joined the rest at the table. "No call yet?" "No brother-in-law. She hasn't called." Just then the phone rang. Steven picked it up. "Hello. Mrs. Walton?" "Steven is that you? This is Letha." "Oh, hi aunt Letha." Letha detected the disappointment in his voice. "Is everything ok?" "Yes, mam. We're expecting an important call. I'm sorry. Can I help you?" "Oh, no. I won't keep you long. Did Kirk Walker deliver a rose bush to your house?" "Yes mam. He did." "Good. Would it be okay if I come by tomorrow afternoon and plant it?" "Sure. We didn't know whose it was." "I'll be there about three thirty. See you then."

Sarah asked, "What did aunt Letha want?" "She asked about the rose bush that Kirk delivered. It must be hers. She's coming by tomorrow afternoon to plant it." Steven turned to Jim and asked, "Well, what are we supposed to do? It's six thirty and she hasn't called." "I don't know, son. The lady may not want to talk with you or maybe she doesn't

know anything about your mother." Steven said, "But Mr. Walton knew mother. He told me what she looked like and he remembered that she played ball. Just let me call. I won't bother them with a lot of questions. I'll just ask Mrs. Walton if she remembers mother. Nothing else. How about that?"

Jim could see the desperation on Steven's face. He agreed to let him call Mrs. Walton. "Okay, son. You can call her. But don't badger her with a lot of questions if she doesn't want to talk with you." "Thanks, dad." Steven picked up the phone immediately and dialed the number. It rang several times and then someone picked up. "Hello? Mrs. Walton?" No one responded and the line went dead. Steven just stared into space. Sarah asked, "What happened?" Steven picked up the phone again and started dialing. "Maybe I called the wrong number." Again, someone picked up on the other end but hung up almost immediately.

Steven was confused. "I don't understand. I checked the number. It's the one I called yesterday. Somebody picks up but they won't answer. Sarah looked at her father and Richard. Everyone but Steven understood that Mrs. Walton didn't want to talk to him. Richard spoke up. "It's okay bud. Your momma was a wonderful person. She helped people all her life. Nobody cared as much as she did." Steven appreciated the sentiments but something was wrong. Why didn't Mrs. Walton want to talk with him about Anne? Why did she come by the farm? What did she know? More questions. No answers.

Sarah and her family left at about eight thirty. Jim went to bed early and Steven finished his homework around ten. After a late night snack, Steven went to bed but wasn't able to fall asleep. All types of scenarios kept running through his mind. Maybe Mrs. Walton had a secret that she didn't want exposed. But what did it have to do with Anne? Perhaps she and Anne were related. Maybe they were sisters. Steven wasn't going to give up but his body finally gave in and he fell asleep.

The past few days had been fascinating. The unexpected rose was still a mystery. The unexpected visitors ended up being an unexpected lead. The developments had reenergized the family in their search for answers about Anne. What they did not realize was that soon they would learn an unexpected truth.

My Field of Roses

Part 2

8   *The Rose Tells Her Story*

The next morning, while Steven was getting ready for school, the phone rang. "Hello." "Good morning little brother. How are you?" "I'm ok." Sarah could hear the lack of enthusiasm in his voice. "Are you still down about the Waltons?" "Yes. I just don't understand why she didn't call or wouldn't answer the phone." "I know. Oh well. Hey, I called to let you know that I'm coming by this afternoon to meet aunt Letha and help her plant the new rose bush. You're not working after school today, are you?" "No. I'll be here." "Good. I'll see you then. Have a great day. Love you bigger than big." "Love you too, sister. Bye."

Jim came in the kitchen and asked, "Who was that?" "It was sister. She's coming by this afternoon to help aunt Letha with the new rose bush." "Good. Are you ready for the day?" "Yes, sir. Nothing special. How about you?" "I have a meeting at four to show the Main Street building. I'll pick up some Chinese for us if that's good with you." "Yes, sir. That's fine." "Enjoy your day, son." "You too, dad."

Steven's Monday was filled with the routines of class,

teachers, assignments, and more. Early in the semester, Steven's grades dropped below his normally high average. Anne's death had certainly affected his focus on school work. He was doing better now and seemed to be back on track with his grades. He also had his eye on a new girl named Tonya. She was from south Louisiana. Her family moved to Pine Hills in January. Tonya was in Steven's eleven o'clock speech class. He considered it the highlight of his day.   After school, Steven headed home to help Sarah and his aunt Letha plant the new rose. When he arrived home, Letha and Sarah were inside at the breakfast table. Steven gave them both a hug and went to the refrigerator for some milk and a snack. "Are we ready to plant the new rose?" Sarah spoke up and said, "Yes. But aunt Letha has something to share with us first."

When Steven sat down he noticed that Sarah and Letha looked as if they had been crying. "Is something wrong? Is dad okay? What's going on?" Sarah spoke up and said, "No. Nothing's wrong. Aunt Letha wants to tell us about the new rose." "Oh. Okay." "Steven, you know how much your mother loved roses." "Yes, mam." "Well, when Anne first knew how sick she was, she wanted to do something for you and Sarah that would help you remember her and how much she loved you." Sarah and Steven both began to cry. Every day of their lives their mother expressed her love for them. Now, even though she was gone, she was still sharing her love.

Letha continued. "So, your mother contacted a grower in California who develops new varieties of roses. She told him what she wanted in the rose and he started working on it. The bush that is outside is the first one the grower produced. It's called Anne's Love." Steven was simply overwhelmed

with emotion. Memories of his mother's love flooded his mind and filled his heart. "She was always thinking about us, helping us, loving us. I miss her so much." Sarah hugged her little brother as he continued to weep.

After a few moments, Letha reached into her purse and retrieved an envelope. It was addressed to Steven and Sarah. Steven immediately recognized his mother's handwriting and looked at Sarah. "Yes, Steven. It's a letter from mother." Steven took the envelope and rubbed it gently with his fingers. It was as if he was holding Anne's hand. He took the letter out and began reading.

My dear Sarah and Steven. I love you with all of my being. I am so sorry that we have been separated from one another. I cannot imagine how difficult it is for you. Remember what I shared with you on countless occasions. God is always as close as the mention of His name. The rose that you have received is named Anne's Love. It represents my love for the two of you and your dad. I pray that it will remind you of my love when you enjoy its blooms. I promise you that God is going to see you through this time. Enjoy the rest of your life knowing that I am watching down from Heaven and waiting for the day when we can be together again. My love to you forever.   Mother

Steven finished the letter but could not take his eyes off it. Tears fell from his cheeks onto the page. Finally, he looked up at Sarah and Letha. His anguish had subsided. He had a smile of contentment on his face. "I'm so glad that she wrote this to us." Sarah agreed.

After a few more moments, Letha spoke up and said,

"Why don't we go out to the field and I'll show you where your mother wanted the rose planted." They gathered up everything they needed and headed to the top of the ridge next to where the first rose had been planted twenty years before. It was a perfect place for Anne's Love. The spot overlooked the entire field. Steven felt that his mother chose the hill as a sign that she was watching over them.

Sarah gently unwrapped the covering and checked the plant to make sure that everything was okay. Steven dug the hole and helped Letha set the bush in place. Once they covered the roots, Sarah gave the soil a good watering. They were done. The three stood silently for a long time. Each reflected on the life of a good friend and a wonderful mother. After a while, a cool, refreshing breeze came down the hill. Steven closed his eyes and said under his breath, "Yes, mother. I love you too." Soon they walked back through the field, crossed the bridge, and stored their tools. Letha said, "I'm going on home. I'll talk with you soon. I love you." "Love you aunt Letha. Thanks for everything."

When Sarah and Steven went in, Jim had arrived with supper from the Peking Palace. Steven asked, "Dad, did you know about the rose?" Jim nodded. "Yes. Letha told me about it this morning when she came by with a letter from your mother." Anne had also written to Jim. The three enjoyed the meal, spending most of their time talking about Anne. When they finished, Sarah and Steven noticed that Jim went out the back door and headed to the field. They watched as he made his way up the ridge to the place where they planted Anne's Love. Jim stayed there until the sun went down.

On Saturday, dozens of friends from the community

came to tend their roses. The field had actually become a place where everyone could come together and enjoy life. Pine Hills was just like every other small town. It had its problems. People are people you know. But the field seemed to bring folks together. No fussing there. No disagreements. It was a place of calm and peace. Often when people finished working on their roses, they would sit by the stream or up by the house and visit for a while. The field seemed to be like an oasis, a refreshing place for the soul.

Steven was always intrigued by the way the field had that calming effect on people. He concluded that it was something more than just the roses. The field evidently had some special meaning to everyone. He couldn't understand what it was but he was glad that it drew people to the farm.

As Steven helped friends that morning, he told them all about the rose that Anne sent. Mrs. Beth Breland came by at about nine o'clock. "Hi, Mrs. Breland. How are you this morning? "Oh, I'm fine Steven. How about the Carpenters?" "We're well. Can I help you with something?" "You sure could. I need a little fertilizer for my roses up on the hill."

Mrs. Breland was one of the first to plant a rose in the field. She actually had three. They were some of the most beautiful in the field. One was a dainty, soft pink English tea rose. Another was a damask rose which had white and lavender petals. The most notable Mrs. Breland planted was a dazzling yellow, apricot and red floribunda variety. It attracted several photographers and even one artist who stayed in the field all day trying to capture its beauty on canvas.

Steven filled the wheelbarrow with fertilizer and followed Mrs. Breland to the top of the ridge. On the way, he shared the story of Anne's Love. "Mother had a rose commissioned for us before she died. I'll show it to you when we get to the top of the hill. She named it Anne's Love." "That's so nice. You know, Steven, your mother was an incredible woman. She and I taught Sunday School together for years. You were just a baby back then. She was so proud that she finally had her little boy." Steven smiled. Mrs. Breland continued. "I remember when she first brought you to church. I've never seen a more proud mother in all my life. We all understood because, Lord knows, she had waited for you long enough. Yes, she was sure proud of her little Steven."

When they reached the top of the ridge, Steven helped Mrs. Breland with the fertilizer. When they finished, he took her to see his mother's new rose. "Here it is. Isn't it beautiful? The two stood there for a moment in silence. Anne had been such an important part of their lives. At one point, Beth could see that Steven was overwhelmed with emotion. The two embraced. Beth let Steven know of her continued prayers and promised that time would help with the hurt.

After the two made their way back to the barn and said their goodbyes, Steven headed to the house. When he went in, his dad and Sarah were sitting at the kitchen table. "Hey little brother." "Hey sister." Steven grabbed a coke from the fridge and sat down. He noticed that Sarah had been crying. "What's wrong?" Jim said, "Nothing's wrong, son. We just have something to give you from your mother." Steven was confused. "Something from mother?" "Yes. It seems that the last month before she died she wrote down some things about her life when she was younger."

Steven was in shock. "Have you read it? Does it tell us

what happened with her name? Where is it?" Sarah took the notebook from her lap and laid it in front of Steven on the table. It was a simple, yellow spiral notebook, the kind a child uses for school. Steven picked it up and just stared at it for a moment. "How did you get it?" "Aunt Letha brought it when she came to plant the rose. Dad read it first and then I did."

Once again, Steven turned his attention to the notebook. He opened it and immediately recognized his mother's handwriting. Tears came to his eyes. For the past several months he had felt so disconnected from his mother. She was gone and wasn't coming back. Now, it seemed as if she was close to him again.

"Go ahead, son. You can take it with you. Keep it as long as you want to." Steven asked, "Does it answer our questions? You know, about her name?" "Yes. It provides all the answers and so much more." Steven couldn't believe it. He thought that he would find someone who knew his mother's story not knowing that she would tell it herself. He took the notebook and went on the back porch.

Steven sat in his mother's favorite rocking chair and opened the notebook. He placed his hand on the first page and began to read his mother's story. "Most of what I know about my early life I learned from my aunt, Mabel Henry. She and her husband, Robert, took me in when I was three years old. The Henry's owned the general store in Norman, Mississippi. Mabel was the finest Christian woman I have ever known. She treated me as if I was her own daughter. She was a great listener and had a peaceful, calm spirit about her.

Uncle Robert was a kind and gentle man who loved to talk with people. His gift of gab and warm personality were a rare combination that endeared him to everyone who knew him. But from time to time, he also enjoyed a bit of mischievousness, pulling practical jokes on aunt Mabel, the girls, and me. His girls are your aunts. Willie, Jennie, and Ellie. They were the best part of my life as a child. I can't tell you how much they meant to me. They made me feel like I was their fourth sister. I'll tell you more about them later.

Now, my story. When I was about ten years old, I remember asking aunt Mabel about my mother and father. I assumed that they died when I was young. Several in my class at school lost their parents when they were young. In those days we didn't have the health care that we have today. People died from infections, the flu, pneumonia, and other diseases that were fatal then. Some died from tuberculosis. It was not unusual for people to die in their forties or fifties.

So I asked aunt Mabel to take me to the cemetery where I could see my parents' graves. She told me that my father died in the war and that his body was never recovered. She said that my mother couldn't handle the loss and just left one day. She never came back. My mother's name, by the way, was Emma.

Evidently, I lived on a farm with my grandparents and aunt Macy for a while. I really don't remember much about them but aunt Mabel told me that they were wonderful, godly people. Grandpaw George ran the local cotton gin and had a small farm of his own. Grandmaw Eliza raised their five children. My mother was the youngest of the children. By the time I was born, my grandparents were well into their sixties. When grandpaw died and grandmaw started having health problems aunt Mabel and uncle Robert decided to let me live with them.

I do remember being sad about the whole situation but I

also remember that over and over again, aunt Mabel would say, "Honey, the only thing that matters is that we love you, the Lord loves you, and God has a wonderful plan for your life." Aunt Mabel was right. Love was all I needed. I just didn't realize it then.

9   *Four Little Rascally Roses*

The fondest memories of my childhood were the times I spent with Willie, Jennie, and Ellie. We were inseparable. Willie was the oldest but she certainly wasn't the boldest. That title was held by Jennie. She talked all the time and was the most likely one to get us all into some kind of trouble. Ellie was the steady one. Ellie had more common sense than the rest of us put together. Me? Well, I don't know if I can provide an objective opinion of what I was like as a child but I was always thinking about how I could help people in need. Maybe it was because I was the one in need and people took care of me. I don't know. But life sure was good in those early years.

It's funny what you remember about your childhood. Sometimes you can recall the details of little insignificant things more than you can the important events of your life. When I think of us girls, I think of all the fun and funny times we had. Every morning aunt Mabel would wake us up at six o'clock. I was always the first one to get dressed and ready for breakfast. I would help set the table and bring uncle Robert

his first cup of coffee. He would take that first sip and say, "Anne, you make the best coffee in Taylor County." He knew that I had not made the coffee but he always tried to make me feel good about myself. I could never repay that man for all he did for me.

When everyone finally got to the table for breakfast, uncle Robert made us hold hands and pray. Every morning he led us in the same prayer and we all said it out loud. "Heavenly Father, we thank you for this day. Please help us along our way to be faithful, kind and true, and to live our lives for you. We thank you for this meal, for the farmers and their fields. Bless us all today, in Jesus' name we pray."

At that time, like most young children, I just said the prayer without thinking about it. Later, of course, it meant much more to me. Uncle Robert and aunt Mabel were an important part of my faith journey. I thank God every day for their influence on my life.

After breakfast, aunt Mabel would check us over one more time to make sure that we were ready to go. Then she gave us our lunch bags and we walked to the bus stop. If it was raining, she would load us up in uncle Robert's old truck and drive us to the bus stop. The old truck was actually an old delivery truck that uncle Robert kept so aunt Mabel could join him at the store about mid-morning. It was the truck that all of us used to learn how to drive. I'll tell you more about that later.

Our ride to school took about thirty minutes. Mrs. Harriet Stoner was our bus driver. She was a wonderful lady. She was about the same age as aunt Mabel and had two boys of her own, Dale and Ricky. Mrs. Stoner would let us talk on the bus but she didn't allow any foolishness. She was always looking in that big mirror to see what was going on.

I remember one day when she caught Ben Stewart pulling Ellie's hair. She stopped the bus, marched back where Ben was sitting, and yanked him up by his ear. All the way to the front of the bus she was fussing him out. Ben was jumping around like a catfish caught on a hook. "Ouch! Ouch! Oh, I'm sorry Mrs. Stoner. I'm sorry. I'll never do it again." Mrs. Stoner acted as if she didn't hear a word he said. She drug him to the seat right behind hers and yelled, "You're going to sit here for a week Ben Stewart, all by yourself! Now apologize to Ellie."

Ellie was bent over, laughing as hard but as quietly as she could. We all were. Ben, still holding his blood-red ear, said, under his breath, "I'm sorry." Mrs. Stoner said, "I don't think she heard you." Jennie spoke up and said, "No mam we didn't hear him." Mrs. Stoner turned and gave Jennie one of those looks, you know, like, if you say another word I'm going to come back there and get you too. Jennie buried her face in her sweater and got real quiet which was a rarity for her.

Ben spoke up and said, "I'm sorry for pulling your hair." Mrs. Stoner said, "Say it again." Ben apologized again. Then Mrs. Stoner said, "Stand up. Say it one last time and this time call her by name and tell her that you'll never do it again." Ben hesitated at first but then stood and said rather quickly. "I am sorry for pulling your hair Ellie Henry and I will never do it again." "That's good", said Mrs. Stoner. "Now, let's get to school and have a great day."

Well, it was a great day for all of us girls. We told everybody in school what happened. For several months after that, when we saw Ben in the hallway at school, we would

smile at him and pull our ears, reminding him of the day that he got caught in more ways than one.

I really loved school. I guess I loved learning. Jennie loved school because she had people to talk with all day. I remember thinking that I'd love to be a teacher one day. Sometimes in the afternoon when we were at the house, I'd get the girls to play school with me. Of course, I was always the teacher. I don't think that they really enjoyed being students after a full day at school but they went along with it anyway.

One thing that most of us remember about school is our teachers. Like everyone else, I had some great teachers, some not-so-great teachers, several nice teachers, some mean teachers, and a few teachers who were just strange.

One of my favorite teachers was Mrs. Hancock, my fourth grade teacher. Back in those days, elementary teachers taught every subject to their class. Your history teacher was also your math teacher and your English teacher. Mrs. Hancock was smart and she made learning fun. She said things that made us think. One day during a history lesson she said, "All of you in this class are going to make history. As a matter of fact, you're making history right now." At first, we didn't understand what she was saying, but soon she explained what she meant. I remember going home that day thinking, I am making history.

Another one of my favorite teachers was Mrs. Bynum. She taught physical education when I was in the 8th grade. Back then, eighth grade was the beginning of high school for us. We only went to school for eleven years. In Mrs. Bynum's class we exercised a lot and played basketball and softball. For some reason, I was very good at sports. I didn't consider myself a tomboy but I loved playing ball. Mrs. Bynum was a great encourager. I had self-esteem problems in high school and she helped me through those tough days.

One of the strangest teachers I had was Mrs. Collins. She taught fifth grade. She was, evidently, sick a lot and had to take cough medicine during class. After lunch she talked real slowly and would sometimes fall asleep while we were reading. One day I mentioned it to aunt Mabel. She got an odd look on her face and said that we should pray for Mrs. Collins and that we shouldn't talk about people's illnesses. Later I found out that Mrs. Collins' cough syrup was mostly alcohol. Mrs. Collins wasn't sick. She was drunk.

The girls and I had so much fun at school during lunch. We would quickly eat our sandwiches and either talk or play. At our school the girls stayed on one half of the yard and the boys stayed on the other half. There was a sidewalk that separated the two sides. Teachers served as yard monitors to make sure that no one crossed over. If you ever got caught on the wrong side, you had to clean erasers after school.

Jennie, of course, always pushed the limits on the rules. When she was in the sixth grade, she had a crush on Billy Talbot. He was in the seventh grade. Jennie talked about him all the time. One day she told us that she developed a plan that would get Billy's attention. I think it was on a Tuesday when she decided to put her plan into action.

When Jennie saw that Billy was close to the sidewalk, she had one of her friends throw a ball that way. She ran after the ball, crossed the sidewalk, and ran right into Billy. She went to the ground and acted as if she had hurt her ankle. Billy, of course, reached down to help her up. Well, she thought that she was in Heaven. Billy was holding her up, felt

sorry for her, and was apologizing for running into her.

About that time, Mrs. Wilson, Jennie's teacher, showed up to assess the situation. She bent down to look at Jennie's ankle. "Well, it isn't bruised or swollen Jennie." "Oh, it hurts real bad Mrs. Wilson." "I don't know. See if you can put some weight on it." All this time Billy was still holding her up. Jennie acted as if she just couldn't put any weight on her ankle.

It was then that Doris Swilling came running up to the scene of the accident. Doris was Jennie's partner in crime. She was the one who threw the ball Jennie's way. Doris was a sweet girl but she was not the brightest star in the sky. Without thinking she shouted, "It worked Jennie! It worked!"

That's when Mrs. Wilson stood up. Doris, of course, had not seen Mrs. Wilson. Mrs. Wilson then asked, "What worked, Doris?" Well, Doris almost had a heart attack. She made up some story but we could tell that Mrs. Wilson didn't believe a word of it. Mrs. Wilson looked over her glasses, raised her eyebrow, and said, "Let's get you to the nurse's station Jennie. Doris, you come along with us."

I don't know how the conversation went at the nurse's station but that afternoon Jennie and Doris were outside cleaning erasers. They cleaned erasers for two whole weeks. Every day, when they got on the bus, they had chalk all over them. It was on their clothes, in their hair, everywhere. Jennie told us later that Mrs. Wilson gave them a tongue lashing like they never had before. It didn't cure Jennie but it kept her out of trouble for several months which was pretty good for her.

Every day after school, the bus dropped us off at uncle Robert's store. We would each get a soda pop and a snack. I can still remember everybody's favorite flavors. Of course, we all liked Coca Cola but some new drinks came out about that time. Ellie and I liked what was called Grape Nehi. Willie liked Hire's Root Beer, and Jennie just loved Orange Crush. Sometimes she would walk around the store with her orange tongue poked out saying, "I just had an orange crush. Do you want an orange crush? I just love orange crush."

After we had our snack, we helped aunt Mabel stock the shelves. We took groceries to the car for older customers, and we spent the rest of the time saying hello to everyone. On slow days when we didn't have much to do, we would play games like hide and seek. Uncle Robert didn't mind. He loved to see us having fun. He often called us his Four Little Rascally Roses.

I remember one afternoon at the store when it was pouring down rain. Ellie came in from the back with a dog. It was a very large hound dog. He was a white and grey Catahoula with blue eyes. You could tell that he had been on his own for a while. He was scruffy and thin and soaking wet. Ellie just couldn't help herself. She loved animals. She was always trying to find homes for stray cats and dogs and she just couldn't let this dog sit out in the bad weather.

Well, Ellie knew that uncle Robert wouldn't want a dog in the store but she brought him in anyway. Uncle Robert was at the meat counter slicing some ham and aunt Mabel was at the register. Ellie tried to find a place to hide the dog. She planned to take him home with her after closing time but had to hide him until then.

Ellie tied the dog to a rack of little girl dresses and bonnets. Why, I don't know. She was headed to get the dog some meat scraps from the back when the chaos began.

Evidently, the dog was hungry and could smell the meat that uncle Robert was cutting. He started pulling on the clothes rack. Pretty soon he was dragging it through the store. Oh my goodness. He turned over several displays and knocked over the women's glove rack.

Then he started barking and scared all the customers. Ladies were screaming. Little children were crying. Others were running for their lives. Uncle Robert came out from behind the meat counter to see the dog running toward him with one of the little dresses draped all over him. I was sitting on the stairs in the back of the store watching the whole scene. Aunt Mabel panicked and jumped up on the counter. She started hollering, "Catch him Robert! Catch him!"

Well, Uncle Robert wasn't going to have to catch him because the dog was running straight for him. He wanted some of that ham uncle Robert was slicing. As the dog reached the meat counter uncle Robert lunged forward and tackled the hound. The clothes on the rack flew everywhere. When it was all over, uncle Robert and dog were on the floor wearing little girl's dresses and bonnets. The dog was eating the sliced ham and uncle Robert wasn't happy. It was a sight to see.

Uncle Robert shouted, "Who brought this dog inside the store?" No one said anything at first but then Jennie spoke up and said, "Well it sure wasn't me. I'm not the one who loves animals." That was Jennie's way of saying that it was Ellie. Uncle Robert shouted, "Ellie where are you? Did you bring that dog into the store?" Ellie had run up on the stairs with me to escape from the mayhem. Aunt Mabel called out, "Ellie. Ellie Henry. You get over here right now."

Ellie walked down the stairs and slowly went over to

where uncle Robert was on the floor with the dog. "Is this your animal?" "Well, he's not really mine." "Did you bring him in my store?" "Yes sir. I'm so sorry daddy but it was raining outside and I just couldn't leave him out there to drown." Ellie knew that the dog wasn't going to drown but it was the best she could think to say at the moment.

About that time, aunt Mabel got down from the counter and walked over to where uncle Robert was on the floor. He had a little bonnet on his head and a dress over his shirt. Well, aunt Mabel just started laughing. She laughed so hard I thought she was going to pass out. The sight of uncle Robert dressed in little girl's clothes was hilarious.

Ellie wasn't sure what to do. She just knew that it was one of the funniest things that she ever saw but she also knew that she was in big trouble. After a minute or two, uncle Robert looked down at his newly donned dress. He reached up on his head to find the bonnet, and he started laughing too. Everyone in the store joined in the hilarity. A couple of the men helped uncle Robert up from the floor. He walked over to Ellie, gave her a big hug, and said, "It's okay honey. Just keep the dog outside."

That was certainly a day that none of us ever forgot. I remember that it came up years later at one of our family reunions. Jennie, of course, told the story. Uncle Robert was much older then but when Jennie was finished, uncle Robert smiled, reached up to his head, and tipped his bonnet. By the way, Ellie kept that old hound for several years until he finally died. She named him Buster but uncle Robert always called him Trouble.

10   *The Roses and Old Rusty*

Earlier, I mentioned uncle Robert's old truck. It wasn't like an open pickup truck. It was a panel truck that uncle Robert used to deliver eggs and milk before he opened the store. He had affectionately nicknamed the truck Old Rusty. It had about half of the white paint left on it and the rest of it was red. Not red paint. Red rust. Hence the name, Old Rusty.

When we were little, aunt Mabel would take us out in the field, put us on her lap, and let us steer the old truck as if we were actually driving it. Sometimes Jennie wouldn't watch what she was doing and aunt Mabel would have to take the wheel before we ran into a fence or hit one of the cows.

When we were old enough to reach the pedals, aunt Mabel took us out and let us practice driving. We started on the cattle trails behind the house. It was actually very hard to drive the old truck because it was a standard shift. You had to push the clutch in and change the gear all at the same time. Willie and I had the hardest time getting that right. I know that aunt Mabel thought that we were going to break the old thing before we learned how to drive it. We would either let the clutch out too quickly or we would let the clutch out too slowly and rev the engine to its limit.

Ellie and Jennie seemed to get the hang of it pretty quickly. But Jennie, as usual, found ways to get in trouble with the old truck. One day when aunt Mabel rode into town with uncle Robert, Jennie decided that she was going to get in the truck and drive over to Billy Warren's house. It was actually just down the road from our house but Jennie never drove the truck without aunt Mabel. I tried to tell her not to do it but she was bound and determined to see Billy.

It had rained real hard earlier that day and the old dirt road was very slippery. So, sure enough, Jennie got halfway to Billy's and slid off the road into the ditch. She ran back to our house and got us to come and try to push the truck back up on the road. Well, when we got there we saw that the truck was up to its axle in mud.

Willie just started pacing back and forth saying, "Oh, this isn't good. You are in some kind of trouble Jennie Henry. This is bad." The first thing Ellie said was, "Well, I'm not getting in that mud and ruining my good clothes to save you." All I knew was that we were never going to get that truck up on the road by ourselves. We needed some big time help.

Jennie almost lost her mind. "Oh, Anne, I just don't know what to do. Uncle Robert is going to kill me. I'll never be able to drive again. They'll send me away to some school and I'll never see you all again." That's the way Jennie responded to every crisis that might have some negative consequences for her.

The only thing I thought of was that the Dukes family

lived right down the road between our house and the Warren's place. Mr. Dukes owned a wrecker truck that he used to haul broken down vehicles to his garage. I told Jennie that I would go down to the Dukes' house and ask Mrs. Dukes to call the garage and see if her husband could come and pull the old truck out of the ditch.

I ran as fast as I could to the Dukes' house and told Mrs. Dukes about the situation. She called her husband at the garage and he said that he could come right over. I thanked Mrs. Dukes and ran back to tell Jennie the good news. Jennie said, "That's great! We can take the truck back home and wash it before uncle Robert knows that anything happened."

Well, you're not going to believe what happened. After about fifteen minutes we saw Mr. Dukes coming up the road. What we didn't see was that he had someone with him. When he stopped, guess who got out of the wrecker. It was uncle Robert.

Jennie almost died. She started crying. "I'm so sorry daddy. I'm so sorry. I'll never do it again. I'll never do it again. It was all my fault. Anne told me not to do it but I did." It was one of the only times that Jennie told the whole truth about something that she did wrong. Most of the time she made excuses or said that one of us had done it. This time she knew that we wouldn't take the blame and so she confessed.

Uncle Robert looked to see if the truck had any serious damage. Mr. Dukes started hooking the truck up to his wrecker. Jennie just kept crying and apologizing. I looked at Willie and Ellie and said, "I don't think this is going to end well." They agreed.

After Mr. Dukes pulled the truck up on the road, uncle

Robert thanked him and paid him for his services. Then we all waited to see what was going to happen next. Uncle Robert cleared his voice, looked over the top of his glasses and said, "Jennie, that is one of the dumbest things you have ever done." He was right and Jennie had done some real dumb things but this one took the cake.

Uncle Robert spent the next ten minutes telling Jennie all the bad things that could have happened to her. She just cried. "Yes sir. I know. Yes sir. You're right. Yes sir. I'm sorry." When he was finished fussing her out, Uncle Robert hugged her, told her that he was so thankful that she wasn't hurt, and that he loved her.

For some reason, Jennie thought that uncle Robert's sentiments meant that she wasn't going to be punished. She got a big grin on her face, looked over at us, and winked. Then she said, "I love you too daddy. Let's go home." But Uncle Robert wasn't quite finished. He said, "Jennie because I love you so much, I'm going to help you learn a valuable lesson from this episode." We could see that Jennie didn't quite understand what uncle Robert was getting at because she said, "Yes daddy, I have learned a valuable lesson from this experience." Uncle Robert said, "No, honey, I'm going to teach you an important lesson from this experience."

Well, when uncle Robert was finished with his teaching, Jennie was doing a lot of chores. She had to do everybody's work for two weeks. She had to wash and iron all the clothes. She had to mop the floors and wash the dishes. Jennie also had to work in the store on Saturdays for a month. And she couldn't drive the truck again until uncle Robert said so.

When uncle Robert was finished with his list, Jennie started trying to negotiate some of the terms but uncle

Robert cleared his voice, looked over his glasses again, and Jennie shut up. Ellie, Willie, and I didn't say a word. We knew that if we made fun of Jennie that we might meet the same fate. So, we all hopped in the truck. Uncle Robert drove us home and Mr. Dukes took him back to the store. It was a long time before any of us wanted to drive that old truck because we never forgot the day that Jennie got stuck in the ditch.

Eventually, Willie and I did learn to drive Old Rusty. When we were teenagers we would make deliveries for uncle Robert after school and on Saturdays. Many of the elderly who didn't have family in the area couldn't pick up their groceries. So they would call in their order and we would bring the food to their house.

When we delivered the groceries, people would often ask if we could stay a while and visit. Uncle Robert told us that as long as we made all our deliveries that we could visit because it was good for business. I remember people telling us all kinds of stories. They talked about their families, their ailments, and more. Sometimes they shared gossip about their neighbors, things that we were probably too young to hear. Aunt Mabel reminded us on several occasions not to tell anything we heard to anyone but her. We all knew what that meant. If we got some real good gossip, we needed to tell her. Aunt Mabel was a fine Christian woman but she was as nosy as the rest of us.

Old Rusty was reliable most of the time. I do remember a few occasions when the old truck broke down. At some point, the fuel gauge stopped working and one day we ran out of gas. Mr. Spillers saw us on the side of the road and stopped. He had a can of gas in the back of his truck and put a gallon in Old Rusty that got us back to town.

There was another time when the old truck just wouldn't start. We had delivered groceries to Mrs. Jane Odom's house. Her husband died the year before and no one lived with her except her cats. Mrs. Odom had lots of cats. Jennie was always afraid to go in the house because she said that cats were of the devil. Ellie loved the cats and always wanted to take one home.

When we were about to leave Mrs. Odom's, Old Rusty wouldn't start. We didn't know what the problem was. We had just put gas in the tank. He wasn't making any strange sounds before we stopped. He just wouldn't start. The engine wouldn't even turn over.

We asked Mrs. Odom if we could call uncle Robert. She said we could but she offered a suggestion on how we could start Old Rusty. She said that maybe the battery was dead and that we could push the truck down the road a bit, pop the clutch, and it would start. She had seen her husband do it several times.

So, Jennie hopped in Old Rusty and Willie, Ellie, and I started pushing. The old truck was real heavy. It took us a while to get it moving. When we finally got it up to speed, Jennie popped the clutch and it started. But when the truck jerked into gear, instead of pushing the clutch back in, Jennie pushed the accelerator to the floor and Old Rusty took off like a rocket. Before we knew it, Jennie lost control and drove Old Rusty into the ditch. Here we were again, stuck in the ditch. When uncle Robert and Mr. Dukes showed up this time, we explained what happened and the two of them just started laughing. We all grinned, hoping that the laughter meant that we weren't in trouble. We weren't. Mr. Dukes

pulled the truck out and towed it back into town. Uncle Robert got a new battery and Old Rusty was ready to go again.

The funniest thing that I can remember about Old Rusty was the time when aunt Mabel and I were making a delivery to the Baldwin boarding house. Old Rusty was parked behind the store at the loading ramp for about an hour with the back doors open. We didn't know it at the time, but a critter had made his way up the ramp and into the truck.

About halfway to the boarding house, aunt Mabel and I detected a pungent odor coming from the back of the truck. We both turned around and saw a huge skunk sitting on one of the grocery boxes. Aunt Mabel screamed. I screamed and I think I remember the skunk screaming. Well, before I knew it, aunt Mabel hit the brakes. I jumped out first and she was right behind me. The only problem was that she left the truck in gear. Old Rusty headed off down the highway. I looked over at aunt Mabel and she was just shaking her head as if to say, "I am not going to try and stop that truck. The skunk can have it."

We stood there and watched Old Rusty, once again, go off the road into the ditch. We waited a minute or two thinking that the skunk would jump out of a window but it didn't. We had to call uncle Robert. He came, opened the back doors, and let the skunk out. Aunt Mabel didn't want to get back in the truck, thinking that there might be another skunk that we had not seen. Uncle Robert just laughed and said that he would make the delivery to the boarding house.

Aunt Mabel and I took uncle Robert's truck back to the store. It was several weeks before either of us drove Old Rusty anywhere and we talked about that little episode for years. Neither one of us forgot the day when a stinky old skunk drove Old Rusty into the ditch.

There is one other thing that I remember about Old Rusty. In those days, most families only owned one vehicle. On several occasions, the boys who wanted to take us out on dates didn't have use of their family cars or trucks. So, they would ask us out and we would pick them up in Old Rusty. I'm sure that it was somewhat embarrassing for the boys but it didn't stop them from asking us out. Some of the boy's sisters teased them about the situation. They said things like, "Make sure that the girls get you back home on time."

The thing that was odd to us was that uncle Robert wanted us to let the boys drive Old Rusty on our dates. We didn't understand that when we first started dating but later we understood all too well. Uncle Robert knew that if the boys had their hands on the steering wheel and the shift, that they wouldn't be able to have their hands on us. I'll tell you more about our dating lives later because there are some hilarious stories about the boys.

Old Rusty lasted until Ellie and I graduated high school. He finally bit the dust one day and Mr. Dukes dumped him in the bottom of Indian Cliff. We never understood why people dumped their old cars in the canyon but that's where Old Rusty is today.

The truck was actually an important part of our lives. I think that it gave us a bit of freedom that most girls our age didn't have in those days. We didn't just stay home all the time and wash clothes, cook, or work in the garden. We did those things but we were able to do much more. I think that having Old Rusty contributed to the sense of independence that all four of us developed in our teenage years. Perhaps

uncle Robert and aunt Mabel knew that and gave us the truck to help us grow up. Thank you Old Rusty. You were a good friend.

11   The Roses On The Farm

Before uncle Robert and aunt Mabel bought the store, they had a small working farm. They raised chickens, beef cattle, and dairy cows. Uncle Robert was actually the first one who delivered milk and eggs to homes in Martin County. He also had about two hundred acres of farm land that he leased from Mr. Carlton Doucet. Uncle Robert raised all types of vegetables. He sold the produce locally and at a farmer's market over in rain.

I was young then but I can still remember several of the farmhands who worked for uncle Robert. Mr. Jim Buck was a middle-aged man who had been wounded in World War I. He walked with a bit of a limp but he always had a smile on his face. He supervised the milk operation. As we left for school each morning, on his way to milk the cows, he'd say, "Good morning, girls. Remember, it's a good day to be alive."

Mr. Raymond Johnson was another one of the men that I remember. He was a black man who worked on the farm for several years. Aunt Mabel told us that Mr. Raymond's father died when he was young and that he had to go to work to

help his family survive. Mr. Raymond wasn't married. He lived in a little bunk house that uncle Robert built on the back side of the north field.

Mr. Raymond didn't talk with us very much. That was common in those days. But we could tell that he was a nice man. He would always tip his brown floppy hat and say, "God bless, children." Mr. Raymond was in charge of working the crops. He supervised the seasonal workers during the planting and harvest times. Uncle Robert said that Mr. Raymond was the best worker he ever had.

When Mr. Raymond was getting pretty old uncle Robert gave him a job at the store. He worked there until he got sick and moved in with his younger brother. When Mr. Raymond died, we all went to the black Baptist church for his funeral. Uncle Robert cried during the service. Aunt Mabel told us that it was because uncle Robert really loved Mr. Raymond.

Mr. Jasper Jenkins was another one of the workers I remember. He was in charge of the beef cattle. He was a real cowboy. He wore boots, a big ten gallon hat, and brown leather chaps. Aunt Mabel told us that he was from Texas and that he had been a bull rider until he got hurt at a rodeo in Oklahoma. He ended up in Taylor County because he married Ophelia Finch who lived over at Foxboro.

All I know is that Mr. Jasper was real good with a rope. He could lasso those cows with both eyes closed and one hand tied behind his back. Sometimes he would come to school and show us his rope tricks. Even though he couldn't ride in the rodeos anymore, he loved going to the bull riding competitions and watching the younger guys give it a try. He would often serve as one of the officials and score the rides. Mr. Jasper was a nice man who worked hard and loved what he did.

Jake was the only other one who helped uncle Robert year round on the farm. He took care of the egg production. Jake was actually our older cousin. He was uncle Hez's son. When we were young, Jake was single. He was like a big brother to us. By the time we were in high school, Jake had married Susy Clark. Eventually, they moved to Birmingham and Jake worked at a steel mill. When he came back home during the holidays, he always ran by the house to visit.

It was fun playing with the animals on the farm. Of course, Ellie loved every animal she ever saw. She named each of the cows and the chickens. I don't know how she really knew one from the other but she said that she did. Every time we had to help with the animals Ellie would talk with them to see how they were doing. Of course, every few days, some of the chickens would go missing. Uncle Robert told Ellie that they must have flown away. Sometimes, she would go out in the field to look for them. Uncle Robert didn't dare let her know that they were the chicken on our dinner plates.

Willie had about the same attitude toward the animals as I did. We liked them but we weren't in love with them like Ellie. Jennie was not an animal person at all. She didn't even really like our dogs and cats. Some people are just like that I guess. I think that the main thing for Jennie was that the animals were not real clean. Jennie didn't like dirty. She didn't like for her clothes to get dirty. She didn't like her hands dirty. The only time we ever saw her not worried about getting dirty was when she was trying to catch the eye of some boy she liked. I'll tell you some of those stories later.

But the farm was a fun part of our lives. Uncle Robert

really didn't want us to work regularly with the animals. We had our chores at the house and he always told us that our main job was school. But we did help from time to time. Some of the funniest and craziest things we ever experienced happened while we were working on the farm.

I'll never forget the first time one of us found a snake in the chicken coop. Some of the nesting boxes were pretty high for us to reach. We would just have to feel around and find the eggs without actually seeing them. One day when Ellie was collecting the eggs, she reached in and caught hold of a snake. She screamed so loud that I thought the barn was going to fall down. "Snake! Snake! Snake!" But the strangest thing was that when she pulled away from the nest, she still had the snake in her hand.

That's when we all started screaming and running. The chickens jumped out of their nests. One of them flew on Jennie's head and got tangled up in her hair. She almost fainted. Our old dog, Blue, started howling as if he was on the trail of big buck deer. Mack, our horse, starting dancing around and almost ran over Willie. It was a sight to see.

Ellie ran out of the barn with that snake flying everywhere. The rest of us were screaming, "Let it go! Let it go." Ellie said, "I can't. It will kill the baby chickens." Aunt Mabel came running out of the house. She thought that one of us had been bitten by the snake. She was screaming, "Oh my Lord! Oh my Lord!"

Sometime before she made it to the house, Ellie finally let go of the snake. When Aunt Mabel went to look for it, she found it by one of the fence posts. The snake was as dead as a door knob. Evidently, while Ellie was running along the fence, the old snake hit every single post. It didn't have a chance.

The next day, uncle Robert put some short sticks in the barn for us to check each nest. He also taught us which snakes were poisonous and which ones were not. It didn't matter to me. The only good snake was a dead snake. We all found other snakes from time to time but none of us grabbed one like Ellie did that day to save the baby chicks.

At some point, when we were all entering high school, a new organization was started. It was called 4H. Boys and girls could raise their own animals, take them to livestock shows, and even sell them. Ellie and I asked uncle Robert if we could raise rabbits. He agreed and built us a small rabbit hutch that we put in the back of the barn.

We started with two Appalachian browns. Ellie named the boy Hopper and the girl Honey. We fed them every day, made sure that they had enough water, kept their hutch clean, and took them out of the cage to play with them. Ellie was in heaven and I have to admit that I enjoyed taking care of them.

Everything went fine for the first month or so but then we noticed that Honey was not feeling well. We asked uncle Robert to check her and he said, "Well, girls you are about to be the proud parents of several baby bunnies." We were so excited. For some reason, though, uncle Robert didn't seem to share our joy. Sure enough, one day, when we went to feed Hopper and Honey, we found eight tiny babies in the pen. Ellie ran to the house to tell everyone and all came out to see the new arrivals. They were so cute. We watched every day as they grew. After a couple of months, they were almost as big as their parents.

Our 4H project was moving along well. Our teacher, who

was the 4H sponsor, came out to see the rabbits one day. He told us about the upcoming competition in Hampton. We started grooming Hopper and Honey to make sure that they looked their best. On the day of the show, we won the first place ribbon. We were so excited.

After the show, one of the judges talked to us about raising rabbits for him. He told us that he would pay us well and that he would pick up the rabbits at our house. Uncle Robert said that we could and he built two more hutches for us.

We learned a lot more about raising rabbits. It was actually hard work but we were excited about the prospect of having a little money of our own. Of course, Ellie and I told all of our friends that we were in the rabbit business and that we were going to make a fortune. We were already deciding what we were going to do with all that money. We were going to buy some new clothes, new purses, new shoes, and much more.

All was going well until the day the buyer came to look at our rabbits. As we were talking, Ellie asked the man what he was going to do with the bunnies. He looked over at uncle Robert and didn't say a word. Uncle Robert hem hawed around and finally told us that the rabbits were going to be used for fur coats.

All was well until Ellie asked uncle Robert how they got the fur off the rabbits. That's when everything went south. When Ellie understood that they had to kill the rabbits to harvest the fur, she ran to the house crying. It took aunt Mabel two hours to calm Ellie down. That night, after we went to bed, Ellie snuck out of the house, and let all the rabbits out of the cages. The next day when uncle Robert found out what Ellie had done, he just started laughing. He gave both of us a big hug and told us that he could sell the hutches to Mr. Ralph Carter. That was the end of the Ellie - Anne rabbit farm.

I guess one of the things on the farm that was funny to us girls but not to uncle Robert was when the cows got out in the middle of the night. Uncle Robert and his men always had to patch the fences. Sometimes, though, the cows would find a way to get out and cause all kinds of problems.

I remember one time when the phone rang at two o'clock in the afternoon on a Sunday. Ellie and I went to the door and listened to see if we could tell who it was. Uncle Robert said, "Hello. Yes, reverend. Oh my goodness." Ellie and I thought that someone had died and that the pastor was letting us all know. But that wasn't it at all.

Some of uncle Robert's cows had gotten out and they were in the Baptist cemetery. Uncle Robert got dressed, called Mr. Jasper and drove over to the church. When he arrived, he saw ten of his cows roaming around the graves. The first thing he thought was that they knocked over or broken some of the headstones. All the monuments were okay but a storm had come through the day before and the ground was soaked. The cows had made a mess of the ground. It wasn't a pretty sight.

Mr. Jasper had come over on one of his horses and was trying to get the cows back to the field. They did not want to cooperate. The pastor was out there. He wasn't happy. One of the cows had crossed over the road to the church and was tearing up the flower beds. Another one had found the rope to the church bell. It was ringing and ringing and ringing. Pretty soon, at least a dozen men were at the church thinking

that there was a fire. Uncle Robert apologized to everyone and finally got the cows back to the field.

That wasn't the only time the cows got out. One time, uncle Robert got a call in the middle of night. The cows were on the railroad track. Evidently, a train hit one of them with the cattle catcher. When uncle Robert and Mr. Jasper arrived at the location, sure enough, one of the cows was down and ten or twelve others were still on the track. The conductor said that the cows just wouldn't move. He blew the whistle a few times but they just wouldn't move. Evidently, they were attracted to the big light on the train.

Uncle Robert and Mr. Jasper finally got the cows off the track and back to the field. Aunt Mabel told us later that she had never heard uncle Robert use words like that when he got home. He was mad at those cows. That night he could have killed the whole lot of them with a good heart.

The following week, aunt Mabel and some of her friends planted new flowers in front of the church. That Sunday the preacher thanked the ladies for their work and announced that the cemetery would be fixed as soon as it dried out. He then looked over his glasses at uncle Robert and smiled. Uncle Robert gave the preacher a nod and everything was fine.

I could tell you a hundred stories about the farm but the main thing is that helping with the animals from time to time gave us a sense of what work was all about. Work was good. It gave us a sense of accomplishment and it also taught us about responsibility. I'm glad that we had the farm.

12   *The Roses At Church*

Church was another important part of our lives, maybe the most important part for me. Every Sunday, aunt Mabel would get up early and iron our dresses. We each had about four nice dresses that we wore to church. I really didn't like having to dress up. Maybe it was because I had a little tomboy in me.

One day, when I complained about having to wear dresses, aunt Mabel said, "Well, Anne, we present our best to the Lord when we go to church." I remember wondering if the Lord was actually impressed with what we wore to church but I certainly wasn't going to argue with aunt Mabel. I had seen Jennie and even uncle Robert try that. They lost every time.

Unlike me, Jennie loved to wear pretty dresses because she thought that it caught the eyes of the boys. She would sashay her way into the sanctuary like it was a royal gala. I remember one time when she was strolling down the aisle in a fancy powder blue outfit. She turned to wave at Jimmy Newcomer and ran into Missy Crain. The two of them

tumbled into Mrs. Smith, the preacher's wife. She fell onto the communion table and knocked the vase of flowers and the Bible to the floor.

Ellie and I started laughing but aunt Mabel cleared her throat and we knew that we had better hush. I'm pretty sure that Jennie got a scolding about the whole thing. The next Sunday, Jennie walked into church all quiet and humble. Of course, it didn't last long. A few weeks later she was back to her normal proud self. She was just a little more careful about how she showed off.

We had several different pastors while we were growing up. Some of them only stayed for a couple of years. One day, I heard aunt Mabel say that the church didn't pay enough for anybody to stay very long. I remember feeling sorry for the kids because they had to move so much. But while they were at our church, I became best friends with many of them.

PKs, as we called them, were just like other kids mostly. They were as much sinners as we all were. Some of them, even worse. Penelope Pratt was one of those. She was Willie's age, a little older than me. That girl lied and gossiped almost every day of her life. She was always spreading rumors and trying to get other kids in trouble.

I remember one time when Penelope walked into class and told our Sunday School teacher, Mrs. Billings, that Ellie had said a bad word. When the teacher asked Penelope what the word was, Penelope said, "Well, I can't repeat a word like that." The teacher knew that she was just trying to get Ellie in trouble. Ellie never said bad words.

When we started the class, Mrs. Billings said, "Today we are going to talk about the sin of lying." She opened the Bible to the Ten Commandments and asked Penelope to read the verse. Penelope's voice cracked as she read, "Thou shalt not lie." Mrs. Billings then proceeded to read every verse in the Bible about lying. By the time she finished, Penelope was about to die. She had the look of guilt written all over her face. At the end of class, Mrs. Billings asked Penelope to stay. We don't know what was said but it was a long time before Penelope pulled a stunt like that again.

One of our preachers, Reverend Adams, had four girls just like our family. Every few months, they would come to the house after church for lunch. When all eight of us got together, it was loud. A couple of the Adams girls were screamers. It didn't matter what you were playing, they just screamed. Mrs. Adams could control them for a while but it wouldn't be long before they were screaming again. After a few visits, aunt Mabel made sure that we played out on the porch. She would close the front door so the adults could talk in peace.

Uncle Robert and aunt Mabel were very active in church. Uncle Robert was a deacon and taught the men's Sunday School class. Aunt Mabel led the Women's Missionary Union group, sang in the choir, and took her turn in the nursery with the babies. It seems like we were in church every time the doors were open but I really liked it.

One of the events we had at church was what they called dinner on the grounds. Each fifth Sunday during the year, when it wasn't too cold or rainy, everyone brought food for lunch after church. The men would set up tables outside under the oak trees and the ladies put out the food.

Several of the ladies made specialty cakes and pies for the event. Mrs. Templeton made her mile high lemon meringue pie that everyone loved. Aunt Mabel baked an

apricot nectar cake that was my favorite. Mrs. Overton made a white chocolate bread pudding that people said was the best in the southland. I never tried it because they wouldn't let the children have any. Years later, aunt Mabel told me that the reason it tasted so good was that Mrs. Overton put a little rum in it. Baptists didn't drink alcohol but they sure ate some when they had Mrs. Overton's bread pudding.

One of the funny things about dinner on the grounds was that uncle Robert would only eat aunt Mabel's food. I heard him say to her on several occasions, "You don't know what's in it and you don't know how clean the kitchen is." Aunt Mabel would just laugh and make sure that he knew what she had cooked.

There was one dinner on the grounds that none of us ever forgot. It was in the summer. All the ladies were waving their funeral fans. The men actually cooked the meat outside. Well, evidently, every dog in Taylor County could smell the food. Everyone had just sat down to eat. The preacher said grace and all of a sudden a pack of eight or ten dogs came around the corner of the church full speed. They were ready for some dinner on the grounds too. An old redbone hound dog jumped up on the table and began eating from the chicken platter. A brindle-colored coon dog got into the pork chops and a big long-legged bird dog went for the dessert table. It was pandemonium.

Food was flying everywhere. The ladies started screaming and running for their lives. The men, with little success, were trying to catch the canines. Mrs. Brinson, who was in charge of the dinner, just fainted. Aunt Mabel was trying to revive her. Some of us were running around playing with the smaller dogs and the preacher was trying to calm everyone down. By the time the men had the dogs under control no one wanted any of the food. I remember going back home and helping aunt Mabel fix some sandwiches for lunch.

Yes, that dinner on the grounds was the talk of the county for months. Everyone had their own version of what happened. Some of them went a little overboard but even a conservative telling of that story was something to hear. If I remember correctly, it wasn't long before the men of the church started building a fellowship hall. No one wanted to have the dogs for dinner on the grounds again.

There were other funny things that happened at church. I'll never forget the time when aunt Mabel and I were sitting with Mrs. Phillips at the church. I guess I should explain that we weren't just sitting with Mrs. Phillips. We were sitting overnight at the church with Mrs. Phillips' body. Back then they had the visitation and the funeral at the church. Someone had to stay with the body. All the families in the church took turns and when Mrs. Phillips died it was aunt Mabel's turn and she chose me to stay with her.

Now, aunt Mabel knew that I was afraid to stay at the church with the body. But she made me do it anyway. She tried on several occasions to explain things to me but her words were of little comfort. I just didn't like it. For one thing, the casket remained open throughout the night. I wasn't comfortable being that close to the departed especially when they were in full view.

I had also heard people say that sometimes you could see the body move. I imagined Mrs. Phillips sitting up in the casket and saying, "Hello, Anne. How are you today?" I know that sounds crazy but that's what runs through the mind of a

child.

The other thing I was afraid of was something that I heard from uncle Robert. He said that if a cat came into the room with an open casket that it would run to try and get to the body. Well, that night it happened. The preacher came in about eleven o'clock to check on us and I saw a big black cat come in behind him. I panicked. I screamed, jumped up, and ran toward the casket. Aunt Mabel woke up and wondered what in the world was happening. When I reached the casket I slammed the door down as hard as I could. Brother Smith was in shock. He thought that I had lost my mind.

They both ran up to me and said, "What's wrong? What's wrong? I explained to them what uncle Robert said about cats and dead bodies. Well, they both started laughing as hard as they could. I remember thinking, "How they could be so irreverent at a time like this." After a few moments, aunt Mabel explained that uncle Robert was just joking about the cat. It was like one of his ghost stories, just for fun.

Well, I felt like a fool. Aunt Mabel told me that she would have a word with uncle Robert about his tall tales. Brother Smith assured me that he wouldn't tell anyone about the incident but for some reason I didn't believe him. I could see him using me as a sermon illustration in his next church. I was just glad that the whole thing was over. It was a long time before aunt Mabel asked me to help with a funeral.

As I think about how different church was in those days, I remember our baptism services. Rural churches didn't have baptistries like the larger city churches. We were all baptized in the river. When it was time for the service, the candidates would change into long white robes and they would sing hymns on their way to the river. When they arrived, the preacher would actually deliver a short sermon and offer an invitation just like he did in church. Sometimes people would come down and be baptized right then.

Of course, there were times when the baptism didn't go as planned. I remember that Jimmy Burke fell in the water before he got to the preacher. Everybody said that he was baptized twice. Sometimes the preacher would have a hard time baptizing people who were, well, really big. When Brother Smith baptized Bertha Watts, she drug him down with her. Uncle Robert joked and said, "Well, maybe the reverend needed another cleansing."

One of my most vivid church memories was actually when we all went to a tent revival in Hampton. We met at the church and loaded up in school buses. None of us, including uncle Robert and aunt Mabel, had ever been to an event like that. All the preachers in the area promoted it for several weeks. We were told that it was going to be a revival that we would never forget. Whoever came up with that promise was right. None of us ever forgot the Hampton tent revival.

The meeting was at the new fairground just outside of town. The tent was huge. It was as big as the one at the circus. When we walked in, a mass choir from several churches was seated on the platform. A lady was on the left side of the stage playing the piano. Several preachers, including our pastor, were sitting on the other side. I guess that there were about five or six hundred people in attendance. We sat down near the back.

When it was time for the service to begin, some other people went up on the stage. They were musicians. One of them had a guitar. Another one uncovered a set of drums and the two others had a trumpet and a trombone. We had never

seen those instruments in church before. As soon as they got settled, a man came to the center of the stage and welcomed everyone. He told us to stand up and get ready to worship the Lord.

That's when the band started playing. Oh my. They weren't playing a hymn like the ones we sang every Sunday. They were playing something that sounded like a honkytonk tune from Bourbon Street in New Orleans. I looked over at uncle Robert and aunt Mabel. They were in shock. The people in front of us started dancing and shouting. Soon, there were people running in the aisles. They were waving their arms in the air and saying, "Thank you Jesus. Thank you Jesus."

Well, that's when it happened. Jennie put her hands up in the air and started shouting. "Thank you Lord. Praise you Lord." Before we knew it she was headed down the aisle. "Yes, Jesus. I love you Jesus." Aunt Mabel and uncle Robert were mortified. Ellie and I thought it was funny until aunt Mabel gave us that look. We heard uncle Robert say, "Go get her." That's when aunt Mabel started down the aisle. She was shouting but she wasn't praising the Lord. "Jennie! Stop! You get back here right now!" Jennie just kept dancing and singing. Somehow she ended up with a tambourine in her hand. She made it all the way to the other side of the tent before aunt Mabel caught up with her. Aunt Mabel marched Jennie back to her seat and sat her down. Uncle Robert just stared at Jenny. I thought he was going to have a heart attack.

Willie, Ellie and I weren't sure what was going to happen next but we couldn't wait to see. Brother Pender, our pastor, walked off the stage and started making his way to the back.

Uncle Robert pushed us out into the aisle and we all went to the bus. No one said a word the whole trip back home. Later, aunt Mabel told us that the people who set up the revival were from an off-brand church. Brother Pender got up the next Sunday and apologized to the congregation. Everyone knew that it wasn't his fault but he was certainly embarrassed by the whole thing.

For several weeks after the experience, we all made fun of Jennie raising her hands and dancing at the revival. The funny thing is that, years later, she actually joined the Pentecostal church. We concluded that if the Pentecostals could keep Jennie on the straight and narrow, they must be doing something right.

Other than all the humorous things, there were some very significant, life-changing moments at church that I remember well. I continued to struggle with questions about my parents. I just couldn't believe that my mother had abandoned me. None of it made sense to me. But one day I had an incredible experience at church that helped with that struggle. I had just turned fifteen.

Brother Smith had been with us for about a month. It was a typical Sunday morning. The service concluded and I was on my way out when Brother Smith stopped me at the back door. I had not actually talked with him before and didn't think that he knew me. But he took me by the hand, looked into my eyes, and said, "I know who you are. I know whose child you are. You're a child of God. You are a blessed child of God and the Lord has a wonderful plan for your life."

I went outside and waited for aunt Mabel and uncle Robert to finish talking with everyone. But while I was sitting on the bench in front of the church, I thought about what the

pastor said. I was a child of God and I was blessed and God had a plan for my life. I remember thinking how much my aunt and uncle loved me. Willie, Jennie, and Ellie loved me and it really didn't matter that I didn't have my parents. I was okay and I was going to be okay because I was loved by so many people. I remember going home that day with a smile on my face and joy in my heart.

That night when aunt Mabel came to tuck me in bed, I told her what the pastor said and thanked her for taking me in. She smiled and gave me a big hug. When I said my prayers, I thanked God for everybody just like I always did. But this time I really meant it. For the first time in my life, I realized that what aunt Mabel had been telling me was true. I was loved.

That was a major turning point in my life. God became very real to me. I prayed more. I read my Bible more. I volunteered to help with events and activities at church. I even served as a substitute teacher for the young children's class. I invited my friends to church. I told them about how much God loved them and how they could become a Christian. I still had struggles from time to time but I knew that God was always with me. I was never really alone and I believed that God could see me through any problem I might face in life. I was a child of God.

13   A Very Special Rose

One of the things I remember most about my childhood was helping aunt Macy with her roses. Macy's life had been filled with tragedy. She faced the loss of a child. Not long after her daughter's death, her husband left her. She had nowhere to live. She stayed with her parents until their deaths and then moved in with us at the Henry's.

Aunt Macy real talent was growing roses, beautiful, incredible roses. She had regular bush roses, climbing roses, ground cover roses, and more. She had tea roses, old fashioned English roses, and every other variety you could think of. At the county fair, aunt Macy's roses won all the blue ribbons. She kept her ribbons in a shoebox. Every once in a while she pulled them out and told us stories about each rose.

Every morning, aunt Macy worked on her roses. She was either pruning, fertilizing, watering, or weeding. Then in the afternoon she would work with them some more. I never saw anyone who loved roses like aunt Macy. In a way, I think that she saw them as her children because every once in a while I

actually heard her talking to the roses. I asked aunt Mabel about it one day and she said that it was okay.

Often, after school and in the summer, I helped aunt Macy with the roses. In the midst of all the work, she would tell me stories. Sometimes she told stories about her childhood. At other times she told stories about famous people. She told stories from the books she had read. Every once in a while she would make up a story of her own.

She also told me Bible stories, quoting long passages of scripture from memory. Most people didn't know and would have never guessed that aunt Macy actually had a photographic memory. She never forgot anything she read, heard, or saw. She knew people's birthdays, wedding dates, death dates, and more. She was also a wiz at math. Aunt Macy was an amazing person.

But back to her stories. No matter what the story was aunt Macy would almost always connect it to something about flowers. I know now that she was teaching me lessons about life. Aunt Macy was actually a woman of great wisdom, love, and care. She loved me. She loved me as if I was her own child. I thank God that she was there for me.

I remember her telling me about the time when she and her sisters got lost in the woods. "You know, Anne, in those days we used a lot of natural remedies to treat our illnesses. Momma and grandma Moran made poultices and teas from different leaves and herbs.

When we were little, momma would go with us to show us what to look for. We collected willow bark, beech tree leaves, mushrooms, dandelions, and different types of roots. We even used sassafras leaves to make a sweet drink that tasted like root beer. When we got older, Momma would give each of us girls a burlap sack with a strap on it. We carried it like a purse over our shoulder and we went out by ourselves.

Well, one Saturday, in the fall, we went out real early in the morning. Momma packed a snack for each of us. It was a little chilly and there was a fine mist on the ground. Within a couple of hours we found some ginger, some yellow root, and we even found what the old people called birthroot. We were having a good morning.

Of course, all along the way we found something to talk about. Your aunt Effie loved to talk about the boys, especially Hezekiah Stevens. She would always say that one day she was going to be Mrs. Hezekiah Stevens. Well, we all know that didn't happen. When Hezekiah came back from the war he moved to Texas and married some girl named Doris. Effie had to settle for your uncle Thomas who has treated her like a queen their whole married life."

Aunt Macy got away from her story but she finally found her way back. "Well, we had been talking and walking so much that we found ourselves in a part of the woods that we had never seen before. The trees were large and very tall. There was almost no grass on the ground, just smooth, dark soil. The canopy of the trees let only slivers of light through their leaves. It was a strange place but it was a beautiful place.

We all stopped to listen to the silence that surrounded us. It was so quiet that all we could hear was the beating of our hearts. Then the wind started blowing and we could hear the faint sound of water running through a stream.

We followed the sound until we came to a small ravine. There we saw what looked like the Garden of Eden. Beautiful wild flowers were on both sides of the little brook. The water

was crystal clear. We just stared at its beauty for a long while. We all wanted to go down the hill to the stream but Effie and I were too scared. Your aunt Sally hiked up her dress and started down the ravine. I was worried that if we went down we might not be able to climb back up. But Sally kept making fun of us so Effie and I took the plunge.

When we got to the bottom, we saw several deer tracks. Evidently, this was a favorite watering hole for the animals. We all bent down to get some water. It was cold and it tasted so good. It was just like the artesian well water from Mr. Barker's farm. Effie and I started looking at the flowers. Most of them were the same as those in the woods around the house. But there was one that we had not seen. The plant looked like a small tree with long green leaves. The flower was white and looked like a different type of camellia. The five delicate petals formed a cup around the bright yellow center. We were all amazed at its beauty. A few feet away from the tree there was a small shoot coming out of the ground. I could tell that it was the same plant. I carefully dug the dirt away from its roots and put it in my sack.

After a while, we decided that we needed to make our way back home. It was almost lunch time and momma would be looking for us. We all agreed to keep the location of our special place a secret. We would never bring anyone else to see it. From time to time, we would go back and enjoy its beauty."

When aunt Macy finished her story, I asked her about the plant that she took. She planted it at their old home place near Foxboro. One day a botanist from Virginia was traveling through the area and saw the flowers in full bloom. He told them that it was a very rare Franklin tree flower plant that was thought to be extinct in a natural setting. It was native to a small river valley in Georgia and none had been seen in the wild since the early 1800s. The girls took the man to the stream where they found the plant and he gathered several samples. Later they all learned that an article about the discovery had been written in a scientific journal. The botanist called it the Hidden Beauty.

Aunt Macy often reminded me that I had a hidden beauty inside. I wasn't pretty like the other girls. When she told me that, I always thought that she was just trying to help me feel good about myself. But one day she quoted a passage from the Bible, First Peter chapter three. It tells us that we should let our adorning be the hidden person of the heart with the beauty of a gentle and quiet spirit which is precious in the sight of God. That verse has always meant a lot to me.

One of aunt Macy's funniest stories was about wedding roses. I can hear her telling it now. "Well, Ellen Huxley was marrying Ben Smith. Her folks owned a small dairy farm over in the Hicks community. Ben's family owned a sawmill up by Silver Creek. The wedding was at the Baptist church in Justice. The reverend asked me to make a rose bouquet for the bride and separate bouquets for the communion table and the foyer.

I brought the roses to the church about two hours before the wedding. Everything was so pretty. The service started when Ben came in with his best man and the preacher. It wasn't long after that when things started falling apart. Just before the organist started playing the wedding march, Ben started sneezing. Well, when it was time for the bride to come down the aisle, we could hear someone sneezing in the foyer. When they opened the doors, we could see that it was

Ellen, the bride. Her father had her by the arm and started walking down the aisle. Ellen was sneezing her head off. Ben couldn't stop sneezing. Ellen was sneezing so hard that some of the rose petals from her bouquet were falling to the floor. It took me a while to realize that the bride and groom were both allergic to roses which is very rare.

By the time Ellen got down to the front, both of them were not only sneezing but they had each broken out in an awful red rash on their faces. People in the pews started whispering and snickering. The pianist was grinning from ear to ear as she played. The pastor was having a hard time keeping a straight face himself.

When the service was finished, Ben and Ellen both just left. They didn't even stay for the reception. Ben's dad got up and thanked everybody for coming and asked them to stay for the food. We found out later that Ben and Ellen had to put oatmeal and peppermint oil on the rash. Their honeymoon trip to New Orleans was cancelled and their first days of marriage were miserable." When I asked aunt Macy what life lesson she learned from the wedding roses, she laughed and said, "Honey, there ain't no life lesson to that story. It's just funny."

It was rare to see aunt Macy laugh like that. But every once in a while she remembered that life, even though it is hard, is still good. And sometimes life is so funny that no matter what else is going on, as the Bible says, there is a time to laugh. That's a lesson all of us need to learn.

One of my fondest memories of aunt Macy was the winter of the big snow. That's what we all called it because it rarely snowed in south Mississippi. Most years we had absolutely no snow at all. Once or twice I remember us having a few flurries but by the next morning the snow was all gone. But when I was ten years old it snowed for three whole days. The old people were even amazed. They had never seen six inches of snow on the ground in Martin Country. It was so beautiful. It looked just like the pictures we had seen in books. We just couldn't believe it.

Our schools closed because the buses couldn't run. So we played in the snow for a whole week. Aunt Mabel didn't like the snow very much. She stayed inside most of the time. But aunt Macy loved it. I remember her building a snow man with us. We named him Mr. Shivers. Aunt Macy put one of her knit caps and a plaid scarf on him to dress him up. Jennie, of course, started dancing and talking with Mr. Shivers. While Jennie was acting the fool, Ellie, Willie, and I made some snowballs. When Jennie finished her dance with Mr. Shivers we hit her with everything we had. Aunt Macy jumped in with Jennie and the war was on. It was our first snowball fight and we loved it.

On one of those days, aunt Macy taught us how to make snow angels. We didn't even know what snow angels were before that. She also taught us how each snowflake was unique, that no two were the same. She said that God made each snow flake up in the clouds and sent it down for us to enjoy. She even drew us a picture of a snowflake. We never saw that before. Then she had us draw our own snowflakes in the back of our notebooks.

After that, she taught us that God made each of us special, just like the snowflakes we had drawn. She even had us look at our thumbs and told us that nobody else in the whole world had our thumbprints. Aunt Macy just had the ability to make us all feel very special. She loved us and we

loved her.

One of the greatest lessons aunt Macy taught me was the difference between thorns and prickles on roses. We were working with the roses one afternoon and I wasn't wearing my gloves. Well, sure enough I grabbed one of the stems and, ouch, my thumb started bleeding. It hurt like the dickens. I went over to aunt Macy and told her that one of the thorns caught me.

We sat down on the porch and she put aloe vera from one of her plants on my wound. As she consoled me, aunt Macy started telling me the difference between thorns and prickles. "Anne, roses don't actually have thorns. They have prickles. There's a big difference. Prickles are very small compared to thorns. They are just extensions of the bark. Thorns are like another stem on the tree. They're very long and could actually kill a person. "

When she said that, I remembered seeing a thorn bush out by the barn. The thorns were about five inches long. If someone fell into that bush, it would be very bad. Aunt Macy continued. "You know, when bad things happen to us, we think that it's like having a thorn in our side or through our heart. We think that we're not going to survive. But most of the time the bad things are actually just little prickles. They hurt but we're going to be ok." I can't tell you how many times that one lesson has helped me through difficult situations and challenges.

I could go on and on about aunt Macy. Even though she was my aunt, she was like a best friend to me. She helped me through the times when I wondered about my mother and father. She helped me understand as much as anyone can understand about teenaged boys. She helped me grow up in so many ways. Aunt Macy was and is a very special rose.

14 *The Roses Face A Great Lose*

When Ellie and I were sixteen, a great tragedy came into our lives. I don't even know how to begin to tell you about that day. It was Tuesday. We were all in school. It was the last week of classes just before the summer break. That morning we were taking our final exams. Everyone was excited about finishing another year. Ellie and I were just a couple of days from being seniors. Willie was graduating on Friday.

The bell rang for lunch. Ellie met me at the cafeteria. Willie was sitting with some of her friends and Jennie was with her newest beau, Dickie Pierce. Everyone was real chatty. The stress of finals and the anticipation of summer had us all anxious and excited at the same time. We were so loud that Mrs. Bankston had to quiet us down several times.

Just before lunch was over, I saw Mr. Pittman walk in the cafeteria. He was our principal, a wonderful, kindhearted man who was an encouragement to us all. Brother Smith, our pastor, was with Mr. Pittman. The two of them appeared to be looking for someone. They went to the table where Willie was and in just a moment, she stood up and started coming our way. We didn't know why. When they got to our table, Mr. Pittman said, "Girls, we need to ask you to come to the office." Brother Smith didn't say a word, but he had an unsettled look on his face. We picked Jennie up on the way out and all went to the principal's office.

When we got to the office, aunt Mabel and aunt Macy were there. That's when I knew that something was wrong. It was easy to see that both of them had been crying. Aunt Mabel said, "Girls, I have some bad news." That's all she said before she started crying. Aunt Macy gave her a hug, looked at us, and said, "Angels, your daddy had a heart attack this morning." Ellie said, "Where is he? Where's daddy? Is he at the hospital?" Aunt Mabel started crying. "No honey. Your daddy didn't make it to the hospital. He's gone."

We all just burst into tears. It was so hard to believe. He had just taken us to the bus stop a few hours earlier on his way to the store. He would be there when we came in from school. We'd get a soda and he'd ask us how our day was. We'd ride home with him in the old truck. He'd say grace over supper and tell us to have sweet dreams before we went to bed. But, no, we would never see him alive again. My heart was broken. This man who took me in, provided for me, loved me, was now gone. He was supposed to be the one who walked me down the aisle when I got married. He would have been like a grandfather to my children. Not now.

Brother Smith tried to console us with words of comfort and he prayed with us. After another few moments, aunt Mabel told us that it was time to go home. Someone picked up our books and brought them to the house later. We didn't go back to school that week. The teachers just gave us the

grades we had before the final exams. One of the first things I thought about on the way home was Willie's graduation. It was in three days. I didn't know if she would even want to go.

When we got home, some ladies from the church were there. They had brought food for us. Each of them gave us their condolences. You could tell that they were also affected by uncle Robert's death. Everyone in the community loved him. When times had been hard for folks, uncle Robert let them have groceries and supplies on credit. Most of them paid him back but when they couldn't he just forgave their debt. He was such a wonderful man.

That night, before we went to bed, aunt Mabel and aunt Macy came to our rooms and tucked us in. Aunt Macy quoted a few passages of Scripture about how God never leaves us nor forsakes us, that He is close to those with a broken heart, and how one day there will be a great reunion with uncle Robert in Heaven.

When aunt Mabel and aunt Macy left, Ellie asked if she could sleep with me. She was so sad. After a few minutes, Jenny came in and laid down on Ellie's bed. Willie came in too. We pushed the beds together and found comfort in just being close to one another. The three of them went to sleep quickly. They were so exhausted. I stayed awake thinking, wondering about what was going to happen. Would aunt Mabel keep the store? Would we have enough money to live? I even thought about what kind of job I could get that would help the family survive. I asked God to show me what I should do. I finally fell asleep sometime in the night but I was worried about the future.

The next morning aunt Macy cooked breakfast for us. Aunt Mabel had already left the house before we got up. She had gone into Pearl Valley to make arrangements for the funeral. Later that morning she came back and told us that the funeral was going to be on Thursday. She left again to go to the store. Mr. Tom Fielding had opened the store that morning. Before he retired, Mr. Tom had been the store manager for the previous owner. He actually helped uncle Robert from time to time when he was needed. Mr. Tom would prove to be a great help for aunt Mabel in the coming months.

That evening we had supper together. It just wasn't the same. Uncle Robert wasn't there to give thanks. He wasn't there to ask us about our day. He wasn't there to tell us one of his funny little jokes. His chair was empty and our hearts were empty too. No joy. No laughter. Just a sense of incredible loss.

Afterwards we sat down in the living room and aunt Mabel told us about her plans. "Girls, I know that you are all worried about what's going to happen now that your daddy is gone. I want you to know that we're going to be okay. I'm going to keep the store and run it myself. That means that there will be a lot of changes for all of us. Aunt Macy is going to be taking care of my chores around the house. I want you to promise me that you will be a help to her. In some ways you're going to have to take care of yourselves. This isn't going to be easy for any of us. We're all going to have to work hard to keep things going. But we love each other and that, with the help of the Lord, is going to see us through." We all agreed.

When we started getting ready for bed, Aunt Mabel took Willie out on the porch. We all wondered what was going on. I remember Jennie going around to several windows to see if

she could hear what they were talking about. We found out later that aunt Mabel asked Willie about graduation. Willie decided that she was going to walk on Friday with the rest of her class. She felt that uncle Robert would want her to attend the ceremony. It would be a bright spot in the midst of our grief.

On Thursday morning we got up early, ate breakfast, and started getting ready. Aunt Macy ironed all of our dresses the night before. Aunt Mabel helped us fix our hair. The visitation was to start at nine for the family and ten for friends. The funeral was scheduled for two o'clock. The ladies at the church planned a lunch for us and the rest of the family at noon.

When we arrived at the church, Brother Smith and his wife were there to meet us. Mrs. Smith was a wonderful minister's wife. She and aunt Mable were very close, almost like sisters. When we went in, we saw the casket at the front. A small picture of uncle Robert was on top in the middle of the flowers. Aunt Macy made the wreath from roses in her garden.

We all went to the front and stood there with aunt Mabel. She took the picture of uncle Robert in her hands and held it close to her heart. I know this sounds strange. But it was the first time that I really thought about how much two people could love each another. We all saw it in the little looks and smiles they shared every day. You could feel it when you saw them holding hands or when uncle Robert gave aunt Mabel a quick kiss on the cheek. I knew that she was suffering the greatest loss of her life but she had experienced the deepest kind of love there is this side of Heaven. What a blessing.

It wasn't long before the rest of uncle Robert's family arrived. Aunt Mabel's family came in soon after that. We all shared our grief but also our love. Friends who came for the visitation were a comfort to us. They helped us understand that we were part of a community that cares. The meal that the church prepared was appreciated. Most of that time was spent catching up on family news, kids and grandkids.

I don't really remember much about the funeral that afternoon. We sang hymns. Someone provided special music, and Brother Smith preached. The part I do remember was the graveside service. I'll never forget the pastor's words. He said "Many people call the cemetery a final resting place. But that is not true for a Christian. The Bible tells us that God has prepared a place for us in Heaven where we will live forever in His presence. Heaven is actually our final resting place." That's when I realized that uncle Robert was in Heaven. I never thought much about Heaven until then. I remember the sense of comfort it gave me. I feel that comfort now as I write these words to you. Soon, I will be in Heaven.

The hardest part of the day came when it was time to leave the cemetery. After all the friends and the rest of the family left, we were there by ourselves. At one point aunt Mabel asked us to wait for her in the car. We did. I guess she wanted to say her final goodbyes to uncle Robert.

The next day was Friday, graduation day for Willie. Willie had been real quiet in the days following uncle Robert's death. That's just the way she was. Willie rarely shared her thoughts and feelings with anyone. I was concerned about her but she got through the day pretty well.

We all went to the ceremony that night. Willie looked so nice in her cap and gown. When the graduates marched

down the aisle and went up on the stage, we noticed that Willie went to the podium. We didn't know what she was doing. When all the graduates were on the stage, Willie said, "Please rise and join me in prayer." We were amazed that she was leading the invocation. We were even more impressed with the prayer she prayed. It was like a beautiful poem. A few years later we learned that Willie had written over one hundred poems. That was how she shared her thoughts and feelings.

After the ceremony, we went to a reception for the graduates in the gym. After that we went home and had a party for Willie. Each of us made a gift for her. That's when aunt Mabel gave Willie one of the most special gifts I believe I have ever seen. It was a letter that uncle Robert and aunt Mabel had written the week before uncle Robert died. Willie read the letter out loud. In the letter uncle Robert and aunt Mabel told Willie how proud they were of her and how much they loved her. They promised her their prayers and support for the days ahead. We all started crying. That was forty-two years ago. Willie still has that letter. She showed it to me just last year. It is the most precious thing in the world to her.

The next day, after breakfast, aunt Mabel talked to us about the future. In basic terms, we were all going to have to work at the store. Uncle Robert didn't have any employees. He did most of the work himself. He stocked the shelves. He took care of the meat counter. He even swept and mopped the floors. We were going to have to take on those responsibilities.

Aunt Mabel told us that Willie was going to work at the store with her in the mornings. Jennie, Ellie, and I were going to have to work in the afternoons. It was summer. We were out of school. All of us had helped with the store before so it seemed manageable. Aunt Mabel told us that she was going to pay us by the hour. That was the first paid job any of us ever had.

For the next few weeks everything went along well. We all got in the routine of working. Mr. Fielding was helping aunt Mabel learn how to take care of the bills, the customer credit accounts, and the orders from suppliers. She had a few small problems but for the most part she was doing well.

What we didn't know, however, was that someone was planning to take the business from aunt Mabel. His name was Foster Hickman. Mr. Hickman owned a big general store in Pearl Valley and another one in Hampton. One day Mr. Hickman came in the store to see aunt Mable. She had never met him before but knew of him. After introducing himself, Mr. Hickman told aunt Mabel that he wanted to buy the store. He said that he was prepared to make a lump sum cash payment. He even had the papers with him. All aunt Mabel had to do was sign. When aunt Mabel told him that the store wasn't for sale, Mr. Hickman said some things that weren't too nice. He said that a woman shouldn't be running a store. She should be at home taking care of her children.

When that didn't work, Mr. Hickman threatened to build a store right down the road and put aunt Mable out of business. Aunt Mable was just about to start crying when Mr. Fielding came out from the back and told Mr. Hickman that it was time for him to leave. Evidently, Mr. Fielding had been listening to the conversation. Mr. Hickman told Mr. Tom that it was none of his business. That's when aunt Mabel snapped. She started screaming, "Get out of here! Get out of here right now! Don't you ever come back in my store again!" Later,

aunt Mabel told us that was the closest she ever came to losing her religion. We all knew what that meant.

Aunt Mabel never heard from Mr. Hickman again. Even though he threatened aunt Mabel, he never built a store in Norman. As a matter of fact, Mr. Hickman never built another store anywhere because later that year a storm of gigantic proportions hit our country. It was called the Great Depression.

I really don't think that I can capture in words how bad things were during those years. It started in October with the stock market crash. Some people across the country were wealthy one day and poor the next. Many couldn't handle the loss and took their own lives. Large factories up north closed. People by the thousands lost their jobs. We did not immediately feel that in Norman. But other storms were soon coming our way.

Gradually, we all recovered from uncle Robert's death. It did, however, change each of us in different and significant ways. Aunt Mable became immersed in running the store. She had to. It was the only way for us to survive. It was hard for her as a woman in those days to run a business. Some of the wholesalers tried to take advantage of her. But she held her ground. If one of them raised their prices for no good reason, she would find another supplier. After a few years she had the reputation of being a very wise and successful businesswoman.

Aunt Mabel never married again. As a matter of fact, she never even went out on a date with another man. Several eligible bachelors tried to gain her attention, but none ever did. Some said that she became married to her work. I don't know. But I always remembered how much she loved uncle

Robert. I think, perhaps, that she still considered herself married even after his death. Unlike most people, aunt Mabel never took her wedding ring off. She wore it until the day she died.

I think that many people were worried most of all about aunt Macy. But aunt Macy, in some ways, became the glue that held us all together. She was a calming influence for aunt Mabel when things at the store were tough. She helped the rest of us through our struggles with uncle Robert's death. Years later, Ellie and I were talking about it. Aunt Macy was the only one in the family who had faced such a great loss. Perhaps the reason she was able to help us so much was because she had already faced death in the loss of her child.

One of the funny things that happened with aunt Macy after uncle Robert's death was that she taught herself how to drive a car. It was mostly out of necessity because aunt Mabel had to be at the store all day. I'll never forget the first time I saw her behind the wheel. It was on a Saturday morning after breakfast. We were all on the porch shelling peas. After a while, aunt Macy left and went over to the barn. That's when we heard her crank up old Rusty. We couldn't believe it. In a minute or two here she came. She went out into the field and drove all over the place. We could hear the horrible sound of her trying to change gears. My first thought was, well that's the end of old Rusty. But after a while we could see that she was getting the hang of it, sort of.

A few weeks later, on a Sunday afternoon, aunt Macy left the field and hit the road. Aunt Mabel was so worried about her that we all jumped in the car and followed her. Aunt Macy was going fast. We had a hard time keeping up with

her. She was hunched over the steering wheel like a race car driver. She was weaving from one side of the road to the other. Aunt Mabel was praying out loud. "Dear Lord Jesus, please don't let her hit anybody."

The Lord answered aunt Mabel's prayer. Aunt Macy never did hit anybody and she finally slowed down after the sheriff had a little talk with her. Eventually, she was able to stay in her lane. Well, most of the time. Every once in a while she would drift over the center line and scare someone half to death. When most people saw her coming they would move over as far as they could to make sure that she didn't hit them. Later, whenever we heard someone say, "Keep it between the ditches." we thought about aunt Macy.

Uncle Robert's death did have an effect on each of us girls. For a while Willie seemed very depressed. I was worried about her. She stayed off to herself most of the time. Ellie and I tried to talk with her but she wouldn't. She just went to the store every morning and came home in the afternoon. That's all she did.

But one day everything changed for Willie. She met Mack Bridges. Mack was from Tupelo. He came down our way to work for the new electric company. He was a quiet young man who went to church every Sunday. Willie and Mack started dating and by the next summer they were married. They stayed in Norman for about two years. Willie continued to work at the store for aunt Mable. One day Mack was promoted to manager and they moved to Pearl Valley. That's when they started their family. Mack came into Willie's life at just the right time. I guess he was that blessing from God that aunt Macy always talked about.

Jennie was affected by uncle Robert's death perhaps

more than any of us. She just couldn't deal with the loss. She was an emotional wreck. Every time we went to church, she cried. She refused to go to funerals. Her grades started falling at school. We could all see her slipping away. At one point aunt Mabel was afraid that Jennie might lose touch with reality or worse. She took her to a doctor in Truitt for several weeks. It didn't seem to help Jennie at all.

But one day, everything changed for Jennie. It was almost miraculous and I don't' say that lightly. It was the week of our spring revival at the church. Most of the time our revival preachers were what we called screamers. They were loud and their sermons were mainly about hell. They told us how bad we were and how God was going to punish us if we didn't repent of our horrible sin that nailed Jesus to the cross. Needless to say, we really didn't enjoy revivals very much.

This time, however, Brother Smith brought in an elderly preacher who had pastored for several years and then taught at the seminary in New Orleans before he retired. His name was Percival Hanks. Brother Hanks was a rather tall, slim man. He had silvery gray hair and a rather ruddy complection. He told us that he was from southeast Louisiana and was the first preacher in his family. We could tell right from the start that Brother Hanks was a kind and gentle man.

The first two nights of the revival, Brother Hanks preached about salvation. But instead of talking about hell he talked about how much God loved us. He read passages about Jesus and how he loved people. Oh, he talked about sin and how we need to repent. But he said that we needed to repent and live for God because of his great love for us. We

never heard a revival preacher bring messages like that before.

The next three nights, Brother Hanks preached about how important it was for us to live godly, Christian lives. One of his sermons was on gossip. We had never heard a whole sermon on gossip. Brother Hanks called it the eighth deadly sin. He said that gossip hurt the church more than any other sin. That hit a lot of folks pretty hard especially some of the ladies. It was interesting that no one came down the aisle that night. Later aunt Mable told us that the sermon was the talk of the town the next day.

But Friday night, the last night of the revival, the most incredible thing happened and I think that it saved Jennie's life. Brother Hanks got up and thanked the folks for their hospitality. Then he read the passage in Matthew that has the Great Commission. The main purpose of the message was for us to go out and tell people about Jesus. He reminded us of his sermons from the previous nights. Once we are saved and once we are living godly lives, God wants us to share the good news of Christ with those around us.

The sermon was inspiring and challenging but it was what Brother Hanks shared at the end of the message that changed Jennie's life. Toward the end of the message, Brother Hanks started talking about his life, particularly about his mother. "I grew up with a wonderful, godly Christian mother. She was actually forty years old when I was born. Every Sunday she took me and my sister to church. Almost every night before I went to bed she read a Bible story to me and prayed with me. Mother was a generous woman. When people in the community had needs she was there to help them.

But one day my mother became ill. We didn't know it at the time but she was seriously ill. For two years she was in and out of the hospital. She faced one treatment after another. But nothing restored her health. Little by little she got weaker and weaker. Then one day my father came to get me out of school because my godly, Christian mother had died.

I was overcome with grief. I actually became angry with God. I felt that He had just taken my mother from me. Why had He not saved her from her illness? She was living her life for Him. My anger turned into despair. I felt hopeless and helpless. I thought that when her life ended that my life ended.

For two years I just walked aimlessly through life. I went through the motions of living but I wasn't living at all. I was just existing. I was a straight A student. But after my mother died my grades fell. I was a junior in high school. I should have been enjoying life. But there was no life to enjoy. My father and sister must have been concerned about me. I know that they were worried if I would ever come out of my despair.

But one Sunday morning something happened to me. Our pastor preached a sermon on Romans 8:28 where the Bible tells us that all things work together for good to those who love God and are called according to His purpose. I had heard sermons on that passage before but none like this message. It was as if my pastor was speaking directly to me that day.

He started by telling us what the verse did not say. The verse does not say that all things are good. He reminded us that life is sometime very bad and hard. He said what the

verse says is that all things work together for good. He told us the story of Joseph and his brothers who sold him into slavery, that what they meant for harm, God used for good. Then the pastor quoted Jeremiah 29:11 which tells that God knows the plans he has for our lives.

That's when God spoke directly to my heart. My mother's death wasn't a good thing. But God could make good come from it just like He did with Joseph. And God had a plan and purpose for my life. My life wasn't over. It was just beginning. And I needed to commit myself to whatever God wanted me to do with my life. I went down the aisle that night and recommitted my life to God. I told God that I would go wherever He wanted me to go, that I would do whatever He wanted me to do.

I started working in the church, helping people in the community. My pastor even let me teach a Bible study one night. I started going on visits with the pastor, inviting people to church. Soon, I started discovering God's purpose for my life. He wanted me to be a minister of the Gospel.

I remember the Sunday when I shared with the church my sense of call to ministry. All the ladies in the church came down and told me about my mother praying for the day when she would see me behind the pulpit. She had never talked to me about becoming a preacher but she had prayed and had everyone else praying that I would answer the call. I cannot tell you what that did for my soul. That's why I'm here before you tonight. God took a tragedy and turned it into an incredible blessing in my life.

I don't really know why I shared my story tonight. I didn't plan on doing that. But maybe there's someone who needed to hear it. You've been facing trouble and heartache.

You know the Bible tells us in Psalm 34 that God is near to those with a broken heart. I can tell you from experience that whatever it is, God can see you through it if you trust Him. He loves you so much. He has a wonderful plan for your life. He's not going to tell you what it is all at one time. You have to walk by faith and live a godly Christian life. But if you do, in time, He will show you His purpose for your life."

When Brother Hanks finished his story, there wasn't a dry eye in the church. Grown men were weeping. The pastor was weeping. I looked over at aunt Mabel. She was crying. But when I turned and looked at Jennie. I couldn't believe my eyes. She was looking up toward Heaven. Tears were streaming down her face. Over and over again she was saying, "Thank you God. Thank you God. Oh, thank you Lord. I love you God. I love you Lord." Then I heard her say, "Thank you so much for sending Brother Hanks. Thank you so much for helping me see."

I didn't realize at first what had happened to Jennie. But evidently Brother Hanks' story touched her deeply. It helped to free her from the burden of uncle Robert's death. I think that she also understood for the first time that God had a purpose for her life that was beyond being focused on herself.

When the invitation was given almost everyone in the church came down. The pews were almost empty. Some came forward to confess their sins and accept Jesus as their Savior. Others came down to recommit their lives to the Lord. Still others went to those they had wronged and asked for their forgiveness. Relationships were restored. One of our young men, Bobby Bateman, surrendered to full time ministry. I had never seen anything like it before. God did something incredible that night with us all.

After church, when we got back home, Jennie told us what she experienced in the service. She talked like I never heard her talk before. It was as if she grew up almost in an instant. From that day forward, Jennie helped people in need. She volunteered at the church. She didn't gossip about people anymore. She quit trying to gain the attention of all the boys. Jennie had a genuine, life-changing encounter with God. It was real and it never left her. We were all so grateful to God for saving Jennie's life.

Uncle Robert's death affected all of us in significant ways. But with time, the help of friends, and the Lord, we all survived. Our loss of uncle Robert actually drew us closer to one another. We no longer had arguments over little, insignificant things. We valued each other in deeper and more meaningful ways. We realized how precious life was and how short life could be. We cherished just being together. All of those things became important in the next few years as we faced more troubling times.

15   *The Roses Face Tough Times*

Just as we were recovering from uncle Robert's death everyone began to feel the effects of the depression. The girls and I didn't understand what was happening but aunt Mabel did. People didn't have money to buy things at the store. Many families lost their homes and their farms. Some had to move away and live with relatives. Times were bad.

Just when we thought that things couldn't get worse, they did. A great drought came across several states. It just stopped raining. In Oklahoma it was so bad that people died from the dust storms that the drought created. In Mississippi, cotton and food crops were scorched in the fields. We had never seen anything like it. One thing led to another and soon we were in serious trouble.

I remember one night when we were already in bed. Aunt Mabel and aunt Macy were talking. Ellie and I went to the stairs and could hear the conversation. Aunt Mabel was crying. She said that she was going to have to use her savings to keep the store open and to keep the farm going. Uncle Robert and aunt Mabel were very frugal. They didn't waste

money on anything. If they had not been so careful, aunt Mable would have surely lost everything.

I did hear her say that it was going to be hard to keep all the workers on the farm. We had a dairy farm, beef cows, and chickens. The milk, beef, and eggs were sold in the store. Mr. Jim Buck managed the farm. He had worked there for as long as I could remember. He was a good man who was always nice to us girls. He had three or four men and a couple of high school boys working for him. All of them were considered part of the family. I remember thinking how sad it would be if some of them were no longer with us.

I learned a lot about myself, life, and people that year. In many ways I grew up. At some point, I remember thinking that I was no longer a child. I started seeing myself as an adult. I was only seventeen but somehow when you face adversities like the ones brought on by the depression, you grow up quickly. That was true for all of us. Ellie was like me. She just did what she had to do. I remember at times that we were so tired that we just came home, ate supper, and went straight to bed.

Early on, Jennie had a harder time with things. Just when she was doing better with uncle Robert's death, all these problems came. You could see the worry on her face. She talked about it all the time. "What are we going to do if we lose the store? What if we lose our house? We wouldn't have anywhere to live." We were all afraid that she might go back to that dark place where she had been before. If that happened again, she might leave us forever.

To our surprise, after a while, Jennie was okay. She stopped talking about losing everything. She stopped crying all the time and she actually helped the rest of us when we got down. You see, each of us had times when we were overwhelmed by the situation. Everyone was working so hard. But it looked as if the hard work wasn't going to be enough. The depression was getting worse. Even with all of us working at the store, aunt Mabel still had to use her savings to keep everything going. At one point she almost closed the doors.

But back to Jennie. One night after supper, she went to her room and came back with her Bible. She started sharing verses with us. She said that God promised to supply all our needs according to His riches in glory. She read a story from the Old Testament about a widow who was eating her last meal when God filled her house with food. She reminded us that God fed five thousand with a few fish and loaves of bread.

We were all in shock. We were so worried about her, hoping and praying that she was going to be okay. It was obvious that night that Jennie was not only going to be okay but she was the one who was going to help us through. It was as if the preacher had come to the house and delivered an encouraging sermon. At one point, aunt Macy said, "Amen!" When Jennie finished, Aunt Mabel hugged her and thanked her for lifting our spirits.

Jennie's reminder of God's care was a word that we were going to need over and over again during those days because things did not get better. On the last day of March we all faced a devastating tragedy. That morning when we left for school, we could tell that it was going to be a stormy day. Clouds were rolling in and the rain started just as we got off the bus. About nine o'clock the rain got real heavy and the wind started blowing. The teachers had all of us get in the

hall. They looked real scared. We had never seen a storm like this before.

At about ten o'clock all the lights in the school went out. That's when we heard some of the windows breaking in our rooms. Some of the girls started screaming. The teachers tried to calm us down but it wasn't working. The wind was howling. I don't remember who it was but one of the boys shouted, "It's a tornado!" None of us had ever been in a tornado. Uncle Robert had built a storm shelter at the house. Aunt Mabel would sometimes store different items down there. Sometimes we would play in there. But we never used it for a storm.

I'll never forget that sound. It was as if a train was coming right though the building. All of a sudden we heard a loud noise what sounded like the roof being torn off. That's exactly what happened. The roof of the gym was taken completely off. We were so afraid. Then, within just a few minutes, it was over. Our teachers made us stay in the halls for a long time. We didn't know if any of our friends had been hurt or worse. We were all worried about our families, wondering if they were okay and if our homes were hit by the tornado.

The teachers finally got us out of the halls and took us to the auditorium. It was not damaged. Mr. Bickham, our principal, told us that parts of the school had heavy damage. The gym was practically gone. He did tell us, however, that everyone was accounted for and that no one was seriously injured. We all thanked the Lord for that. He told us that most of the buses had been completed demolished. When we finally went outside we saw buses turned over. Some were in a field across from the school and others were just gone. Only one wall of the gym was still standing. Most of the beautiful trees around the campus were uprooted or total stripped of their new spring leaves. We just couldn't believe it.

That's when we really got worried about aunt Mabel, aunt Macy, and Willie. At the time the tornado hit, they should have all been at the store. Hopefully, they made it safely through the storm. I can't tell you how anxious we were to get home. The problem was that there was no way to get home. Mr. Bickham told us that they were trying to have buses brought in from other counties. They were also trying to find people with cars who could take us home.

We were at the school until two o'clock. That's when aunt Macy showed up in old Rusty. We were so glad to see her. We immediately asked about aunt Mabel and Willie. That's when aunt Macy started crying. Our first thought was that aunt Mabel or Willie had been hurt or worse. We all just held on to each other waiting for the news.

After a while aunt Macy said, "Your momma is okay but the storm came right though Main Street. We got down behind the big front counter and held on. Jennie asked, "Well, where was Willie?" Aunt Macy started crying again. "Willie had gone to the house to pick up the morning eggs from the farm. On my way to pick you up, I went by the house. She wasn't there. The delivery truck wasn't there. We don't know where she is."

We couldn't believe it. Surely she stopped somewhere to get out of the storm. I was worried though. If something had happened to Willie, I didn't know if we could take another loss. On the way home we just prayed and prayed that Willie was okay.

As we made our way back to Norman, we saw the awful

devastation left by the tornado. Whole houses had been ripped from their foundations. A large part of one house was actually in the middle of the road. Others were simply demolished, reduced to a pile of splinters. We saw horses and cows dead in the fields. Huge trees were uprooted or snapped in half. Debris was all over the road. Mr. Johnny Langston lost his barns and his home. We saw him with his family going through the rubble trying to find family photos and other memorabilia. I felt so bad for them.

When we got to our house we saw that it had been spared. There were a few shingles missing on the roof and the chairs we had on the porch were in the yard. But the barns and the house were okay. When we got to the house, the first thing I did was check the storm cellar. I thought that Willie might be in there. She wasn't.

Aunt Macy took us on into town to see aunt Mabel. When we got there, we saw that several stores were damaged. Mr. Mitchell's bakery had been hit the worst. The whole roof and the front of the store were gone. The next week, aunt Mabel made room in the store for Mr. Michelle. He stayed for about three months while his place was repaired. Every day when we came in from school we could smell the aroma of fresh baked bread.

Mr. Childers' barber shop had also been hit pretty hard. His place was next to Ganny's Restaurant. Mrs. Aaron, who was affectionately known as Ganny, owned the only restaurant in Norman. She was a wonderful lady who laughed all the time. Her husband had started the restaurant years ago but he was killed in an accident. Mrs. Aaron continued the business just like aunt Mabel after uncle Robert's death. The restaurant had weathered the storm well and actually became a feeding station that helped those families who lost their homes.

When we finally saw aunt Mabel, we were so relieved that she was okay. Then, all our thoughts turned to Willie. Where could she be? Aunt Mabel told Jennie and Ellie to stay at the store with aunt Macy. Aunt Mabel and I went to find Willie. We stopped at every home between the store and our house. Of course we saw that many had lost everything they owned. The tornado cut a path of destruction that was over a mile wide. Almost everything in its direct path was gone.

We asked everyone along the way if they had seen Willie. No one had seen her or the delivery truck. There were only two farms left to check. When we got to Mr. Willard Jones house we saw him in the front yard. His house was heavily damaged. We asked Mr. Jones if he had seen Willie. He had not. We only had one more home to check. It was our neighbor's house, Mrs. Dollie Goodson's. Her home was also heavily damaged. We checked to see if she was home. No one answered our calls.

We went around back. That's when we saw our delivery truck turned over on its side. We quickly checked to see if Willie was in the truck. She was not. Mrs. Goodson didn't have a storm cellar so we both thought the worst. The storm had taken them away. That possibility was too much for aunt Mabel and me to take. We just started weeping.

But that's when we heard voices. They sounded familiar but they seemed far, far away. That's when we looked up and saw Willie and Mrs. Goodson waving at us from the barn. Aunt Mabel and I ran to meet them. It turned out that Mrs. Goodson's milk cow, Mollie, was having a calf. Willie and Mrs. Goodson were in the barn when the tornado came

through. Mollie had a difficult delivery that lasted hours after the storm. Just before we arrived, Mollie delivered her little boy. Of course, Mrs. Goodson named him Stormy.

Aunt Mabel told Mrs. Goodson that she could stay in the room on the second floor of the store as long as she needed it. We gathered some of her things together and went back into town. When Ellie and Jennie saw that Willie was okay, they were elated. That night at supper, each of us prayed, thanking God for his protection. We also prayed for each family we knew who had not fared so well.

In the next few weeks it was amazing to see how people pulled together to rebuild our little community. Work crews from around the state came in to help. I remember hearing the sound of hammers every day as homes and businesses were brought back to life. We went back to school about four weeks after the storm. They made us attend classes through June because we had missed so many days.

Ellie and I graduated on Friday, July first. At our graduation, Brother Smith delivered the baccalaureate message. He noted how we all came together and helped those in need after the storm. He challenged us to live the rest of our lives in service to the Lord and each other.

Aunt Mable had a party for all the Norman graduates after the service. We went to Ganny's and enjoyed a wonderful meal together. Mr. Mitchell baked a graduation cake for us and aunt Mable presented each graduate with a little gift from the store. When we went home, aunt Mable had special gifts for Ellie and me. The most precious of the gifts was a letter aunt Mable wrote. In my letter she told me how proud she was of me. She said that I was just like another daughter to her, that she loved me, and that she would pray for me every day as I grew into a young woman.

I can't tell you how much that letter meant to me. After graduation I again began to wonder about my real parents. Were my mother and father still alive? Who was my father? Where did they live? Why did they leave me? One day, perhaps, I would learn the truth. Until then, I had a second mother and a family that loved me with all their hearts. I was truly blessed. For now, that was enough.

16 *Hard Decisions For The Rose*

After graduation I had an important decision to make. Most girls were married by the time they were eighteen. I wasn't interested in anyone and no one seemed to be interested in me. I actually didn't want to get married then. I had become rather independent. Working in the store gave me a different perspective on life. I was considering college.

Mrs. Bynum encouraged me to think about becoming a teacher. She had attended Mississippi College for Women in Cedarville. She told me that the college had just organized a basketball team. She felt that I could play at MCW. Since I had no parents, Mrs. Bynum told me that I would be eligible for special scholarships and a work study program. She thought that I would make a great teacher and coach.

In those days you received a teaching certificate after completing two years of college. I could return to Norman after graduation and teach. I could help aunt Mabel with the store in the summers and be close to my family. That was my plan. Even with a plan and a dream I was still torn between going to college and helping aunt Mabel with the store. She had done so much for me. I didn't want to abandon her if I was needed at the store. The depression still had its grip on the nation. There was talk of how a new President might be able to turn things around but that was down the road and it might not happen any time soon. I just didn't know what to do.

I finally decided to talk with aunt Mabel about my struggle and my dream. She was so supportive. She told me not to worry about the store. I couldn't believe it. She made my decision much easier. Mrs. Bynum took me to the college and helped with my application. Within a couple of weeks, I was accepted. Orientation was just three weeks away. I had so much to do to get ready.

The girls all wished me well and gave me a going away party the week before I left. Aunt Macy told me to make sure that I went to church every Sunday and to write every week. I promised that I would. The Sunday before I left, Brother Smith had a special prayer at church for all of us who were headed to college. Everyone let me know of their prayers. I was blessed.

None of the other girls from my class were going to MCW. Actually, I was one of only five girls who were going to any college that year. The depression robbed so many of that opportunity. If it had not been for my family situation, I would not have been able to attend.

The day I left for school, aunt Mabel took me to the train station in Hampton. I told her how grateful I was for her love and care. She told me that I was a blessing to her and the family. Just before I boarded the train, aunt Mabel gave me a gift that was wrapped with a pretty red ribbon. She asked me not to open it until later. We hugged each other one more

time. The conductor gave his last call. I grabbed my travel bag and got on the train. My seat was close to where aunt Mable was standing. I waved at her until I couldn't see her anymore. When I opened the present, I found a beautiful jewelry box. It was a musical jewelry box that played the song, Roses From The South. It became one of my most prized possessions.

When I arrived at the train station in Cedarville, a small bus was there to take me and several other girls to the campus. One of the new students was Julie Bates. She was from Meridian. Her family owned a general store that was like aunt Mabel's store in Norman. Julie and I soon became good friends. Margaret Weathersby was another new student who came in on the same train. She was from Picayune. Margaret was one of the other girls who planned on playing basketball. Both of us ended up making the team. We also became good friends.

When we arrived on campus, the Dean of Women met us and took us to our dormitory, Callaway Hall. During orientation, we were told that Callaway was the oldest building on campus. It was named after Mary Calloway who served as a professor of mathematics and as acting President of the college on two occasions.

When we received our room assignments, I met Beverly Garrett. She was from Yazoo City. We roomed together our first year. Beverly also came for the two year teaching certificate. She wanted to serve as a missionary to Oklahoma and teach children on one of the Indian reservations. Since both of us were dedicated Christians, we went to church together and had a Bible study in our room every week.

In those first few weeks of school, I didn't have much

time to reflect on the experience. I was busy with classes, basketball practice, and just learning to be on my own. All of a sudden, my life became rather hectic. It was all good. But there was just so much I had to do. I noticed that several of the other girls felt the same way. We had to learn to manage our time. At one point I thought about aunt Mable and all the work that she had to handle with the store, the farm, and the family. My appreciation for her was growing every day.

At the end of my first semester, I took the train back to Norman. It was so good to see everyone and to have some time away from study. One day I was able to see Mrs. Bynum, my old coach. We talked for three hours straight. I also got to see a few of my friends who went to other colleges. Mary Beth Stoker was home from Blue Mountain College. Jane Ingram came in from Whitworth. All of us were glad to be home.

Of course the best time was spent with the girls, aunt Macy, and aunt Mabel. Ellie and I stayed up late most nights talking. She told me about a young salesman who came to the store about once a month. His name was Gene Morton. They actually went on a date. Well, he took her to Ganny's for supper and then they went to Indian Cliff to watch the sunset. She really liked him. He was rather quiet and seemed to be real nice. Ellie never talked so much about a boy.

Willie and Mack Bridges were dating all the time. I was so happy for her. Willie had not dated at all in high school. She was so shy that the boys never paid any attention to her. But now she was lively, talking, and enjoying life with Mack. Willie did tell me that they had started talking about marriage. When I asked her how she felt about it, she smiled as if she had already made up her mind. I expected that by

the time I came home again, Willie and Mack would be engaged.

Jennie and I didn't have much time to talk. She was very busy. She was practicing for the church Christmas program, wrapping toys for the children at the orphanage in Truitt, and spending time with Jeremy Miller. Jeremy was the son of the new preacher at Pleasant Hill church. His family had moved to the church in August. Jennie met Jeremy at a Baptist youth meeting at Oakmont church. When I was able to talk with Jennie, I could tell that she was doing well. She seemed more mature than I ever thought she would be.

All the girls were enjoying life and love. They were still helping aunt Mabel at the store and helping aunt Macy with chores at the house. Aunt Macy seemed so glad to see me. We spent a lot of time out on the porch just talking. She wanted me to tell her everything about college. When I asked how she and aunt Mabel were doing, she said, "We're doing as fine as frog hairs." That was a saying that older people used a lot back then.

She did tell me that things had settled down some. The store was doing okay and they were getting by. She was a bit concerned about aunt Mabel because she never had any time off. Before, aunt Mabel and uncle Robert shared that load. Now, everything was on her shoulders.

Over the break I helped as much as I could. I tried to get aunt Mable to take a day off but she wouldn't. I could see that she was tired. When I asked how she was doing, she smiled and said, "Honey, don't you worry about me. God's going to see us through." She was a strong woman but everyone has their limits. I was just hoping that the depression would end soon and give everybody some relief.

I went back to school the first week of January. The time off had been good for me. Getting back in the routine of study and all the rest was also good. Basketball season was starting and I loved it. It was actually my stress relief from studying.

Miss Madeline Parker was our coach. She had taught English at Judson College in Alabama before coming to MCW. This was actually her first coaching position in college. She had coached high school in her hometown, Milford, Mississippi. She was only twenty eight years old.

Miss Parker was incredible. She demanded our very best every minute of every game. But she demanded the same of herself. She actually played with us during practice. If she wanted to teach a player a new move, she made that move rather than describe it.

She came to almost every practice with a new formation or play. She required each player to keep a notebook with all the plays. I had never come to practice with a pencil and pad. But I did for Miss Parker. She had a system of codes with numbers for each formation and play. Of course we had to memorize all of them. In practice she would call out a play and ask each player about their position and move. If you didn't know, well, it wasn't good. If it happened more than once, you were going to be running bleachers after practice.

The best part of having Miss Parker as our coach was the life lessons she taught us. One of those lessons we learned in game six of our season. We had won our first five games. Some were close but we won them. We were feeling pretty good about ourselves. Then we played a small school in northern Alabama. I don't know if we thought that we were so much better than them that we didn't have to play hard

but we lost that game.

We all wondered what Miss Parker was going to say about the game. She met us in the locker room and said, "Women, in basketball, failure is inevitable. You are going to lose games. You're going to lose games sometimes because the team is better than you. You're going to lose some games because you didn't play your best. The question is whether or not you're going to learn from those loses. What did you learn from this lose tonight."

At first we thought that it was a rhetorical question. But Miss Parker wanted us to answer the question right then. None of the other girls spoke up so I said, "Miss Parker, I learned not to take anything for granted." Miss Parker replied, "Exactly, Anne. Whether it's wins in basketball, family, or friends we don't need to take anything for granted. We need to do our very best all the time and we need to appreciate people, especially people who love us.

I was in awe of the wisdom Miss Parker shared with us. She did that quite often. One day when we were playing a home game, Hillary Caldwell started shooting the ball every time it touched her hands. She thought that she was the best player on the team and she was good but not that good. Her antics caused us to fall behind by ten points at halftime.

When we left the court I noticed that Miss Parker and Hillary did not immediately follow us to the locker room. The two of them sat down on the bench. In a few minutes Hillary came in with Miss Parker and said, "I'm sorry for the way I've played. It's my fault that we're behind. Obviously, I have a lot to learn about being on a team. I am not the team. I'm sorry."

All of us just sat there in shock. We had never seen Hillary humble before. Whatever Miss Parker told her worked. Hillary never hogged the ball again that season. She became a different person off the court also. It was amazing.

A few weeks later, Miss Parker was talking with us about teamwork. She noted the differences between team sports and individual sports. Again, she related sports to life. "Basketball is like life. Both are team sports. None of us can be successful in life without other people by our side, helping us along the way. The prodigal son thought that he didn't need his family but he did." Every once in a while Miss Parker tied her lesson to the Bible. She helped me see things in Scripture and in life that I would never have seen on my own. A few years later, when I returned to the college for a team reunion, I thanked Miss Parker for the blessing she had been in my life.

All of our games were on Saturdays. Some of the schools we played had men's teams. We would play in the afternoon and the men would play at night. Of course, more people attended the men's games. Most of the teams we played were in Mississippi, Alabama, Georgia, and Tennessee. We traveled on one of the school buses. It was a rough riding vehicle which, of course, did not have air conditioning. Sometimes the ride to the game was tougher on us that the game itself.

Most of the time we left early in the morning on Saturday to get to our games. We would stop somewhere for lunch and then make our way on to our destination. Of course, we had a few eventful trips that season. One day we were headed to play Alabama State College for Women in Montevallo. About half way, we stopped at a little restaurant just outside of Tuscaloosa to eat. The waitress noticed our jerseys and asked us where we were playing. We told her and

didn't think anything else about it. In a few minutes she brought our food and we enjoyed the meal.

Well, about twenty minutes after we left the restaurant, we all started getting sick. I mean real sick. We pulled in to a rest area and, well, we were sick. I never felt that bad in my life. One by one we all mentioned how the food tasted a little funny. That's when Julie Bates shouted, "We've been poisoned! We've been poisoned! That waitress poisoned us!

Margaret Weathersby started crying, "Are we going to die?" I don't want to die. I'm too young to die." After a few moments of hysteria I finally got everyone to calm down and started thinking through the situation. We had not eaten anything else that could have made us sick. It had to be something that all of us ate. The food did taste a little different.

There were only two possibilities. The food at the restaurant was just bad. If that was the case, everyone who ate there got sick. Or the waitress had sabotaged our meal so we would lose the game. Surely not. But it was a possibility. Whatever the case, we finally made it to Montevallo but we were in no shape to play our best. Fortunately, our opponents weren't very good and we won the game. On the way back home, some of the girls wanted to stop at the restaurant and confront the waitress, but Miss Parker wouldn't allow it. Needless to say, we never ate there again.

We had a few other incidents on the road that season. Everything from a flat tire to hitting a deer one night. I guess the funniest thing that happened was on our way to Belmont College for Women in Nashville. We had to leave very early on that Saturday morning. It was the longest trip on our schedule. Somewhere just across the Tennessee line, we stopped for a rest break at a little general store. We used their facilities and each of us bought a candy bar and soda pop.

We got back on the road and headed toward Belmont. We had all run out of things to talk about and were reading one of our books. After about an hour, somewhere around Franklin Tennessee, coach Parker asked Millie Higgins to come up to the front of the bus. We didn't pay any attention to it but evidently Millie didn't hear Miss Parker so she called for Millie again. When Millie didn't respond, Miss Parker pulled the bus over and said, "Millie I need to talk with you. Come up here." We all looked up and to our surprise, Millie wasn't on the bus. Miss Parker almost lost her mind. "Where's Millie? Oh my goodness! Oh my! Oh no. Lord help us."

That's when we realized that we had left Millie at the store. Well, we were almost to Nashville. Our game was in an hour and we didn't have time to go back and get Millie. Miss Parker took off. We stopped at the first place that had a phone. Miss Parker called the store. When the owner answered the phone Miss Parker said, "Hello, this is Madeline Parker. Is one of my basketball players there at your store?" Later Millie told us that the store owner started laughing and almost couldn't stop. Finally, he said, "Yes mam. She's here."

Miss Parker was so relieved. There was still one problem. We would not be coming through that little town until after the store closed. The owner said that he and his wife would stay until we got there. When Miss Parker hung up the phone, she started praying. "Thank you Lord. We praise you Lord." One of our Pentecostal players later said

that she thought Miss Parker was about to get the Holy Ghost.

We played our game with Belmont and made our way back to the little store. When we arrived, Millie was sitting behind the counter with a candy bar and soda pop. She said, "Welcome ladies. What can I help you with?" Actually, we were all glad to see her safe and sound. After that little episode, Miss Parker did a role call every time we got on the bus. When she got to Millie's name, we all yelled, "Millie's here."

That semester was one of the most memorable of my life. The relationships that were built in those few months have lasted for all these years. We write each other and occasionally call to stay in touch. Several of them have been very supportive during my illness. I love those girls and always will.

At the end of the semester, I headed home to Norman. I was so glad to see everyone and I was ready for a break from school. All the girls were doing well. Ellie was going out with Gene Morton every time he came into town. Jennie was still dating the preacher's son and Willie was about to be engaged to Mack Bridges. They were all happy and I was so glad for them.

Aunt Macy was fine. She was busy taking care of her roses and helping aunt Mable. We spent time out on the porch most nights talking about everything in the world. She told me how proud she was that I was in college. Of course, she ask me if I was seeing anyone. I wasn't. I was too busy studying and playing basketball. She told me not to get so serious about school that I didn't have some fun every once in a while. I just smiled and went on. Aunt Macy was a great encourager for me at that time.

Everyone was doing well except aunt Mable. I couldn't put my finger on it, but something was wrong. Oh, she put a smile on her face every day but you could see that she was struggling with something. I actually asked her one night when we were alone. She grinned and said that she was just getting older. To me she looked weary, at times, almost exhausted.

I spent most of my days helping at the store. There was always something to do. Business had actually picked up rather substantially. The federal government started a new work program called the Civilian Conservation Corps. Young single men were hired to work on forestry projects. The Mississippi CCC built a camp just outside Norman. They shipped in most of the specialty equipment they needed but they bought everyday items locally. Aunt Mable had a contract with the government for things like gloves, hats, shovels, and more. The increase in revenue actually saved the store from going under.

The young men in the CCC were from all over the country. Many of them were from northern states. They had never traveled in the South. They seemed particularly fascinated with our southern accent. At times they would mock us in a way that we didn't appreciate. Like, "How y'all doing?" We would come back with, "We're doing fine, yous guys."

The back and forth was mostly fun but sometimes it got a little out of hand. Our boys had not worked very much with big trucks and road machinery. They could take a tractor apart and put it back together in their sleep. But they were not familiar with the new equipment. The northern boys

would call our guys dummies, ignorant, and worse.

Well, one day our boys got the best of them. A group of the men were going up toward Silver Creek to plant some trees. They left Norman early that morning. Somewhere around Oakmont the truck lost one of its tires. It just fell off. They couldn't find the bolts and the supervisor, who was from New York, just threw a fit. What were they going to do?

He told the men that they were going to have to walk back to camp which was ten miles away. One of our boys spoke up and said, "Sir, some of us better stay with the truck. Somebody might try to vandalize it." The supervisor agreed. So all our boys stayed with the truck while the northern boys headed back to camp. Well, in just a few minutes, to everyone's surprise, our guys came down the road driving the truck. How in the world did they put that tire back on?

The supervisor was stunned. He looked at the tire and it had real bolts on it but he didn't look close enough to see what the boys had done. He said, "Where did you find the bolts for that tire?" One of our guys spoke up and said, "Well, sir, they were there all the time on the other tires. We just borrowed one bolt from each tire and put it on the one that had fallen off." The supervisor couldn't believe it. As they were all getting back in the truck, one of our boys said, "Not bad for a bunch of ignorant southern boys, huh chief?" The supervisor growled and thanked the boys for fixing the truck. That little incident put an end to the thought that we southerners were just a bunch of dumb, backward folks.

The community faced a few additional challenges with the influx of CCC workers. Our county was a dry county. That meant that alcohol was not sold in Taylor County. If you wanted to drink, you had to go over to Martin County toward

Hampton. The men at the camp didn't have cars and they had very little money. So, moonshiners and others from around the area would bring liquor to the boys on the weekends. I remember Brother Smith preaching several sermons on the evils of alcohol.

Well, the Taylor County Sheriff had a big problem on his hands. He didn't have enough men to deal with all the illegal bootlegging that was going on. So the Sheriff came up with a unique solution. He let it be known that a big buyer was coming in to purchase a large quantity of liquor. Anyone who had good stock could come to a certain location at night and sell all the alcohol they had. The Sheriff, of course, was going to confiscate the liquor and deal with the sellers.

The night of the operation, dozens of people came to sell their alcohol. One was a Baptist deacon and two were twin sisters who sang in the choir every week. Can you imagine how embarrassed they were? I would have been mortified. Of course, the Sheriff knew all the sellers and none of them were arrested. But they got the message. Don't sell alcohol to the CCC boys.

I guess the other problem that I could mention was the romance issue. It was huge. These young men had their eyes on every girl in town and some of the girls liked the attention. A few of them felt that their boyfriends weren't paying enough attention to them. So they let the CCC boys think that they were interested in them. Mary Ellen Pigott played that little game. She was dating Bobby Turner who was from Hicks. Mary Ellen was working that summer at Ganny's Restaurant. Whenever Bobby came in she would flirt with the CCC boys to make Bobby jealous. Well, that little trick backfired on Mary Ellen and Bobby started dating Sue

Richardson. They were engaged within a few months and married the next year.

Sometimes the girls were just innocent bystanders when trouble came. A guy was cozying up to Ellie in the store one day when Gene Morton came in. It wasn't good. Gene walked up to the guy, tapped him on the shoulder, and told him to leave Ellie alone. The guy just kept talking to Ellie. Gene tried again to get the guy's attention. He didn't respond. That's when Gene grabbed the guy by the belt, ran him out the back of the store, and threw him in the street. None of us had ever seen Gene act like that. He was a rather mild mannered guy. But he wasn't going to let some fellow steal Ellie away from him.

The episode I remember most that summer was the one at the church social. Every summer, all the churches got together and had a special fellowship. We had all types of events at the social. Choirs sang, we played games, and, of course, we had dinner on the grounds outside. It was always a great time to see folks from different communities.

Well, some of the CCC boys came to the social. Most of them were nice enough but a couple of them started talking to the girls. One of them was particularly interested in Ella May Knapp. She had just graduated from high school and was dating Billie Bennett who was from Justice. Well, one of the CCC boys sat down next to Ella May for lunch. Willie and I were across the table from them. Willie kept looking at me like something is going to happen. And it did. Billie came out to sit down by Ella May. He said to the CCC boy, "You're sitting in my seat." The boy looked up at Billie and said, "I don't see your name on it."

That's when Willie and I got up. We didn't want to be in

the line of fire. I thought that Billie was going to punch the guy. Instead, he emptied his plate and his drink on the guy's head. Oh my goodness. The CCC guy jumped up and lit into Billie with all he had. Billie gave it right back to him. A couple of Billie's friends went to his aid and that's when the other CCC boys joined the ruckus. They were knocking over tables, throwing food at each other, and more. It was like one of those fight scenes from a western movie. Before Brother Smith and the other men could stop the fight, we lost all the desserts and half of the fried chicken. Everybody was mad. Later we learned that Brother Smith and the other pastors met with the CCC camp supervisor. After that, the romance conflicts ended.

On the fourth of July, aunt Mabel closed the store and we drove over to Pearl Valley for the celebration. At the big gazebo on the town square there were signing groups, bands, and politicians making speeches. On the outside of the square there were carnival games, food, and more. Aunt Mabel gave each of us two dollars but she told us not to spend it on the carnival games because that was gambling.

Jennie, Ellie, and Willie met their boyfriends and I spent time with some of my friends from school. We had fun watching the boys try to win dolls for their girls. Joseph Aaron won a little teddy bear for knocking down some milk bottles. He had been a pitcher on the high school baseball team and could throw a ball harder than anyone else in the county.

Joseph didn't have a girlfriend at the time and it would have looked funny for him to be walking around with a teddy bear under his arm. He looked at me and said, "Miss Hill would you hold this bear for me." I took the bear not

realizing that he had given it to me. He said, "I think that bear likes you. Why don't you take him home?" I thanked him for the bear and we shared smiles. Later, all the girls starting saying silly things about me and Joseph. I just laughed and went on.

When we all met to go back home, the girls asked me where I got the bear. I told them and they started in on me with that old kissing song, "Anne and Joseph sitting in a tree, K I S S I N G. First comes love. Then comes marriage. Then comes Anne with a baby carriage." I started to fuss them out when Aunt Mabel broke in and said, "Well, I think you girls are just jealous." She always knew how to end one or our arguments.

We got back home about seven o'clock that night. Just before bedtime, I went to see aunt Mabel and thank her for taking us to the celebration. Unfortunately, that's when I first discovered how ill she really was. When I walked in, aunt Mabel was holding a rag over her mouth and coughing. When she removed the rag I was shocked. I ran to her and helped her sit on the edge of her bed. She was hot with fever. She kept holding her chest as if it hurt to breathe. I knew what was happening. Aunt Mabel had Tuberculosis.

TB was a horrible disease. I had seen so many people with it when I was younger. Hardly anyone survived more than a few years. Most of them had to leave their families because it was so contagious. Doctors had worked for years to find a cure but none had been found. There were specialized hospitals all across the country for those who contracted the disease.

I just burst into tears. I couldn't help it. Aunt Mabel tried to calm me down. After a moment or two she talked to me about her situation. Doctor Everett suspected that she had TB weeks earlier. She had a persistent cough for over three weeks and none of the medication the doctor prescribed worked. She had also been having fevers and chills off and on for about two months. I knew that she looked fatigued but I had no idea that she was so ill.

Aunt Mabel told me that none of the girls knew how sick she was. She planned on telling them soon. The doctor told her that the only real option she had was to be admitted to the TB hospital in Truitt. Thankfully, the hospital was only an hour away from Norman. The doctors there were experimenting with some new drugs which might cure the disease.

We just sat there together for a while. I told her that I loved her and that I would do anything she needed. I prayed with her and went to bed. I couldn't go to sleep. At first, I didn't realize what all this meant for the family. I didn't understand what it would eventually mean for me. That night I begged God to heal aunt Mabel. I told Him that I would do anything for her to be well. I cried myself to sleep.

The next morning I got up early and went out to the rose garden and continued my conversation with God. I was actually praying out loud, pleading for a miracle. As I looked up to Heaven and cried out to God, I heard a voice, a very familiar voice. Aunt Macy had been on the side porch the whole time I had been praying. She asked me to join her on the swing. She put her arm around me and I just fell apart.

After a few minutes, aunt Macy started talking with me. "Honey, this is just another storm that we're all going to have to go through. We've made it through worse. But we have to hold on to each other and hold on to God to get through.

Mabel is in the Lord's hands and that's the safest place she can be." I knew that everything aunt Macy was saying was true. We had made it through uncle Robert's death. God sent Mr. Fielding to help aunt Mabel in the store. We had all made sacrifices and worked hard to keep things going.

But this time was different. Mr. Fielding couldn't run the store by himself. He was old and losing his health. Willie didn't know how to order goods from the wholesalers and keep the books. Ellie was doing her part but she couldn't take aunt Mabel's place and aunt Macy wasn't able either. No, this was different than before. This was more serious. This could mean that aunt Mabel would have to sell the store which would have a significant impact on all of us.

As I finished thinking through all of those realities, something happened. I had a revelation of sorts. You see, I had left myself out of the equation. I was going back to school in a few weeks. I was going to be a teacher. I had my whole life planned. I just couldn't face the truth that I was probably the only one who could actually run the store.

I started weeping. I didn't know what to do. This was the greatest decision I ever had to make. It could change my whole life. If I left school, I might never have the opportunity to return. If I took over the store for aunt Mabel, it might be permanent. She might not survive her illness. I would be responsible for everybody. I cannot express in words what a burden this was on my heart. I can remember thinking about Jesus in the Garden of Gethsemane when He prayed that He would not have to face the cross. But I remembered also how He said, "Not my will but thy will be done." I just didn't know what God's will was. I needed someone to help me make this decision. I couldn't talk with aunt Mabel about it. I knew that she would just tell me that everything would be fine without me. I considered going to my former coach, Mrs. Bailey. She was a good Christian woman. But I decided to talk with Brother and Mrs. Smith. I'm so glad I did.

We met one morning at their house for breakfast. Mrs. Smith made some fresh biscuits with eggs and sausage. I explained the situation. They already knew about aunt Mabel's illness. She told them early on. When I finished sharing my dilemma, Mrs. Smith turned to Brother Smith and said, "Dear, why don't you share your story with Anne.

I had no idea what she was talking about but Brother Smith did. He said, "Anne, I was the oldest boy in my family. I had a younger brother and three sisters. My father was a lumberjack. He cut trees and drove a timber truck. When I was fifteen years old my father was killed in a logging accident. I had to quit high school and go to work to help my family.

I had so many different jobs in those few years that I can't even count them. I worked on a farm for a while taking care of cows and bailing hay. I sold car batteries. I sold Bibles. I sold just about anything people could buy. Sometimes I had to work away from home and send money back to my mother. It was hard but I had to take care of my family.

Eventually, all my siblings graduated and moved on with their lives. I worked hard to finish my education and then went on to the seminary. That's where I met my sweetheart, Mrs. Smith. If all those things had not happened, I may never have met her. You see, Anne, sometimes bad things end up being good things. That's what the Bible says. It doesn't say that all things are good. It says that all things work together

for good to those who love God. And I know that you love God.

I certainly can't tell you what to do. That's what I did and I have never regretted that decision. Mrs. Smith and I will be praying for you. We're confident, because of your strong faith, that you will make the right decision for yourself and your family. If you need to talk with us again, please feel free to come at any time. We love you Anne and God loves you. He will see you through all of this and I believe that God has a special plan for your life because you're a special young lady. God bless you dear."

Mrs. Smith gave me a hug and I left. All the way home I thought about Brother Smith's story. I couldn't imagine how hard it must have been for him to leave school and take on such a heavy responsibility. But he did and God blessed him. Later, I thought that maybe Brother Smith went through all that so he could share it with me, to help me. Whatever the case, I had to make my decision very soon. School was starting the first week of September.

The next week, I could see that aunt Mabel's symptoms were getting worse. Aunt Macy looked real worried about her. The girls could now see that something was wrong. Ellie asked me if I noticed how sick her mother was. It was time for aunt Mabel to go to the hospital in Truitt and it was time to tell her about my decision.

We were all working in the store one afternoon. I told the girls that they needed to go home early and bake a chocolate cake for aunt Macy's birthday. I told aunt Macy that I was going to the office to talk with aunt Mabel. She and Mr. Fielding watched the front. When I came in, aunt Mabel was doing some paperwork. I asked if we could talk and she said, "Sure honey. What do you need?" That's how aunt Mabel always greeted people. Her first words were an offer of help.

I said, "Aunt Mabel, God has given me a clear vision of what He wants me to do with my life." She smiled and said, "That's wonderful dear." I knew that she thought I was going to share something about school or a future vocation. I continued. "I'm going to run the store for you while you're at the hospital in Truitt." Once again she smiled. But it was different. I knew what was coming next. "Now honey, don't you worry about the store. You're going to finish your next two semesters and start teaching. I can take care of all this. You don't worry about a thing."

It was going to be the first time that I went against her will. "Aunt Mabel, I'm not going back to school." She said, "Now, honey, you are. You have to. We're going to be just fine." That's when I put her hands in mine and looked at her with all the love in my heart. "Aunt Mabel, you have to go to the hospital. You have to go now. We need for you to get well."

She started crying. "Anne, I'm not going to get well. People don't get well from TB. They die. Some live longer than others but nobody survives this." I just started weeping. I didn't even know what to say. Aunt Mabel started coughing. I went and got her a towel. Aunt Macy ran in to check on her. She saw that we were crying. She took us both by the hand and started praying. It was an incredible prayer. She asked the Lord to calm our hearts and take away our fears.

The Lord answered her prayer. In just a few minutes, an unbelievable peace came to my heart. I can't explain it but I believed that the Lord was going to see us through. Aunt

Mabel even felt it. She actually stopped coughing and seemed to be able to breathe better. That's when she looked at me and said, "Honey, are you sure? Are you sure you want to run the store?" I said, "Yes, mam. I do." When I said that, she looked as if the weight of the world had been lifted from her shoulders.

That night we celebrated aunt Macy's birthday. It was the first time in weeks that I had seen aunt Mabel laugh. A few days later, she told the girls about her illness. They were upset but they seemed glad that I was going to be at home with them. I spent the next two weeks getting a crash course on how to run the store. Mr. Fielding agreed to work a few hours a week to help me with the transition. Aunt Mabel notified her suppliers about the changes and they were all very supportive.

I knew that this wasn't going to be easy. I was afraid and wondered if I really had what it took to run the store. In those two weeks before aunt Mable left, she encouraged me in every way possible. She quoted Scripture verses about being strong and courageous for the Lord is with us everywhere we go. She reminded me of the verse that says we can do all things through Christ who strengthens us. I soon found out how much I needed those words.

17   *The Rose Grows*

Aunt Mabel left on a Sunday afternoon. Brother and Mrs. Smith took her to the hospital in Truitt. We took care of a few chores and had an early supper. Aunt Macy said the prayer. All I can tell you is that aunt Macy knew how to talk with God. She asked the Lord to take care of aunt Mabel and to help us with all of our new responsibilities. She prayed for me particularly, asking the Lord to give me everything I needed to run the store.

We were all so emotionally drained from saying goodbye to aunt Mabel that there wasn't much conversation around the table. After supper Willie went to her room. Jennie took a walk with old Buster. Aunt Macy, Ellie, and I went out on the porch. It wasn't long before we were blessed with one of those late afternoon rain showers. You could smell it in the air. It was refreshing for us and for aunt Macy's roses.

Well, Monday morning came and I was in charge. I tried to remember everything aunt Mabel had shared with me. I got to the store at seven. Mr. Fielding was there to meet me. We went in and got things ready for the day. I filled the cash

register with the money aunt Mabel gave me. I checked to make sure that the refrigerator units were working. Mr. Fielding met Mr. Beakman in the back and brought in the milk and eggs. By then it was time to open the doors.

I'll never forget how I felt when the first few customers came in. I knew all of them and had waited on them before but somehow today was different. Instead of aunt Mabel welcoming them, I did. I answered their questions. I took their money or put the purchase on their account. I said, "Thank you. See you soon." I remember saying to myself, "You're twenty years old and you're running one of the biggest stores in town." I didn't say it boasting. I was scared to death but I was determined not to let aunt Mabel down.

Mondays were normally very busy at the store. Most of the housewives did their weekly shopping on Monday morning. Before I turned around twice it was lunchtime. Mr. Fielding took over the counter while I went back to the office for lunch. Aunt Mabel took a lunch break every day at noon. She would eat a ham sandwich, go over the morning sales, put some of the money in the safe, and look at her inventory needs. I don't know how she did all that in thirty minutes but she did.

When I went back to the front, Mr. Fielding asked me if I needed anything. I told him that I was fine. He told me to call him if I needed anything and then he left. Willie, Ellie, and I just looked at each other as if to say, "Well, it's ours now."

We decided beforehand which sections of the store each of us would manage. Aunt Mabel made some suggestions and we followed exactly what she said. Willie took care of the meat, produce, and canned goods. Ellie worked with all the clothing and the general items on the floor. I took care of everything behind the counter.

Before aunt Mable left, she hired Thomas Thornton to work in the afternoons. He was a senior in high school. We all knew him. He was a quiet boy who was really nice. The school bus dropped him off every day just after three o'clock and his daddy picked him up at six. Thomas helped us with heavy items and swept the store clean every day. He also took the trash out to the burn bin and did other things as needed.

That first evening when we closed the store, I felt pretty good about everything. The girls and I were proud that we had managed everything well. When we got home we enjoyed a great meal that aunt Macy cooked. She asked us about the day and told us how proud she was of us. When I went to bed that night I thanked the Lord for helping us through the first day. I asked Him to bless aunt Mabel and to bring her home as soon as He could.

That first week Mr. Fielding showed me a little more about keeping the monthly account records and the girls did a great job helping customers. Almost everyone who came in asked about aunt Mabel and told us of their prayers. On Friday I handed out my first payroll. I told everyone to check and make sure that it was right. I also made my first deposit at the bank. Mr. Jensen checked to make sure that the amount was correct. He told me how proud he was of how we were helping aunt Mabel.

The next day was Saturday, the busiest day of the week. That's when families came from all around the area to shop. Of course, they brought their children with them. The children were always a challenge. For one thing, they could never make up their minds on what kind of candy they

wanted. We had about twelve different jars of candy to choose from. Sometimes children would just take the lid off the jar, grab a piece of candy, and pop it in their mouths before their parents saw it. I remember many times when I had to tell a customer that little Bobby or little Susy had taken some candy.

The kids would also run through the store chasing each other. Most of the time Ellie did a good job of corralling those little critters. But every once in a while, she would have to talk to the parents. I remember once when little Billy Carter was running through the store. He was one of the worst. He was also a mean little kid. He got in fights at school all the time. We just knew that Billy was going to grow up and be some kind of criminal.

Well, one day, Billy was running down the tool aisle when he ran into Mr. Hank Powers. Mr. Powers was one of the biggest men I had ever seen and he was strong as an ox. In spite of his size and strength, Mr. Hank was known as the Gentle Giant because he was so mind mannered. Well, when Billy ran into Mr. Powers, he knew that he was in trouble. Ellie saw the whole thing. She said that when Billy looked up at Mr. Hank, he just froze. He didn't run. He didn't say anything. He just froze. Ellie said that she thought Billy was going to pass out.

Mr. Powers looked down at Billy with the meanest face he could make and he said, "Son, you need to stop running in this store." Billy said, "Ye, ye, ye, yes si, si, si, sir." Billy had evidently developed a stuttering problem. Mr. Powell said, "I want you to promise me that you will never run in this store ever again." Billy didn't say a word. He just nodded his head. Then Mr. Hank said, "Well, good. Then let's shake on it."

Billy put his little hand in Mr. Powell's big bear paw and they shook on it.

Ellie said that Mr. Hank walked away and Billy just stood there with eyes as big as fried eggs. That was the last day that Billy Carter ran in our store. Every time he came in after that, he stayed right by his mother's side. Billy didn't get in many more fights after that either. The funny thing is, Billy grew up to be a preacher. We all figured that Mr. Powers not only saved Billy from a life of crime but also helped him hear the call to ministry. And it all started one Saturday at the Norman General Store.

For about three months, I felt like I was running the store by the seat of my pants. I had a lot of firsts in those early days including my first irate customer. Mildred Baker brought a hat back that she purchased the day before. We had the same policy that every other store had. Hats were not returnable and Mrs. Baker knew that. This wasn't the first time she had done something like this. Aunt Mabel warned me about her. Mrs. Baker was not the nicest person in town. Aunt Mabel said that all the ladies had a nickname her, Mrs. Mil Dread. They called her that because they all dreaded having to deal with her.

Well, this day Mrs. Baker wanted to return a hat. She said that the lining had a tear in it. She was correct. The lining was torn. The problem was that we inspected every hat before we placed it on the rack. I asked Ellie if she was sure that she had checked all the hats. She said that she remembered checking that particular hat because she thought about getting it for herself. Mrs. Baker probably snagged the hat on something and tore the lining.

I didn't know what I was going to do. I checked in the

back to see if we had any more of that style hat. We did not. Then I thought that I would offer to have the hat repaired by Mrs. Fredricks, a local seamstress. So that's what I did. I said, "Mrs. Mildred, I don't have a replacement in the store and we don't have another order for that style hat. Would it be okay if I have the hat repaired at our cost? Mr. Baker spoke up and said, "I just want my money back. That is a defective hat. If the lining is bad the rest of the hat is probably bad too."

I was just about to tell Mrs. Baker that we couldn't give her a refund when Ellie spoke up and said, "Mrs. Mildred, we'll be glad to give you a refund on that hat. It is our most popular style and so few of them were made. I want one myself." I didn't realize at first what Ellie was doing. She went on and on about how pretty that hat was. She took Mrs. Mildred over to the mirror and put the hat on her head. She told her how good it looked and how it brought out her beautiful hazel eyes.

When everything was said and done, Mrs. Baker decided to keep her hat and agreed to let us fix the lining. When she left the store, I said, "Shame on you Ellie Henry." Ellie said in a heavy southern drawl, "Well, I was just helping her to see how pretty she looked in that hat. Ain't nothing wrong with that, is there?" We both laughed our heads off. I couldn't believe that Ellie outsmarted Mrs. Mil Dread. When we told aunt Macy that night she just cackled.

Another one of my firsts came when a salesman tried to pad an order we had for nails. Just before aunt Mabel went to the hospital, she ordered ten cases of sixteen penny nails. The CCC men were building something over at Darbonne. When the nails arrived the salesman gave me the bill. It was for fourteen cases of nails, not ten. I immediately saw the discrepancy but didn't say anything. I went in the back and checked our order sheet. Sure enough, it was for ten cases. The salesman had changed the second one of the eleven to a four.

When I went back to the front, I counted out the money for the ten cases and said, "There you are sir. Have a nice day." The salesman, of course, spoke up and said, "That's not what's on the bill." I smiled and said, "No sir it's not. It's what's on the order sheet aunt Mabel and you signed. It's so nice to see that you're donating three cases of nails to the CCC project. You are a patriotic American sir. God bless you."

He started to open his little weaselly mouth and argue with me but I raised my eyebrow and showed him the order sheet. He didn't say another word. He grabbed the money, gave me a disgusting look, and stormed out. Of course he took his three cases of nails with him. I told Mr. Fielding about the incident later that morning and he started laughing. He said, "Anne, you are just like your aunt Mabel, a velvet brick." I didn't really know what a velvet brick was. I guess Mr. Fielding was saying that I was nice but tough. The truth is, I was becoming more like aunt Mabel every day.

One of the fun aspects of the store was having salesmen come in with new products. I will never forget the first time I saw scotch tape. You could fix just about anything with it. Torn pages in a book. Window shades. Dollar bills. We used it to put pictures in memory books. We taped signs all through the store with it. Of course, someone found silly things to do with the tape. Jennie taped her eyelashes up to her forehead one day and went around the store with a goofy

look on her face. She scared little Tommy Tuttle half to death. He thought that she was a monster and went screaming to his mother. I made Jennie apologize.

Then one day Jennie put some tape on Mittens' paws. Fortunately, no one was in the store at the time. I have no idea how or why that thought popped into Jennie's mischievous little mind but have you ever seen what happens to a cat when you put tape on its paws? It is cruel but it is hilarious.

That cat started jumping and shaking like nothing we had ever seen. She was bouncing off the walls, running into displays, and making the strangest noises I have ever heard. Ellie got mad at Jennie and started fussing at her. Willie eventually caught the poor cat and took the tape off her paws. If she had not, I think that Mittens would have lost her mind. It was several weeks before Mittens got anywhere close to Jennie.

I just knew that the next thing I would see was old Buster running through the store with tape on his paws. I told Jennie that if she did that again, I was going to tape her to the wall. She never did it again at the store but I would bet that she showed her friends with their cats. There was never a dull moment with Jennie Henry around.

Another one of the new products that came out then was bubble gum. We had hard candy and chocolate bars in the store but nothing like bubble gum. I remember the salesman coming in the store with a big pink bubble on his mouth. I didn't know what to think. When he got to the counter he mumbled, "Watch this." Then he popped the bubble which scared me. He started laughing and gave me one of the new candies to try. I did. He said, "Blow a bubble." Well, I didn't really know how to blow a bubble but after a while I got the hang of it. It was like candy with a little extra fun. When the girls tried it, they loved it. Of course, we got it in our hair and Willie got it on her glasses. I had to warn Jennie not to give it to the pets.

The salesman told us that the gum was good for ladies because it helped to tighten the face muscles and reduced wrinkles. That was the lamest sales pitch I had ever heard. He told us that we had to tell everybody not to swallow the gum. Evidently, it did not digest well in the human body and could cause, as he said, "Some unintended consequences." I didn't ask him what those consequences were, but we taped a sign to the box of bubble gum, telling people not to swallow the gum.

I ordered one box of the gum to try it out. We sold that entire box in four days. It became our most popular candy item. Kids just loved it. Adults too. Some of the ladies believed the rumor about the gum removing wrinkles and bought several pieces each week. The schools eventually put a ban on the gum because the kids were popping bubbles in class. But that didn't hurt sales at all. Everyone was going to have their bubble gum.

I guess that the most profitable new product that came while I ran the store was nylon stockings. Before nylons, ladies wore stockings made of silk. They were not very practical and they were easily torn. One day a salesman came in the store with a suitcase full of the new nylons. Of course he was happy when he saw that a lady was running the store. When I examined the hoses I just couldn't believe it. They were so sheer and light weight. The salesman said, "Why don't you go in the back and try some on." Well, I wasn't

going to do that so I said, "No. Just leave some samples and when you come back by I'll let you know." Well, as soon as he left, I went to the back and tried them on. I called for Ellie and she tried some on too. We just loved them.

There was no dress store in Norman at that time. I thought that a most of the ladies would prefer to buy the new hoses from us rather than having to drive to Pearl Valley. So when the salesman came back, I ordered several dozen. The day they came in, Willie asked me how we were going to display the hoses. I had not thought about that. Hoses were actually almost like underwear. We didn't need to have them out on a rack for everyone to see. We finally decided to keep them behind the counter and place a sign by the register. We all started wearing them at the store and the ladies just went crazy over them. The nylons sure helped business back then and the ladies loved the new look.

In spite of all the challenges with the store, we were doing pretty well in aunt Mabel's absence. Jennie was a junior in high school. Her spiritual fervor had faded to some degree but she was still doing better than before. I think that she finally came to grips with uncle Robert's death. She was still struggling with aunt Mabel being away, but we did all we could to help her with that.

On Sunday afternoons when we called aunt Mabel, we let Jennie talk with her first. The call time was limited, so sometimes the rest of us didn't get to talk with her much. But that was okay. The phone calls really helped Jennie make it through the week. When I was able to talk with aunt Mabel, she, of course, asked about how things were going at the store. I told her about the funny things that were happening and how Mr. Fielding was a great help to me.

In addition to the phone calls, each of us wrote aunt Mabel a short letter every week. We mailed them at different times so she would have one to read almost every day. We hoped that the letters helped her through the long days at the hospital. Every once in a while aunt Mabel sent a letter to all of us. She had a line or two for each of us. Every one of her letters ended with the same words. "I love you all. I'm praying for you all. God bless you all."

Four months after aunt Mabel went to Truitt, it was Christmas time. All the merchants dressed up their places with Christmas cheer. We decorated our store in green and red ribbons. Jennie had a good eye for design so we put her in charge. Each of us chose a special present for aunt Mabel. Ellie gave her three pairs of hose. Aunt Macy knitted a beautiful scarf for her. I chose some of the new makeup items we had just gotten in. Willie put together a bag full of chocolate and other candies. Jennie decided to give her a pair of gloves and some warm wool socks.

It was probably the hardest Christmas for us as a family. It was our second Christmas without uncle Robert and our first with aunt Mabel in the hospital. We all tried to make the best of it but it was obvious that we were struggling. Each of us had tearful moments. I went back in the storage room one day and Ellie was just weeping. She missed her father so much. I had to ask Mr. Fielding to take the counter one day while I went back to the office. The stress of the work and the absence of aunt Mable just got the best of me.

On Saturday, before Christmas Eve, we closed the store at noon. That night aunt Macy took us to Pearl Valley to see the new Christmas lights on Main Street. It was the first year the town had decorated with lights. Several church choirs

sang at the gazebo and they had a live nativity scene at First Baptist Church. It was a special time for everyone.

On Christmas Eve we all went to church. Jennie and Ellie sang in the musical. Brother Smith preached an incredible sermon that day. He talked about how the world in Jesus' time was a hard world, a dark world. It was much like the world we were facing with the depression. But there, in the middle of the darkness, was a light, a light for our hearts and our souls, a light that is still shining today. The light is the Lord and He is telling us that no matter how dark things may seem, He will always be with us. The Lord will never leave us. We can lean on Him for strength. We can lean on Him for wisdom. He is going to see us through to a brighter day. Just trust Him and let Him carry you through.

At the end of the service, almost everyone came down to the altar and prayed. I went down and asked God to give me the strength to keep everything together. At some point, two or three people touched my shoulders and began to pray for me. I had never experienced that before. A peace came over me like none I had ever known. For some reason I felt sure that our family was going to be okay.

On Monday, Christmas day, all the stores were closed. We were glad to have a day off and a morning where we could sleep late. Aunt Macy played Santa Claus. She went upstairs at about eight o'clock and said, "Ho, Ho, Ho. Merry Christmas!" The girls and I went downstairs to find fresh, hot cinnamon rolls on the table. They were a special treat back then and aunt Macy made the best in town. They were big and drenched in melted sugar cinnamon. Oh my goodness.

After breakfast, we all went to the living room to open our presents. Aunt Macy handed them out. Ellie had drawn my name. She gave me a beautiful wool coat that she ordered from the Sears catalog. It fit perfectly. When Jennie opened her present from Willie, it was a nice coat also. I knew that I had gotten a coat for Willie and when Ellie opened her present from Jennie, it was a coat too. We couldn't believe it. We had all gotten each other coats.

When aunt Macy opened her present from the four of us, we all knew that it was also a coat. Later we found out that each of us had gone to aunt Macy for gift advice. She told every one of us to get the other a coat. And then I guess we all had coats on our minds when we decided to get aunt Macy one. For years we referred to that Christmas as the Crazy Coat Christmas.

After we opened gifts we waited for aunt Mabel to call. When the phone rang and Jennie ran to answer it. "Momma, is that you?" Jennie looked at us with a big smile and a nod to let us know that it was aunt Mabel. "Merry Christmas momma. We love you. Did you get your presents?" Aunt Mabel told us how much she loved the gifts.

We all got to talk with her for a few minutes. Ellie and Willie told her about their boyfriends. Jennie talked with her about school. Aunt Macy told her that everything was good at the house. When I talked with her, she asked about the store. I told her that everything was fine. She thanked me for the makeup. It was good to hear her voice even though she sounded a bit weak.

The rest of the day was wonderful. It had been a long time since we just enjoyed each other's company. That night aunt Macy made a fire in the backyard and we toasted some marshmallows. She fixed some hot chocolate for us and we all went to bed early. Tomorrow was coming and life would

be back in full gear.

Early Tuesday morning Willie and Ellie took down the Christmas decorations while I got everything ready to open the store. We had the same routine every day. Get the furnace running. Make a pot of coffee. Open the safe. Fill the register and unlock the back door for deliveries. Since Christmas had been on Monday, this was delivery day. Our first deliveries for the week were always milk, eggs, and butter. Everything else was delivered by Wednesday.

This Tuesday was no different from any other. Customers were in and out. The CCC supervisor made another big order for gloves. But a man came in the store that morning and asked to speak to the owner. I said, "Well, if you're a salesman, I'm the one you need to talk to." He gave me a little grin and said, "No mam, I'm not a salesman. I have this flyer about a countywide meeting in Pearl Valley next week. Can I put it in your front window?"

I took a look at the flyer. The meeting was about a manufacturing company coming to Taylor County. Major Hughes was asking business owners and anyone else who was interested to come. The next week, I attended the meeting. Major Hughes said that he had contacted a manufacturer about opening a garment plant in Taylor County. The company agreed to come if the town could raise eighty-five thousand dollars for construction. The major said that anyone could be a part of the investment. The company would use local men to build the plant and hire over three hundred women to work in the facility once it was completed. This was great news for everyone.

When I got back to the store, I called aunt Mabel and told her about the opportunity. She told me to invest three hundred dollars in the project. When all was said and done, the town raised the money needed and the company began construction on the plant. Young men and not so young men who had been without work for over two years finally had hope that better days were on their way.

When the plant finally opened, Willie was one of the first hired. She and Mack wanted to get married but never had the money for their own place until then. That was true for so many couples during the depression. Within a few months of getting her new job, Willie married Mack and moved to Pearl Valley. We were all so happy for them.

The store continued to do well because of the CCC camp. But times continued to be hard for so many families. All across the state people were losing their homes and land because they couldn't pay their mortgages. The Mississippi Sentinel in Truitt reported at one point that almost twenty-five percent of all the property in Mississippi had been auctioned off for unpaid taxes. The depression hit the South with a vengeance.

I was always afraid that the camp was going to close. If that happened, we would have to close the store. But, thank the Lord, the camp continued to start new projects in the area and we had plenty of business because of that. We did have one problem at the store, however. It was a growing problem that was directly related to the depression. Before the depression hit, uncle Robert allowed customers to set up accounts and buy things on credit. He rarely had anyone who could not pay their bill each week. If that happened, he extended their payment period and they almost always paid their bill in full.

The depression was not just a time when a few people

were a little down on their luck. It was a sustained period of time where almost no one could find a job. People were trying their best to grow their own vegetables but they still needed other life essentials and they just couldn't pay for them. I talked with aunt Mabel about it at some point because several families owed over one hundred dollars on their bill.

Aunt Mabel said that our cash flow was still good enough for us to let most of the families continue charging their groceries. She did say that we had to stop allowing credit for non-food items. She was so smart. I implemented the new program and no one complained. We did have to forgive the debt for a few families but that was okay. We wanted to help everyone as much as we could.

Before we turned around twice it was May. Aunt Mabel had been in Truitt for nine months. Our weekly phone visits were good but it was obvious that she wasn't getting any better. In fact, aunt Mabel's health was worsening. Every once in a while the doctor would give aunt Macy an update on her condition but she never shared anything with us. We were all so worried about aunt Mabel.

Jennie finished her junior year of high school and started working at Ganny's as a waitress. We really didn't need her at the store and I think that she wanted a little independence. The only thing that she had to put up with was the attention of the CCC boys. They would ask her out on dates and tell her how pretty she was.

I told Aunt Mabel about it and she asked me to have a little talk with Jennie. I did and Jenny understood the situation. Unfortunately, her boyfriend, Jeremy, did not understand. One day he walked in Ganny's to pick Jennie up for a date. Just about that time one of the CCC boys grabbed Jennie's hand. Well, that wasn't good. Jeremy marched over there and took Jennie's hand away. He didn't say a word to the guy but he stared him down as if to say, "That had better be the last time you touch my girl."

Jennie went to the back to get her coat while Jeremy waited at the door. As they were headed out, the CCC guy stood up and yelled, "Hey darling. I'll see you tomorrow." Then he blew Jennie a kiss. Well, that was too much for Jeremey to take. He headed back in the restaurant toward the guy's table. Now, Jeremy was only sixteen and he didn't weigh much over a hundred pounds. The CCC guys were much bigger and stronger. Besides that, there were four of them and only one of Jeremy. But we all know that love causes you to do strange things.

As Jeremy crossed the room, the CCC boys all stood up. Everyone in the restaurant was expecting to see a rather short but painful fight. Jeremy, of course, was going to be the one in pain. What the CCC boys didn't know was that Mr. Hank Powers had been watching the whole thing from his table. They had also not noticed that Mr. Powers had gotten up and was standing right behind them.

When Jeremy got to the table, Mr. Powers spoke up and said in that huge voice of his, "Now, Jeremy, there is no need to hurt these guys." The CCC boys turned around expecting to knock somebody else out when they saw this giant of a man towering over them. Everyone said that the look on their faces was priceless. They were scared out of their minds.

Mr. Powers slapped his big bear paws down on the shoulders of two of the boys and continued. "No Jeremy, you're not going to have to beat these boys up because they're

going to apologize right here and now." Jeremy didn't understand what was happening at first but the CCC boys sure did. They started apologizing for their behavior and promised that they would never do anything to disrespect Jennie again.

Jeremy was shocked. When he realized what had happened, he looked up at Mr. Powers, grinned a little grin as if to say thank you, and walked away. The CCC boys looked back at Mr. Powers one more time and sat down. Everyone in the restaurant gave Mr. Powers a thumbs up. Once again, the Gentle Giant had saved the day.

I guess I learned a lot that year. I learned a lot about myself. I found out that I could actually run a business which surprised me beyond belief. I never thought that in a million years I would be able to take aunt Mabel's place at the store. I learned that I had a knack for dealing with people, even difficult people. God gave me the confidence I needed and the courage I needed to lead. I had never seen myself as a leader before then.

I didn't know what the future would bring but, for now, things were good even in the midst of the difficult. I still worried a lot about aunt Mabel and wondered what I would do, what we all would do if something happened to her. But I gave that to the Lord also. I knew that she was in His hands and that was the safest place she could be.

18   *The Rose And The Donut Man*

The summer heat was brutal that year. Temperatures hit the one hundred degree mark at least once a week. This was just a year or two before the introduction of air conditioning for businesses. We had big fans in the store at the front and the back. It was tolerable but still very warm. Several of the CCC boys were having trouble with the extreme temperatures. They had never worked in triple digit heat before. I think we sold more soda pop that summer than any other time I can remember.

This was also the year when several new food products came out. It seemed as if a new candy bar was introduced every month. I remember the first time the salesman showed me a tootsie roll. Pay Day and Three Musketeers bars came out about the same time. Kids were coming in the store every day after school to enjoy their favorites. Back then, a candy bar only cost a nickel. Kids would actually keep their milk money and drink water at lunch so they could buy a candy bar after school. It was crazy.

Back then, most of the candy bars were in two pieces. Little boys would come in the store with a girl they liked, buy

a candy bar, and split it with her. For fifteen cents you could buy two cokes and a candy bar. If you really wanted to impress your girl, you could spend the extra nickel and have two candy bars. Either way, a coke and a candy bar was a pretty cheap date.

Several other new products came to market that year. But the one that literally changed my life was the donut. I know you must be thinking, "The Donut?" Yes, the donut. Let me tell you why. We had just opened the store. Ellie and I were straightening things up behind the counter when a young man came in with a flat, brown cardboard box. He was rather tall, and I thought, very handsome. He was wearing a blue and white seersucker suit with a navy and white striped tie. He was also wearing a dark blue summer business hat.

He came to the counter and said, "Hello, ladies, I would like to introduce you to the food hit of the century." Before I could say anything he opened the box and offered us a fresh, hot donut. We all knew what a donut was. Aunt Macy made them every once in a while. I actually said to the man, "You're selling donuts?" He said, "Yes mam. Just try one please." Well, I took a bite of the donut and to my surprise it was the softest, lightest, best tasting donut I ever had. When aunt Macy made donuts, they were heavy and doughy. These were different.

The salesman said, "Isn't that the best donut you've ever had in your life?" I had to agree with him. It was delicious. But I had never thought about having donuts in the store. We had no room for the machinery. I couldn't hire any new employees. Just then, it was almost as if he had read my mind. "Mam, what would you say if I told you that you don't have to buy any expensive equipment and you don't have to hire any new employees to have hot, fresh donuts in your store every day?" I said, "Well, that would be wonderful."

That's when he told us about his company. A man by the name of Levine had invented a new process for making donuts. He introduced it at the World's Fair in Chicago. The Gallup family in Hampton had just purchased five of the new machines. They would start making donuts in two weeks. The salesman was setting up route deliveries to stores like ours. They would deliver the donuts three times a week.

My first question was, "Well, how do you keep the donuts warm like these?" That's when he asked me to come outside to his delivery van. He opened up the back door and showed me a small tabletop glass enclosure that had a high powered lamp in it. I had never seen anything like that before. All you had to do was plug it in, put the donuts inside, and they stayed warm all day. I know that sounds simple to you all, but it was incredible to us back then.

Then the salesman said, "If you buy ten dozen a week for at least one year, we'll put this warmer in your store at no cost." Well, that was too good to be true. I told him that I would have to talk with aunt Mabel about it but that I could have an answer for him by Wednesday. I knew that would give me another opportunity to see him. He thanked me for the consideration and was on his way out when I said, "Sir, you never told me your name." He said, "Well, mam, my name is Jim Carpenter." That's right, Sarah and Steven. Your dad was the donut man.

When he left, Ellie looked at me and said, "Well, that is certainly a nice young man, isn't he?" I said, "Yes, he sure seems to be." "And nice looking too isn't he, Anne?" I said, "Well, yes." I guess Ellie could see that I was in a bit of a

daze. That had never happened to me before. Oh, there had been boys in school that I liked but this was different. Ellie just grinned, raised her eyebrows, and started humming the kissing song. I didn't care. My mind was already thinking about Wednesday when Jim would return to the store.

That night I called aunt Mabel. Since it wasn't one of our normal weekend calls, she thought that something was wrong. I assured her that everyone was fine. I told her about the donut proposal and she agreed that it would be good for business. I also mentioned the nice young man and she started telling me about the time when she met uncle Robert. In other words, we had a good girl talk. I think it did aunt Mabel good to have one of her girls confide in her. We had all missed that since she had moved to the hospital.

Well, Wednesday came and your dad showed up just before noon. We went over the details of the contract and the delivery schedule. He also set up the warming cabinet for the donuts and showed me how to operate it. That's when he told me that he would be coming by every month with our bill and to make sure that we were happy with the product and their service. Well, needless to say, that was music to my ears. I would get to see him at least once a month.

When we wrapped things up, Jim asked if there was a good restaurant in town. I told him about Ganny's and he thanked me for the recommendation. When he left, I asked Ellie to go to lunch with me. We normally ate sandwiches for lunch but I couldn't help myself. Willie and Mr. Fielding could handle the store for an hour. I told Ellie on the way to Ganny's why we were going out to lunch. She said, "I knew it. I knew it. I just knew it. You are sweet on that salesman. I can see it now, Anne Carpenter. Well, here we go."

When we got to the restaurant we saw that Jim had taken one of the tables close to the front. He waved at us when we came in. I whispered to Ellie, "Go over there and ask him if he would like some company for lunch." "No. You go and ask him." About that time your dad got up out of his seat and walked right over to us. He said, "Ladies, I would love to have you sit with me at my table for lunch. I just hate eating alone." I said, "Well, we don't want to intrude." I don't know why I said that. There was no one else eating with him. He extended the invitation again and we accepted.

During lunch your dad told us about his family and how he got the job with the donut company. Ellie and I told him about aunt Mabel and the store. We found out that he was a little older than us but that he had never married. His family lived mostly in the Pearl Valley area. He had just recently rented an apartment in Hampton.

After an hour of talking and laughing, it seemed like we were sharing lunch with an old friend. Your dad was so personable and nice. He offered to take care of our lunch but we insisted on paying for our own. When it was about time to leave, he thanked us for eating with him. Of course, the pleasure was all ours. Well, mine. Later I thanked Ellie for going with me. She just grinned and started humming that kissing song again.

The rest of the day, all I could think about was lunch with Jim. I hoped that I would enjoy many more times with him. I had always asked God to give me a good man for a husband and I started thinking that Jim might be that man. I couldn't wait to see him again.

In the few weeks some strange things happened. One of my classmates from high school showed up at the store,

Walter Givens. Walter moved to Pearl Valley to work in the garment plant as a cutter. His job was to cut the large bolts of fabric into the shapes needed to make the men's shirts.

Walter told me that he had come back into town to see his folks. He asked how aunt Mabel was doing and how I was getting along running the store. We chatted a bit and then Walter asked me if I would like to go to a movie in Pearl Valley Saturday night. The Martin Theater had just opened and people by the hundreds were going every night.

I didn't know what to say. For one thing, Walter had never shown any interest in me. I didn't know why he was asking me out on a date. The other thing was, I had Jim on my mind. I sort of stumbled around for a second. That's when Ellie started waving at me from the other side of the store. She had evidently heard Walter ask me out. She was mouthing something like, "Go. Go. Go." Well, I told Walter that I would be glad to go to the movies with him. We agreed that he would pick me up at the store around closing time on Saturday.

Walter picked me up and we headed for Pearl Valley. On the way, Walter told me about his new apartment and what it was like to live on his own for the first time. One of the funniest things he shared was about washing his clothes. Walter couldn't afford a washing machine so he had to wash his clothes at the new laundromat that had just opened. He said that it really wasn't the best situation for a young man. I asked him why. "Well, you know, you have your clothes and other people have their clothes and..." I asked, "And what?" "Well, you can see other people's clothes. You know what I mean?" I knew what he meant and I was giggling inside. Walter was talking about, or not talking about, people's unmentionables. I thought it was kind of cute. He was embarrassed to talk with me about it. I spoke up and said, "Oh my. You mean..." "Yeah, that's what I mean."

We moved on to other subjects and soon arrived at the theater. The lines were very long. I would guess that over a hundred people were there. Two movies were showing. One was a comedy, *It's A Gift*. The other movie was *The Man Who Knew Too Much*. It was more of a thriller. Walter asked which one I wanted to see and I chose the comedy.

As we were waiting in line, I looked around to see if I knew anyone. I saw Trudy Wallace. She graduated the year before me and went to business school. She was with two girls that I didn't recognize. I also remember seeing Judd Casey. He worked at the big Stewart's Dairy plant. He was with Eleanor Taylor who lived in Justice. Eleanor had a different boyfriend every few months. She thought very highly of herself and I guess she couldn't find a guy who could meet her expectations. The funny thing is that she didn't get married until she was thirty. None of the boys around home could deal with her overwhelming opinion of herself. She finally married some guy from out of state. I was told that they didn't stay together long. We all knew why.

I saw a few other people that I knew. But just as we were about to go in, I saw your dad. It was not good. He was with a tall blond girl who looked like a movie star. My heart just sank. They were laughing and carrying on. I guess that I had no right to be upset. I mean, well, Jim had never asked me out or indicated that he was interested in me. But it sure hurt. All kinds of thoughts passed through my head. I wasn't pretty enough. I wasn't this and I wasn't that. I was mad but I was mad mostly at myself for having a pity party.

Walter and I found some seats and settled in for the movie. It wasn't two minutes later when I heard someone call my name. I turned around and there was your dad and his date, headed our way. If there had been a rock to crawl under I would have done it in a heartbeat but there was no way to avoid the inevitable. "Hey, Jim. Funny seeing you here." Again, I said something that didn't make sense. "Hey, Anne. Can we sit here with you all?" What was I going to say? "It's okay with me if it's okay with Walter. Walter, this is Jim Carpenter." The two of them exchanged greetings. That's when your dad spoke up and said, "This is Jennifer." She smiled and said, "Nice to meet you." I was about to die. The two of them sat down next to us and watched the movie.

As we were all leaving, Jim said, "Hey, why don't we go across the street to the ice cream shop." Well, I didn't know if I was up to seeing your dad and Jennifer sitting together much longer. But Walter spoke up quickly and said, "We'd love to join you."

So there we were together at the ice cream shop. Jim and Walter started talking about guy things and Jennifer asked, "Anne, what do you do?" I told her about the store and the family. Then I asked about her work. "I work at Williams Pharmacy over on Second Street. I actually live in an apartment above the store."

The longer we talked the more I could tell that Jennifer was a nice girl. Still, I avoided asking her how she knew Jim. When we finished our ice cream, your dad said, "I'll buy us some sodas." He asked Walter and me what we wanted and then he said, "Sis, what do you want to drink?" She said, "Grape Nehi big brother." At first, I just sat there with my eyes going back and forth from Jim to Jennifer, Jennifer to

Jim. Had I heard them call each other brother and sister? That's exactly what I heard. Just to make sure I asked, "Is Jim your brother?" "Yes." Then she laughed. "You thought that we were dating? Oh no. We go to the movies together once a month. It's about the only time that we can see each other. Right now neither one of us is dating anyone and we both like movies, so, voila."

Well, you can imagine how I felt. I was elated. We ended our time together and Walter took me home. Ellie was waiting for me and asked how things went. I told her about Jennifer and she laughed at me for the longest. When I finally went to bed, I couldn't go to sleep. All I could think about was the next time I would see Jim at the store.

When I did see your dad again, he had our bill as usual. He asked about the donuts and the warmer. I told him that everything was fine. Then he asked me about Walter which I thought was odd. "How is Walter?" "I guess he's fine. I haven't seen him since we went to the movies." "Oh, I thought that maybe you saw him on a regular basis." That's when I understood Jim's questions, at least I thought I did. I said, "Walter and I are just old high school friends. We aren't dating." That's when I saw a little smile on your dad's face.

We finished our business and Jim went on his way. Of course, Ellie came out from the back and starting questioning me about our little visit. I told her and she started humming that song again. I gave it right back to her and we had a good laugh. Both of us were in love. She already had her guy and I was still working on mine.

The next time I saw your dad was probably the best. It was not on the day of his regularly scheduled visit. I said, "Hi Jim. What are you doing here?" He said, "Oh, I'm just

passing through. I'm on my way back to the office." I asked if he would like a soda. "I sure would Anne. Thanks." We sat on the bench that was by the counter and talked for several minutes. He told me how well things were going with sales and I talked with him about the store and the family.

At some point, we ran out of things to talk about and your dad said, "Well, I better be getting back to Pearl Valley." I told him to be safe," That's when he spoke up and said, "Anne, there's a great movie at the theater this weekend. It's with Fred Astaire and Ginger Rogers. It's called *Top Hat.* If you're free Saturday night, I'd love to take you to see it." I cannot tell you how excited I was. My heart was beating ninety miles an hour. I said, "Well, I would love to go to see it with you Jim." We set a time for him to pick me up and he was on his way.

When your dad got in his car, I checked to make sure that no one was in the store and I screamed. Ellie came from out back and I told her that Jim had asked me out on a date. Then she screamed. We started talking about what I should wear and how I should fix my hair. I just couldn't believe it. I was going out with Jim Carpenter.

Of course, we had a wonderful time on our date. After the movie, your dad took me to the ice cream shop. We both had coke floats. Jim talked with me about his dream of becoming a business owner. He wasn't sure what kind of store he would have but it was obvious that he didn't want to sell donuts the rest of his life. I told him how much I enjoyed running aunt Mabel's store. I shared some of my funny customer stories and he told me about some of the crazy store owners on his route. Oh, I had such a great time that night.

On the way home, your dad asked if he could take me out again. Of course, I said yes. I don't know exactly how to describe it. Both of us seemed to be comfortable with each other. It was like we had known each other for years, like we were already good friends. Jim was so nice and so funny. I know you won't believe it but both of us were jokesters and kidders in those days. Most children don't realize that their parents were different people when they were young. We both loved to laugh and enjoy a good time.

Well, there is much more I could tell you about those early days but you know the end of this story. A lot happened in both of our lives before we got married but none of it drew us apart. If anything, the storms drew us closer as we relied on each other for strength. I am so thankful for the day when God introduced me to the donut man.

19 *A Rose Fades Away*

The red hot days of summer finally ended. Fall that year was wonderful. Mild days and cool nights. By the end of October, the rose bush leaves were changing color and dropping. I always loved to see those yellow and burgundy leaves. Sometimes I would use one as a bookmark for my Bible. Before aunt Mable was ill, she would put some of them in her Thanksgiving floral arrangements.

Aunt Macy started preparing her plants for the winter. She covered them with pine straw and mulch every year to protect them from a freeze. Some said that it didn't really help but aunt Macy won more blue ribbons for her roses than anyone else in Taylor County. So I think she knew what she was doing.

Things at the store were going well. I was in my second year as manager. Aunt Mabel and Mr. Fielding were very encouraging. They told me that they were very proud of my work. I guess that my confidence had grown to the point that I felt I could handle most situations we had to face. It was a good feeling. Even though she was still working in the afternoons at Ganny's, Jenny helped us with the holiday decorations for the store. Ellie had the stock of winter coats on display. Our order for gloves and scarves came in on time. Everything was looking good.

The depression had eased somewhat. The new garment factory opened which gave many people the jobs they had been looking for. The new WPA program, which was similar to the CCC, created construction jobs for the building of schools, post offices, and other municipal buildings. A new program for farmers provided subsidies which helped those families get back on their feet. Overall, President Roosevelt's New Deal seemed to be working.

On Thanksgiving Day, the first thing we did was talk to aunt Mabel. She called at nine o'clock sharp. Even though her voice was weak, she sounded happy which was refreshing to all of us. She told us that she was most thankful for the family and how we were getting along with each other while she was gone. She asked Jennie how school was going and asked Willie about her new job at the garment plant. Aunt Mabel joked with her a little and told her that she loved her.

When I talked with aunt Mabel, she asked me to call her the following week. She said that she wanted to talk with me about something that was very important. I was curious as to what we were going to discuss. Several things went through my mind but aunt Mabel didn't want to give me a preview of our conversation. I would have to wait until next week. We set up a day and time. Monday at ten o'clock. I told her I loved her and that I was still praying for her every day.

Aunt Macy cooked an incredible Thanksgiving meal for us. We had baked sweet potatoes, ham, turkey, cornbread

dressing, and aunt Macy's famous chocolate meringue pie. We all ate so much that we couldn't move. It wasn't really that cold outside so we went out on the porch with our blankets. Aunt Macy told a few of her crazy stories and we just drifted off to la la land.

Around three o'clock I woke up to the sound of a car coming up the driveway. It was Jim and Gene. Ellie and I ran inside to fix our hair and put on some makeup. We went for a drive with the guys over to Indian Cliff. It was the first time that the four of us went out together. We had so much fun. Your dad had never been to Indian Cliff. We went as far down as we could and were able to see the old cars. Jim was amazed. When we got back up to the top, we laid out on blankets and did some cloud watching. We got home around six o'clock and the guys ate supper with us.

On Monday, I opened the store and spent the next three hours anticipating aunt Mabel's call. What was she going to say? Was something wrong? Was it about her health? Was she going to tell me that she was dying? I just didn't know. Maybe she was going to sell the store. If she did that, I didn't know what I was going to do. Could I find a job? Where would I live? How could I support myself?

At ten o'clock the phone rang in the back office. I ran to get it. It was aunt Mabel. "Hey, honey. How are you doing?" "I'm fine." "Did everyone enjoy Thanksgiving?" "Yes mam." She sounded the same as she had a few days earlier, weak. We talked for a few minutes about the family. I told her that all were doing well. Then she said, "Anne, I am having some legal papers drawn up for the store and the house." I didn't know what kind of papers she was talking about. "I'm going to give aunt Macy the house. You all, of course, will still be able to live there. I'm putting the store in your name, Anne, with the stipulation that as long as you run the business, half the profits will go to you and half to the girls and aunt Macy. I know that they probably won't work there much longer but it is their birthright. If things change along the way, I'm sure that you all can work things out in a fair way."

I didn't understand at first why she was doing that. It didn't make sense to me. But then she continued. "Honey, the doctors have told me that I am not a candidate for the new medication and treatments." I didn't know what to say because I knew what that meant. I closed the door to the office. "Honey, are you there?" "I'm here." I knew that she could hear my struggle. "Anne, listen to me, honey. It's all going to be okay." I just couldn't hold back the tears. "Aunt Mabel, I love you so much." "I love you too, dear. The doctors tell me that I may have another two to four months. The problem is that the last month or so is going to be really tough and I won't be able to see you all."

At that point I fell apart. I was weeping uncontrollably. I had prayed so hard that God would heal her. I had hoped for so long that she would be one of the few who survived. I had wished for a miracle but that wasn't going to happen. There was nothing I could do to save her.

After a minute, aunt Mabel spoke up and said, "Anne, I know this is going to be hard for you, honey, but I promise you that the Lord is going to help you and the girls get through this. Brother Smith and his wife are going to be right there by your side. When uncle Robert died, I didn't think that I was going to make it. It was so hard. But I found out what the Lord can see you through and He's going to do the same for you."

After another moment or two, I calmed down enough to continue our conversation. "Aunt Mabel, what do I need to do?" She told me that she was going to call and tell the girls that night. She had already told aunt Macy. In a few days, a lawyer would come to the house and have everyone sign the papers. Aunt Macy and Brother Smith were going to make the arrangements for the memorial service. I asked if we would get to see her before she passed on. She told me that the hospital was going to set up a family visit real soon. I told her that I loved her one more time. She did the same.

I just sat in the office for the longest time. I'm sure that Ellie wondered what was going on. I finally went to the front knowing that I would have to do my best not to let anyone know about the bad news. I guess I did okay with that. I got busy doing my work and just waited for closing time. I knew that the call at the house that night was going to be very difficult for the girls. I hoped that aunt Mabel was right, that God was going to see us through the storm.

Aunt Mabel was going to call at seven o'clock. She had asked Brother Smith and his wife to be at the house. I closed the store at six o'clock and went home. We had just finished supper when the phone rang. Aunt Mabel asked the girls to get close to the phone and then she told them about her condition. Well, you can probably imagine that it was more than the girls could handle.

Aunt Mabel told them that we were all going to be able to visit with her at the end of the next week and maybe one more time. She talked with each of the girls and told them how much she loved them. Then she asked to speak to me. Once again she assured me that God was going to provide. I told her that I would try to be strong and take care of everyone else. Aunt Mabel asked Brother Smith to lead us in prayer while she was still on the line. He asked the Lord to give us courage for the days ahead. When he finished, Aunt Mable said one more goodbye and ended the call.

Brother and Mrs. Smith stayed with us a little while longer and let us know that they were available any time we needed them. When they left, we just sat there for the longest time. It was as if aunt Mabel had already passed on and our mourning had begun.

After a while the girls all went to bed. Aunt Macy and I stayed up and talked. She knew that I was feeling the weight of the world on my shoulders. At some point, aunt Macy said, "Anne, let me tell you about the time when I lost my child." When she first said it I thought, "How in the world does she have the strength to tell her story especially after learning about aunt Mabel." But this was one of those moments when aunt Macy showed just how incredible she was.

"Ben and I married right after I graduated high school. He was twenty one. Ben worked on his daddy's farm and was going to take it over in a few years. He was the only boy in the family. He had two sisters, Margie and Susan. They were a close knit family. Ben's mother was a gracious lady and she was nice to me. We lived in a small home that Ben's daddy built for the farm manager. It wasn't much but it was all we needed.

That first year, Ben and I truly enjoyed life together. Ben worked hard every day and I kept the house and cooked. Ben was a good young man and he treated me well. He didn't go to church too much. He used that Bible verse about an ox in the ditch as an excuse not to go to church. He always found something around the farm to fix on Sunday.

We had been married about a year when I found out that I was pregnant. Everyone in the family was so happy for us. I was hardly sick at all during the pregnancy. Ben's mother helped me with the house and cooking during the last few months. Ben's dad made a baby bed for us. The family gave me a shower that loaded us down with everything we needed to take care of our new baby.

The day I went into labor, we called for Dr. Williams and he came to the house. He examined me and I could tell that something was wrong. He just kept listening for the baby's heartbeat. I could see the worry on his face. After a few minutes he stepped out of the room with Ben. When they came back in, Ben told me that the baby would be stillborn.

I couldn't believe what they were telling me. I asked the doctor to listen again. With a tear in his eye, he told me that there was no heartbeat. Later, after the delivery, Dr. Williams placed the baby in my arms. It was a little girl. She was so beautiful. She looked like a little doll. I named her Sophia after my grandmother.

Ben had called the preacher when Dr. Williams told him the bad news. When the pastor came in, I asked him if we could have a graveside service for Sophia. He agreed to conduct the service. We buried her on a Tuesday morning in the Angel Memorial section of the cemetery.

I can't even express how much grief I felt. I went from depressed to angry in a matter of a few hours. I cursed God. I cried to God. I questioned God. For a while, I left God. I cried myself to sleep for over two months. Everyone was worried about me. Ben tried to talk with me but I wouldn't let him. The preacher tried. My parents tried. But I guess that I wanted to hurt. I felt that my hurting for my baby showed how much I loved her. I became ill in my mind and in my soul.

When spring came, I was numb with pain. There was no joy in my life. I was so depressed that I thought about ending my life. Ben poured himself into his work on the farm to avoid facing our loss. After a while, we quit talking with each other and grew apart. Everyone around us tried to help but there was no helping our marriage. Ben came home from work one day and packed up his clothes. He moved back in with his parents and never came back to me. About a month later we divorced and I moved back in with my parents. I had not only lost my child but I lost my husband too.

I didn't do very well after that. I sort of checked out mentally and emotionally. My parents found me one day back at the house where we lived. They tell me that I was in a bad way. My parents took me to a hospital. I stayed there a few months and got better. I moved back in with my parents and started trying to put my life back together. I know that people think I'm still crazy. They look at me funny and won't talk with me much. Maybe I'm not completely well but I'm so much better than I was.

Let me tell you how I was able to cope with my child's death. When I was in the hospital, I started reading the Bible. Over a two or three week period, it seemed that the Lord led me directly to the passages of Scripture that I needed. I read over in Psalm 34 that God is near to those who have a broken heart. I read in Psalm 147 that God heals the brokenhearted. In the Sermon on the Mount I read that those who mourn will be comforted. I read verse after verse about Heaven. One day a pastor's wife came to visit us in the hospital. I guess that she knew my situation. Maybe she didn't. But she gave

me a little card with Psalm 23 on it. I had never read those words in the light of my loss. They were so comforting to me.

After a while, I realized that God had not forsaken me but that He was as close as the mention of His name. I spent hours a day in prayer. I told God everything that He already knew about what I was thinking and feeling. In the midst of those conversations and my renewed relationship with God, my broken heart was healed.

Since then, God has been so real to me that sometimes I'm, well, I'm a little different than most people. I'm not closer to God or more spiritual than anybody else. I just feel His presence in my life. That's how I'm getting through Mabel's illness. I've been here before and I figure that if God could see me through the loss of my child, that He can see me through this. He can also see you through it Anne."

I just started weeping. I had not trusted God with our situation. I was so busy trying to face it on my own that I hadn't let God in. I was afraid that He wouldn't understand what I was going through. Then I was reminded that, in a way, He lost His loved one too when Jesus died on the cross.

Aunt Macy was right. God was near to us. He wanted to help us through aunt Mabel's illness. We just needed to go to Him when we were tired and weary. I asked aunt Macy to pray with me. She said, "Lord, you know why we're here. You know how our hearts are breaking. We claim your Word, Lord. Hold us close Father. Let us feel your comfort. Wrap your arms around Anne. She loves you Lord. She lives for you Lord. Help her in her time of need. Give her strength. Give her courage. Give her peace. Let her know that she is in your hands and that that is the safest place she can be. Bless her Lord as she faces this struggle. Keep her mind and heart focused on you. Thank you Lord for answering our prayer."

I can't explain it but while aunt Macy was praying I could feel God's love just filling my heart. I know that sounds odd but it was very real to me. It was as if God had taken this heavy burden off my shoulders. I could breathe again. I felt for the first time that no matter what happened with aunt Mabel, the family was going to be okay. I was going to be okay.

The next week, on Friday, we all went to see aunt Mabel at the hospital. Mr. Fielding ran the store for us. When we arrived, we had to put on hospital gowns and masks. We went to a little sunroom which was on the back of the hospital. It overlooked a garden that was filled with rose bushes. It was too late in the year for flowers but it was a nice sunny day. Aunt Mabel told us that it was her favorite place to stay during the day.

We each gave her a hug and sat down in some rocking chairs. We talked for a while about little things. Aunt Mabel asked about a few people back home. I talked with her about the store. Aunt Macy caught her up on some of the gossip in town and made her laugh. The girls talked about their beaus.

After a while, aunt Mabel, said, "Girls, I want to talk with you about the days ahead. I'm not going to be with you much longer. I'm going to see your dad and my parents and so many more who have gone on before me." Of course, that's when we all started crying. The reality of aunt Mabel's pending death was finally before us. Until then, we had hoped that something would change, that she would get well and come back home. Hearing her talk about leaving and going Heaven made us face the inevitable. Aunt Mabel wasn't going to be with us much longer.

After several minutes of tears, we all settled down a bit. Aunt Mabel talked with us about the future, our futures. She talked about us getting married and raising our own children. She talked about how important it was for us to stay in church and raise our children to know the Lord. She told us that she would be looking down from Heaven, that the Lord would be with us, and that we were all going to be okay.

I can't explain it but as aunt Mabel was talking, I felt the same way that I did when aunt Macy was praying. It was as if God was talking to me through aunt Mabel. I think that it was the calm in her voice. It was obvious that she had come to terms with her death. She knew that God was going to carry her through that valley. There was something else too. Even with the mask on I could tell that she had a peaceful look on her face. Her eyes were full of love. It was one of the most incredible moments of my life.

We finished our visit with more hugs and, yes, a few more tears. We asked aunt Mabel if she wanted us to bring her anything when we came back. She told us that she was fine. On the ride back home we didn't talk much. Jennie leaned over on me and fell asleep. She was emotionally drained from the visit. Willie just looked out the window. I could tell that she felt the same loneliness that all of us had experienced. Ellie put her arm around Willie just to be close to her. Aunt Macy was driving. She hummed some old gospel hymns all the way home.

We didn't know it then, but that would be our last visit with aunt Mabel. She died two weeks later on a Wednesday morning. We had her funeral on Saturday. Brother Smith delivered the sermon. He said that aunt Mabel was like the woman in Proverbs 31. Her worth was far more than rubies.

She watched over and provided for her family. She opened her hand to the poor. She was clothed in strength and dignity. She spoke with wisdom and faithful instruction. She loved God. Brother Smith was right. Aunt Mabel was just like the virtuous woman.

When we got home from the service, Mrs. Sarah White and some other ladies from the church were there. They provided a wonderful meal for us. That afternoon we all just sat out on the porch. Like all families who face the death of a loved one, we grieved aunt Mabel's passing. It was hard. I was carrying this huge burden of running the store. I didn't know if I was ever going to get back and finish school. Most of all, I still had so many unanswered questions about my parents. Who was my father? Was my mother still living? It was just a very difficult time.

The only thing I had were those words that aunt Mabel shared with me when I was a little girl. God loves you and has a plan for your life. I believed that but I was hurting too much for those truths to give me peace. Soon, however, everything changed.

20   *A Letter For The Rose*

The next day, Sunday, we didn't go to church. Everyone understood. We were all so exhausted from the funeral. I was the first to get up that morning. I made some coffee and went out on the porch. It wasn't long before aunt Macy joined me. We had always been the early risers in the family. Many of the best conversations we ever had were in the morning on the porch before everyone else got up.

For a while we just rocked and enjoyed watching the sun come up over the hill. Out in the field we saw a mother deer and one of her spotted fawns. They danced around for a while before going back into the woods. The birds started chirping and we heard from one of the roosters as he welcomed the morning. It was going to be a beautiful day. More importantly, it was going to be a day that changed my life forever.

Aunt Macy asked me how I was doing. I was honest with her. I felt lonely and I was fearful about the future. She smiled and said, "Honey, there was a time when I felt the same way." I knew that she was referring to the loss of her child and her marriage. She continued with a question. "Tell me, Anne, why do you feel so lonely?" I hesitated for a moment because I knew that if I talked about it, I would start crying and I had already cried enough.

That's when aunt Macy reached over and put her hand on mine. She looked at me with those loving eyes and said, "It's your parents, isn't it?" It was as if she had read my mind again. I just looked at her and said, "Please tell me how you know these things." She smiled and said, "Honey, God helps me with that." I didn't doubt her answer for one minute. I had experienced it too many times. Evidently, aunt Macy and God were very close friends.

I told her that since uncle Robert's death, I had been thinking a lot about my parents. I let her know how grateful I was for her and aunt Mabel. I told her that I loved the girls and felt like they were my sisters. Aunt Macy interrupted me and said, "Honey, you are as much family as family can be to us." I started crying and said, "Yes, mam. I believe that but I just have to know the truth about my parents.

That's when aunt Macy got up and said, "Stay right here. I'll be back in just a minute." She picked up her coffee cup and went inside. A few minutes later she came back with an envelope in her hand. It was addressed to me. I recognized the handwriting immediately. It was from aunt Mabel. Aunt Macy said, "This is for you, dear. It's a letter from your aunt Mabel. I believe that it will help you with your struggle."

I opened the envelope and found a very long letter from aunt Mabel. It began with, "My dearest Anne. I love you so very much." I looked at aunt Macy with tears in my eyes and said, "Aunt Mabel loved me, didn't she? She smiled and said,

"Yes, honey she did, with all her heart."

I focused again on the letter and read aunt Mabel's words. "I am so sorry that I had to leave you but as I have always told you, God has a plan, a good plan for our lives. I am now experiencing God's great gift of Heaven and enjoying time with my loved ones who passed on before me. I no longer need faith. I no longer need hope. I am in the presence of the one I trusted with my very soul, the one who promised that He would never leave me or forsake me. I am in perfect peace and rest.

I imagine that you and the girls are struggling right now. You are probably concerned about the future wondering what is going to happen with the family and the business. I promise you this – God is going to see you through. I have all the confidence in the world that you are going to accomplish great things in the days ahead. You are strong. You are smart. Best of all, you love people and you love the Lord. You are a very special and gifted person Anne."

I stopped reading for a moment and thought, sometimes we live our whole lives not knowing what people really think about us, even our family members. We wonder if they actually care about us. Do they believe in us? Do they think that we will ever amount to anything in this world? Then we have a hard time sharing our own feelings with others. We hold back. We don't have deep, serious conversations about our love for them and how we feel.

Well, I was overwhelmed by aunt Mabel's words. They sounded so genuine and they were so encouraging. I returned to her letter. "I am so sorry that you had to leave school to help with the store. I know that you had to lay aside your dream of teaching. I can never thank you enough for making such a sacrifice for the family. I hope that someday you can return and finish your studies. You would make a wonderful teacher.

Anne, I am so proud of what you have done with the store. You are actually a better manager than I was. Uncle Robert would have been proud of you. You're tough with those pushy salesmen and your kind to the customers, even the ones who cause a little bit of trouble from time to time. I don't know if you realize this or not but you are the one who has kept our family together these months since I have been at the hospital."

About that time, Ellie came out on the porch and said, "Breakfast is ready." She and Jennie had baked some biscuits and fried some bacon and eggs. At the table, aunt Macy said the blessing. "Dear Lord, we still need you to help us with our loss. We know that Mable is in Heaven with you but we sure do miss her here. Please help us with our hurt. Help us with our heartache. Help us to carry on. Thank you for our food and our family. Please bless this meal in Jesus' name."

Our time together at the table was rather solemn. Aunt Macy did her best to try and comfort us and she tried to talk with us about the future. It was just too soon for us to even consider what our lives would be like without aunt Mabel. She wasn't coming back and we were all having a difficult time facing the reality of it all.

After breakfast, the girls went in different directions. I went back out on the porch to finish reading aunt Mabel's letter. I sat in the big swing that uncle Robert had made. "Anne, I know that one of the greatest struggles of your life has been knowing about your parents. Even though it has been a while since we talked about it, I know that it stays on

your mind. I don't know how that feels but I can understand why you continue to wonder about your mother."

Aunt Mabel was right. When I was a little girl, she told me that my father died in the war and that his body was never returned home. She told me that my mother could not deal with his death and just ran away one day. As I got older I remember thinking that part of the story just didn't make sense. Why would my mother leave her family, the people who could have best helped her with the loss of her husband?

I remember feeling angry at times because my mother left me. How could she do that? How could she abandon me? I wondered, at times, if she even loved me. I felt that if I had been in the same situation I could not have left my family, much less my daughter. It hurt thinking that maybe she didn't want me.

I still had some of those feelings within me but I spent most of my time wondering if she was still alive. If so, where was she? Did she know anything about me and my life? Had she remarried? Did she have other children? Did aunt Mabel or aunt Macy know where she was? If so, why hadn't they told me? I had so many questions and no answers.

At one point, I even asked God to take me to her. When that didn't happen, I asked Him to talk to her and tell her to come back home. I was so desperate that I would go into town and try to find a woman who looked like me, who had my features and my hair. One day I almost stopped a woman in a department store to ask if she was my mother. That may seem rather extreme but that's just how it was for me. I think that most people in my situation would do everything they could to find their mother.

Aunt Mable had tried her best to serve as my mother. If

it had not been for her and uncle Robert, I would have been placed in an orphanage and never experience what it was like to be in a loving, Christian family. I owed the two of them so much. But there was still that longing, that desire to find my real mother. I felt that if I could talk with her, that all my questions would be answered, that she would come back home, and that my struggle would be over.

Just as I was about to continue reading aunt Mabel's letter, aunt Macy joined me on the swing. Before she sat down, she bent over, kissed me on my forehead, and held my face as she looked into my eyes. She had done that before but there was something different. It was her love and her compassion but it was more. Very soon I understood. Aunt Macy knew what I was about to read.

"Anne, it is time that you knew the truth about your parents." I started crying. Aunt Macy held me in her arms. After a little while, I continued reading. "Macy and I are the only ones who know what really happened. No one else in the family was ever told. That's the way your mother wanted it. Macy and I promised her that we would never tell a soul and we haven't. Your mother just asked that when you were grown that we tell you the truth.

The first thing I want to share with you is that your mother loved you with all her heart. There was nothing wrong with you. You were her beautiful little girl and she loved you more than anything in the world. When she left, it broke her heart to leave you. She had actually thought at one point that it would be better for her to die than to leave you but she chose to leave.

This is what happened. One day your mother came to Macy and told her that she was pregnant. Your mother was

not married, at least that is what we thought. When we asked her who your father was, she wouldn't tell us at first. When your grandparents were told that she was pregnant, they insisted that she tell them who the father was. Most of the time in those days when a young woman was pregnant and unmarried, the girl's family forced the young man to marry her. In this case, your mother simply would not tell anyone who the father was.

As the pregnancy continued, people outside the family became aware of the situation. When the pastor heard about it, he visited your grandparents to talk with them. He suggested that your mother move to a maternity home for unwed mothers. He further suggested that she put you up for adoption. That way your mother could return home after the pregnancy and continue on with her life. Your mother chose not to take that option.

Rumors started circulating. Some suggested that the father was the preacher's son. Your mother and he had been dating for several months. Other's said that it was a traveling salesman or someone who was just passing through. People in the community and even in the church were very cruel. I had never seen anything like it. Everyone turned their backs on the family. Your grandparents and your mother faced tremendous ridicule and scorn.

When you were born, things got worse. The pastor told the family that they were not welcome at the church. When your mother walked down the street with you in her arms, people would turn their backs and not speak to her. Your grandparents felt humiliated. At one point your grandfather thought about selling the farm and moving away but they just stayed, ostracized from the community. Your uncle Robert and I were about the only ones who stayed in contact with them and your mother. It was the first time I saw your uncle Robert so mad that he wanted to quit going to church. One Sunday he almost got up to tell them and the preacher how hypocritical they were.

Macy and I continued to talk with your mother but she was growing more and more depressed all the time. We were worried at one point that she might try and hurt herself. With no support from the church and the community, the family was slowly falling apart. The situation was taking its toll on everyone.

But one day, out of the blue, your mother decided to tell us what happened and who your father was. She had been seeing one of the young men who worked for grandpaw George at the cotton gin. His name was Arthur Gray. He was twenty years old. Your mother was only seventeen at the time. She had just graduated from high school. Your mother knew that if uncle George found out that she was seeing Arthur, he would have been so furious that he might have hurt the young man. So your mother kept their relationship a secret.

Arthur played on your mother's affections until one day she found that she was pregnant. When she told Arthur, he talked your mother into going to a justice of the peace a few counties over to get married. He told her that they needed to keep everything a secret until he could find a job in another town. He said that he would return for her when he was settled in. He never came back. Your mother was devastated.

I know we told you that your father died in the war and that his body was never returned home. We're sorry about that. Maybe you can forgive us now that you know the

truth. We were only trying to protect you because you were so young. Your mother asked us to wait until you were grown to tell you what really happened."

I couldn't believe what I was reading. I looked at aunt Macy and just shook my head. She took my hand and said, "Honey, it's okay. You're going to be okay." I turned back to the letter. "Soon after you were born your mother started facing the wrath of the community and the church. That's when she decided to leave. She didn't want you to have to grow up with that kind of ridicule.

We tried to get her to stay. We told her that it didn't matter what people thought. We begged her to tell everyone what had happened but she wouldn't. She was too ashamed of the choice she had made. Right or wrong, she decided to leave. What I want you to understand is that she left for your sake. I know that doesn't make sense but she left so you could have a better life.

Macy and I asked her to write and tell us where she was and how she was doing. She said that when she got settled she would let us know. We never heard from her again. Your grandparents and Macy raised you until you were about three. They loved you with all their hearts. Your grandfather died and your grandmother, Eliza, lost her health not long after his death. That's when uncle Robert and I took you and Macy in. We knew that God wanted us to raise you with our girls and over these years He has confirmed that we made the right decision. I hope that you feel the same.

Aunt Macy can answer any questions you might have about your mother. They, of course, are sisters. She can tell you what your mother was like as a child. I know that you would like to learn more about her. I want to thank you again for everything you've done this past year. I know that God is going to use you to do great things for Him in the future. Never doubt His presence and His power in your life.

Hopefully, one day you will meet a good, godly Christian man who loves you and cherishes you as his wife. I pray that, if God wills, you can experience the joy of having your own children and I know that you will raise them up in the church to know the Lord. Life is good Anne. I know that you've been through a lot of life that wasn't good. But life is good even in the hard times when you have the strength of family and faith in your heart. I love you Anne. God bless. Aunt Mable."

I just sat there for a moment. Many of my questions had been answered but others remained. When I looked over at aunt Macy, she had tears in her eyes. "Honey, I hope you aren't angry with us. We just did the best we could under the circumstances. We love you Anne." I assured aunt Macy that I was grateful for their care and support. I was just so emotionally drained that I told aunt Macy I wanted to go to my room and rest. She understood.

Over the next few weeks, I learned a great deal about my mother. Aunt Macy and I sat out on the porch after supper almost every evening. She would tell me a different story each night. "Your mother was the youngest of five children. I was closest in age to her. We had one other sister and two brothers. Our sister died from polio when she was young. Our two brothers were several years older than us girls. They worked at the cotton gin and on our farm with daddy.

From day one, your mother was what we called a live wire. She had more energy than anyone I've ever seen. Sometimes that was good and sometimes that was bad. She just couldn't sit still very long at all. That's why she got in

trouble at church a lot. I remember one Sunday when she was fidgeting around like she always did and before we knew it, she was crawling on the floor toward the back of the church. I saw her before momma and daddy did and I knew that this wasn't going to end well. You could hear people talking about her as she passed from one pew to the next. At some point, momma turned to me and asked where she was. I just pointed down at the floor.

Well, momma just about lost her mind. She got up, crossed past daddy and marched toward the back of the church. Daddy looked at me wondering what was going on. I just shrugged my shoulders as if I didn't know a thing. In just a minute we heard the slap on your momma's behind. It wasn't the first time and it wasn't the last. As a matter of fact, sometimes your momma got up to five spankings a day. When we were real young, our brother Mason would count the number of spankings your mother had. He would sometimes give us a report and say that more spankings were coming."

I really enjoyed hearing the stories about my mother even if she did get in trouble a lot. One evening, aunt Macy told me about the time when mother decided that old Jack, their dog, needed a haircut. "Your mother went out to the barn and found some shears that daddy and the boys used when they had sheep. Your mother took old Jack out to the barn, tied him to a post, and started shearing away.

It was a fiasco. Jack would howl every time your mother nicked him with the shears. There was fur and hair all over the place. When your mother was finished, old Jack looked pitiful. If that wasn't bad enough, she put a big red ribbon and a little bell around his neck. Then she added some little branches on his ears. I guess the best description would be a miniature skint reindeer. When your mother brought the poor dog in the house, she was so proud to show off Jack's new hairdo. Momma just gasped. Daddy started laughing. I was surprised that they weren't mad. But what could they do. Old Jack didn't know any difference and his fur would grow back in time. So everybody just said to themselves, there she goes again."

Aunt Macy's stories gave me the first glimpses of my mother's personality. She was creative but mischievous. Aunt Macy told me that one of mother's, well, shall we say, talents, was making faces at people. It was the thing that got her in trouble more than anything else. Aunt Macy laughed and said, "She made faces at teachers when they weren't looking. She made faces at our parents. She made faces at people in church.

The thing is, that after she made a face at someone, she would turn around to the people behind her and show them the face she had made. Then everyone would laugh. By the time a teacher or someone else turned around, your mother was back in place with her normal face. She was that quick.

There was one occasion, however, when your mother made a face that got her in big trouble. We were having a revival at the church. When we had regular services, after the music part of the service was finished, the choir members would come down and sit with everyone else in the pews. But when we had revival services there was not enough room for the choir to come down.

At this particular revival we had a visiting preacher whose face was a little, well, different. I'm not saying that he was ugly. His face just looked a lot like a, well, a horse." I

couldn't believe aunt Macy said that but I wanted to hear the rest of the story. "Well, the preacher started his sermon and every once in a while he would turn to the choir that was sitting behind him and preach to them. Your mother, of course, noticed this and decided to seize the opportunity.

One time when the preacher turned to the choir, your mother made the most awful face you've ever seen. It was a crazy horse face. What she didn't realize was that all the choir members saw her. The ladies in the choir were shocked. Their faces looked almost as bad as your mother's. Then, if that wasn't bad enough, as she often did, your mother turned around and showed the congregation the face that she made. The whole church was stunned. When momma looked over at us to see what was wrong, she screamed.

The poor preacher was the only one in the building who didn't know what was going on. When momma screamed he thought that she was a Pentecostal shouting praises to the Lord. Brother Willis, our pastor, was mortified. He just sat there on the platform with his face in his hands.

Your mother didn't realize how much trouble she was in until she was jerked up out of her seat and marched outside by momma. I figured that she was about to get the worst spanking she ever had. The preacher just kept on preaching but I don't think that anyone was listening to a word he said. They were all thinking about what your mother had done.

Well, the service finally ended. As everyone was leaving, I could hear them talking about what had happened. I went out to the car and found your mother sitting in the back seat. It was not a happy scene. When we got home, momma told her to go to her room. They punished her for a month. She couldn't ride her bike. She couldn't leave the house for a month. The next Sunday, momma made her stand up in front of the church and apologize. None of us kids thought that her apology was real. We were right. The next week she was making faces at her teachers again. She was something all right. A mess I tell you, a pure mess."

As the weeks passed on, aunt Macy told me more and more about my mother. I enjoyed hearing the stories but I still struggled with the fact that she left. At least I knew the truth and maybe one day she would come back. Until then, I had to run the store and take care of the family. That is often how life is. You do what you have to do. But sometimes in the midst of living, God blesses in unexpected ways.

21   *New Names For The Rose*

When I learned about my mother and Arthur Gray, I asked aunt Macy if I could see my birth certificate. She found it in aunt Mabel's papers. The first thing I wanted to know was whether my name was listed as Gray or Hill. There it was, Elizabeth Anne Hill. Then I checked mother's name. It was Hill also. When I looked at the space for the name of the father, I was shocked. It was blank. That's why no one knew that Arthur was my father.

Back then, I would have been known as an illegitimate child. I have always hated that term because a child has no choice in how they are born. If anyone was illegitimate it was Arthur Gray. My mother wasn't an adult when she became pregnant. Arthur could have gone to jail for what he did. That's probably why he left and never came back. He was afraid that mother would tell someone what had happened.

I certainly had mixed emotions about the choice my mother made. Most children were proud of the name their father had given them. Under different circumstances, my name would have been Gray. I knew that there was no reason to care for Arthur but he was my father. I know this sounds odd, but soon I would have to make a choice about my name. Let me tell you how that happened.

I remembered that aunt Mabel mentioned in her letter that my mother and Arthur Gray were secretly married. One day I decided to go to the courthouse and see if I could find their marriage certificate. I brought my birth certificate with me just in case I needed it for identification. I asked the woman at the records office for mother's marriage certificate. She didn't even ask to see any identification. When she handed me the document, I saw it plain as day. Mother and Arthur were legally married.

Well, their marriage was not actually legal. Mother was underage. Her parents would have had to sign a document allowing her to marry. They had not. But there it was. I should have been born Elizabeth Anne Gray. I really didn't know how to feel about that. A person's name was important in those days. In some ways it defined who they were. Your name represented your heritage and your character. I can remember uncle Robert telling the girls, "Remember, you're a Henry. Henrys are good people, honest people."

I had never really had a sense of connection with my name. I'm sure that my grandparents were proud to be Hills. They were good and honest people too. But they were gone. Mother was gone. I was raised in the Henry house. I know it sounds like I'm rambling but for several months I struggled with knowing who I was. My identity had been so wrapped up in the Henry family that I felt like I was one of them. I was and that was good. But now I had to consider who I was going to be. Elizabeth Anne Hill or Elizabeth Anne Gray.

For a while I thought that my father didn't deserve for

me to have his name. He had ruined my mother's life. He was responsible for her leaving me. Then I thought, well, I should choose to be a Gray so that one day he would have to accept his responsibility for me. I didn't really know what to do. I guess that deep down inside I wanted to be like everyone else. I wanted to have the names of both my parents on my birth certificate. Eventually, I was forced to decide.

That was the year that the government established the Social Security Administration. Everyone had to go to the courthouse and sign up for a Social Security card. You had to bring your birth certificate as identification. If you didn't have it, they would make a copy from their records.

Now I had to make a decision about my name. Hill or Gray. I talked with aunt Macy about it. She told me that it was my decision, that she would support me whichever one I chose. I made the decision but knew that I would have a problem presenting my birth certificate. No name was listed for my father.

So I went to the courthouse, told them that I didn't have a copy of my birth certificate, and asked them to create a duplicate that I could present for the Social Security card. As the lady in the office was filling out the copy, she noticed that my father's name was missing. She looked up at me with an air of disgust as if it was my fault. Evidently, she had seen this situation before. When she handed me the duplicate, I thanked her and knew what I had to do next.

I took the new birth certificate home and added my father's name. Arthur Gray. I also added Gray to my mother's name and my name. I chose to become Elizabeth Anne Gray. I didn't think, then, that I would ever meet my father. But if I did, he would know that I knew who he was. It didn't bring joy to my heart but I thought of it as justice. You have a daughter Arthur Gray. Her name is Anne, Elizabeth Anne Gray.

The next day, I went back to the courthouse to the new Social Security office. I was pretty nervous. I had run several different scenarios through my mind. I thought that they might be able to tell I had altered my birth certificate. They might go across the hall and find the original. The person at the office might know me or my family and stop the whole process. I was afraid but I was determined.

When I walked in, there was no line. I didn't recognize the clerk and I hoped that she didn't recognize me. I said, "Good morning. I'd like to apply for my Social Security card please." The lady didn't even look up at me. "Fill out this form and attach your birth certificate."

I went over to one of the small desks in the room and completed the form. When I returned, she looked over the document and verified the information from my birth certificate. I was holding my breath the whole time. She pulled out a large ledger book and put my name by the next number. Elizabeth Anne Gray. For some reason the clerk had omitted Hill. Then she turned to her typewriter and completed the card. Again, Elizabeth Anne Gray. She handed me the card and my birth certificate and I was finished.

I never told anyone except aunt Macy what I had done. Soon I started signing documents with my new name. No one ever noticed or said a word about it. I had to be careful, however, when I met new people in front of the girls or my close friends. They would have noticed if I introduced myself as Anne Gray. The main thing was that I had made a choice. I chose to have my real father's name. I didn't know if I would

ever meet him. But if I did, he would know that I was his daughter. Elizabeth Anne Gray. I didn't know it at the time, but very soon I would have to change my name again.

In the year following aunt Mabel's death, our family changed in some very significant ways. Willie married Mack Bridges and moved to Pearl Valley. Jennie graduated and decided to go to nursing school with two of her friends. That left me and Ellie to run the store.

I hired a couple of high school boys to help in the afternoons and we were able to get by pretty well but the work was overwhelming at times. Ellie and I wouldn't get home until seven o'clock at night and we had to get up at five the next morning to open the store at seven. Sunday was the only day we closed the store. I just didn't see how we could keep working such long hard hours without some permanent full-time help.

We had another problem in Norman at that time. Our quiet little town was being overrun by the WPA and CCC workers. Some of those guys were rough and roudy. Ellie and I were often challenged by those who had no respect for women. On more than one occasion I had to get the sheriff to escort some of them out of the store.

I remember one time when I was sorting some ladies hosiery at the counter. A man came in and wanted to set up a credit account. When I asked him where he worked, he told me that was none of my business. I told him that I needed his place of employment to start the account. Well, he started going through the store and taking things off the shelves. He thought that he was going to make me put those items on credit for him.

About that time, Sheriff Dudley Crowell walked in the

door. Sheriff Crowell was a well-respected law officer who had served as sheriff for over fifteen years. He was a fair man but a firm man, and he was a big man, a real big man. Sheriff Crowell and Mr. Hank Powers were always the finalists in the arm wrestling competition at the county fair.

I told the sheriff what was going on and he waited by the counter. When the man plopped all his items on the counter and demanded that I set up an account for him, the sheriff just started laughing. The man asked, "What are you laughing at?" The sheriff asked, "Your name is Bullock, isn't it?" "That's right." "You aren't married and don't have a steady girl do you?" "That's right. What about it?"

That's when the sheriff started cackling. Then he pulled a pair of those ladies hose I had been sorting out from under the items the man put on the counter and asked, "Then who are these for?" The man turned as red as a beet. The sheriff said, "Wait til I tell the boys about this. Old Bullock wears ladies hose." Mr. Bullock started to say something to the sheriff, but that's when Crowell gave him that look like, you better not, and he didn't. The sheriff made him apologize and threatened to put him in jail for disturbing the peace if he did anything like that again.

When Mr. Bullock left the store, I thanked the sheriff for coming to my rescue. We shared a smile about the hose and the sheriff was on his way. That wasn't the last time he had to get me out of a jam but it was one of the funniest times. When Mr. Bullock came in the store after that, he was real nice, didn't say a word, and paid cash for everything he bought. He nor I ever forgot the day when sheriff Crowell put him in his place with a pair of ladies hose.

There was one other problem, however, that was bigger

than all the rest. It was our guys. Ellie and Gene had been dating for over two years. Your dad and I had been going out for almost a year. We both knew that we would love to be married but we had to keep the store going for the family. We had promised Jennie that we would pay her room, board, and tuition at the nursing school. Aunt Macy couldn't support herself. I didn't want Ellie to have to find another job. Most of all, I had made a promise to aunt Mabel.

Ellie and I just didn't know what to do. Ellie knew that Gene would soon ask her to marry him. I felt the same with Jim. We talked with aunt Macy about. She didn't have a solution but she told us that God did. That if the Lord wanted us to marry, He would provide a way in His time. Ellie and I believed that but probably not as much as aunt Macy did.

Well, that spring, Gene asked Ellie to marry him and just a few weeks later, your dad asked me. We were both excited about the proposals but we had to talk with the guys about our obligations and the store. Gene and Jim both said that they would wait for us until we could work something out. Ellie and I were so grateful for that but knew that we couldn't put the guys off forever. What were we going to do?

A few months went by and we still had no answer for our dilemma. The hard work and long hours at the store were getting the best of Ellie and me. We were both making more money than we could spend but we were both showing signs of fatigue. Neither one of us could see an end to it all. We were both afraid that Gene and Jim might start dating other girls. I remember one night as we were closing the store that we both just broke down in tears.

But one day, as aunt Macy would say, "In God's time," everything changed. Your dad took me out for supper after work one night. While we were eating, he started asking me questions about the store, questions about how much money I made and how much Ellie made. At first, I found it a little odd that he was asking about our finances. But then he spoke up and said, "I have the answer to our problem."

Jim's solution was for him and Gene to quit their jobs and work with Ellie and me at the store. I would have to give Ellie a part of my share to make things even but that was okay with me. We would divide up the work so that one couple took a morning shift and the other took an afternoon shift. That way, a man would always be on duty at the store. We would expand the store a bit to offer new products and make more profits. For housing, one couple could live in the apartment above the store and the other couple could live with aunt Macy at the family home.

When Jim finished sharing his plan, I was speechless. It was perfect. Our portion of the store profits were more than all four of us made together. It didn't matter to me where we lived, as long as aunt Macy was okay with that arrangement. We would all be working fewer hours and the guys could, in a way, have their own business. Your dad and I decided to talk with aunt Macy first to see if she would agree. She did. Then we were ready to talk with Ellie and Gene.

We asked them to go out with us in Pearl Valley the next Saturday night. We had a nice drive over and chose to eat at a new restaurant called Sonny's Steakhouse. It was a little more upscale than we were accustomed to but this was going to be a very special night. Ellie and Gene had no idea what we were going to share with them. It had been hard for me not to tell Ellie but I was able to keep the plan secret.

After we ordered from the menu, Jim shared his idea.

He decided to pitch it like a wild salesman. It was hilarious. "Gene, are you in a dead end job like I am with no way to advance? Are you tired of traveling mile after mile every day like I do, working yourself to death so others can make their fortunes? Do you want to rise up and take hold of an opportunity that could change your life like I do?" By this time Gene's eyes were as big as two baseballs. He didn't know what to think. He looked over at Ellie and she was just as stunned as he was. I was hiding my face with the dinner napkin, trying really hard not to burst out laughing.

By the time your dad delivered his last words, he was standing up shouting, "Gene, do you believe it's possible to make a better life for yourself and your loved ones? Do you believe that you can change your destiny?" Gene was so caught up with the whole presentation that he rose to his feet and said, "Yes, I believe. I believe." The people at the table next to ours evidently thought that Jim was an evangelist and that Gene had become a Christian right there and then. One lady stood up and said, "Amen. Thank you Jesus."

That's when I lost it. Ellie looked at me like, "Has Jim lost his mind?" Gene came down from his high and said, "Jim, what in the world are you talking about?" It took both of us a long time to stop laughing. When we did, I said, "Jim and I have been talking and we want to share with you a way that we can all move forward with our lives together."

Gene and Ellie listened to the plan. Gene had a few questions but in the end they were both very excited about the opportunity. After we finished our meal, we stayed until the restaurant closed, talking about as many details as we could think of. When the guys dropped us off at the house, Ellie and I stayed up after midnight talking about what it would be like to be married. It seemed that God was working everything out for us. He had sent us two fine Christian men who loved us and respected us. You can't ask the Lord for much more than that.

We all agreed that your dad and I would take the apartment above the store. Gene and Ellie would live at the house with aunt Macy. Ellie and I asked the guys if we could have a double wedding. They agreed. On the first Saturday in June we were married. That's when I changed my name again. I became Anne Gray Carpenter.

22   *Joy And Trials For The Rose*

Our new lives together began. The first thing that your dad and I had to tackle was the apartment. No one had lived up there for years. It was not a very large space, one bedroom, a living room and dining area, the kitchen, and the bathroom. The best part of the apartment was the porch. It ran the whole length of the apartment. There were doors out to the porch from the living room and the bedroom.

The porch overlooked the woods and field that were right behind the store. Every morning and late afternoon we could see deer and other animals at the small pond that was in the middle of the field. The porch was where we enjoyed breakfast almost every day. At night we would sit out on the porch and talk about our plans for the store and for our family. I'll never forget those early days of our marriage. They were wonderful.

The arrangement with Ellie and Gene was great. The stress of working twelve-hour days was gone. The guys took care of the business end of things. They dealt with the salesmen and deliveries while Ellie and I concentrated on serving our customers. We rearranged the floor space which allowed us to add more items. We expanded the business to include lumber and we even added basic farm supplies. We hired two men to help with the extra work.

After the first year, we were making more profit than we had ever made in the store. The WPA and CCC contracts were expanding. Families were actually moving to Norman and building houses. The four of us even talked about building our own homes across the field from aunt Macy. The future seemed bright for us all.

Unfortunately, that all changed when war broke out in Europe. Rumors were that the United States would soon enter the war. Ellie and I were so afraid that Gene and Jim would be drafted. Every night, we would listen to the radio for news about the war. Every morning, we rushed to read the newspaper for any updates. It was a very trying time for all Americans.

We lived with the fear of war for over two years. Back then couples delayed starting their families, afraid that their husbands would be drafted. I cannot explain in words how that fear controlled our lives. It was all people talked about. Depression was a major problem during that time. Some people simply couldn't cope with the stress of the situation. Pastors tried to encourage their congregations by preaching sermons about relying on God for our strength.

Then one day, all our fears were realized. It didn't happen as we had anticipated. We thought that the President would declare war on Germany. Instead, the Japanese bombed Pearl Harbor. The news was unbearable. So many killed. We knew then that there was no option. America

would be at war.

After the bombing, things changed quickly. Men ages twenty-one to forty-five had to report to their local draft office immediately. Gene reported and was drafted that day. Your dad was not drafted. He received a deferred status because he was just over twenty-eight years old. His status could have changed at any time but it never did.

Ellie was heartbroken. They had only been married for two years. Their plans for the future were in serious jeopardy. Aunt Macy and I tried to calm her fears but all our efforts failed. Ellie was convinced that the day Gene left was the last day that she would see him alive.

One by one the young men of our little town left for war. Within six months, about half of them were gone. Only those whose families owned farms or those who had some physical problem remained. At one point, even the men who were married and had children were drafted. Young mothers were left alone to raise their babies.

The men who stayed did so much to help the families of those whose sons and husbands were fighting. Your dad helped as many as he could. He did little fix it jobs that the women couldn't handle. He even learned to work on cars which was something he had never done before.

There was one thing that was rather humorous during that time. Most of the women back then did not drive their cars. They worked at home and there was no need for them to learn how to drive. But once their husbands were gone, they were forced to learn.

One day the phone rang at the store and Jim answered. I could hear his side of the conversation. "Hi. How are you? You need some help with your car? Well, how can I help you?

Oh my goodness! I'll be there as soon as I can!" When Jim hung up the phone, I asked him what was wrong. As he hurried out of the store, he said, "Mrs. Cecile Brooks just ran her car into Dorothy Farley's front porch!" The Brooks and the Farleys were best friends, well, until then. Your dad told me that Cecile was bringing lunch to Dorothy because she had been a little under the weather. When Jim got there, the two were about to kill each other.

On other occasions some of the ladies would bump into other cars while they were parking on Main Street. Often, they never told the owner of the other car about their little fender bender. Once, at church, Virginia Perkins backed her car into the preacher's truck. The pastor was gracious and told her not to worry about it. Virginia got back in her car, put it in reverse, and hit the preacher's truck again. He just shook his head and asked Virginia if she would like him to get her car out of the parking lot.

Other than the car incidents, there was little else for anyone to laugh about. Every night we huddled around the radio to hear the latest on the war. One night when your dad and I were listening with aunt Macy, we heard what, for us, was very serious news. The government was halting all WPA and CCC construction projects. More men were needed to join the forces in Europe and in the Pacific. We both knew that this was going to have a major impact on the store and our family.

We received notice within two weeks that all the camps in Taylor County were closing. Our government contracts were dropped and sales at the store were cut in half. We didn't know what to do. Jim made contacts with every agency he could think of trying to find some way that we could make

up for the loss. Nothing worked out.

Aunt Mabel had entrusted me with the store. I promised her that I would take care of the family. I now felt helpless to keep that promise. Your dad tried to encourage me. He said that something would work out. But I could see that he was as worried as I was. We talked to aunt Macy and Ellie. We all agreed that we would do whatever we had to do to keep things going. Jim looked into getting a job in Pearl Valley, but no one was hiring. Ellie tried the same with no luck.

Jennie finished nursing school just as the war began. She actually joined the Army Nursing Corps. Before we knew it she was at an Army hospital in England. Gene was injured in a training exercise and never went overseas. He was reassigned as an assistant to the Commander. Ellie joined him and secured a clerk position on the base.

Your dad and I were left to run the store by ourselves. We tried for several months to keep things going but there were simply not enough sales to make ends meet and to take care of aunt Macy. We had to find jobs. One day we noticed an ad in the newspaper. A new shipyard was opening in New Orleans. They were hiring workers for all types of positions.

I asked aunt Macy if she thought that she could take care of the store for a day while Jim and I went to New Orleans. She said she would and we left early the next morning. When we arrived at the shipyard, we were overwhelmed by the number of people looking for jobs. There must have been a thousand people applying. But we got in line, filled out the application, and waited for our interviews.

Eventually, your dad went one way and I went another. When we met up again, both of us had big smiles on our faces. I had gotten a job in the payroll department and Jim had been hired to work as a shipfitter apprentice. Neither one of us was going to make the kind of money we did in the store, but that didn't matter. We just needed to make enough to take care of ourselves and aunt Macy.

On the way back home, your dad and I talked about what we needed to do with the store. We could simply close it down or try to find someone who could run it until the war was over. Maybe after that, we could come back home and all would be back to normal. We eventually decided to keep the store open and we knew exactly who we wanted to run it.

When the government camps closed and so many people left town, Mrs. Aaron, Ganny, had to close the restaurant. She was the perfect one to run the store. We talked with her the next day and she agreed. Because Mrs. Aaron and aunt Macy were such good friends, they looked after each other. Jim and I felt good about the new arrangement.

Living in New Orleans was certainly different than living in Norman. Our first objective was to find a house to rent. We tried to find something near the shipyard but that didn't work out. We had to settle on a duplex that was located in the garden district off Magazine Street. Every day we commuted across the river to the plant. Fortunately, we had the same work hours and the same days off.

On our days off we really enjoyed the city. There was so much to see and do even during the war. City Park was one of our favorite places. We would pack a picnic lunch and spend half the day just strolling through the hundred year old oak trees. The park also had several small lakes that served as a wonderful habitat for all types of water birds.

We also enjoyed going to the French Quarter. Our house was only about a mile from the Quarter. When the weather

was good, we walked. We would buy some beignets and watch all the people as they passed by. We also enjoyed watching the artists who lined the sidewalks on Jackson Square. One day your dad had an artist draw a picture of me. I finally agreed only if he allowed me to have one drawn of him. He agreed. You may have already found those two drawings in the picture box. They served as fond memories for us at a time when good memories were hard to come by.

Once a month we could go back home on our days off. It was always good to see aunt Macy. She had an apricot nectar cake for us every time we came. We were also able to see how Mrs. Aaron was doing with the store. All was well but people continued to leave town to find work. Mrs. Aaron had no family, so sales at the store were enough to meet her needs.

The war continued for four long years. Every month families received the heartbreaking news that one of their loved ones had been killed. Aunt Macy told us about the ones from Normal. In our small town, four young men lost their lives defending freedom. After the war, a small monument was placed in the park that was renamed in their memory.

As the war was coming to an end, your dad and I knew that the shipyard would soon start laying off most of the workers. We had to make some decisions about where we would live and what we were going to do for jobs. By that time, the population of Normal had dropped below one hundred. Norman was just like thousands of small towns all across the country, a shadow of what it had once been. All the stores were closed except ours and the gas station. We sold the store to Mrs. Aaron with the stipulation that aunt Macy would receive part of the profits as long as she lived.

New Orleans, on the other hand, was booming. After the

war ended, your dad found work at a wholesale jewelry company. He handled sales for the larger accounts. That's when we decided to have you Sarah. We continued to live in the little duplex and actually purchased the other side of the property. That's when your dad became interested in real estate.

Sarah, I can't tell you how much joy you brought us in those days. Right after you were born, we bought our first instant camera. As you know, we took dozens and dozens of pictures of you. At one point, I actually thought about putting them all together in a book and calling it, *Sarah Carpenter: The Early Years.*

I loved buying new dresses and outfits for you. Your dad worked on Canal Street which wasn't far from our home. Sometimes we would shop for you during his lunch hour. We also loved taking you to the zoo. You absolutely loved the zoo. Your favorite animals were the monkeys. When they started talking, you would just laugh and laugh. I think that there is actually a picture of you making faces at the monkeys. Those were special days for us all.

About two years after you were born, Sarah, your dad and I had grown weary of living in such a big city. We wanted to move to a small town like Pearl Valley. About seventy miles north of New Orleans, in the town of Pine Hills, a large paper mill was being built. In the next several years, people by the thousands would be moving there to work. Hundreds of homes would be built. We finally saw the opportunity that we had been looking for.

Your dad secured a job at the paper mill and I found work at the bag factory. Those early days were pretty tough. We both worked shifts and sometimes we only saw each

other as we were coming and going. We survived knowing that we had a plan. Jim would acquire his real estate license and begin buying and selling homes part time.

All of those plans eventually worked out but there were serious trials and challenges along the way. Three years after we moved to Pine Hills, the paper mill workers went on strike for six months. We almost lost our home during that time. Every week the banks were repossessing the homes of striking workers. Jim wanted to buy some of those homes but because our income was also limited, we didn't have the money to buy them.

After the strike, it took us a good two years to recover our losses and for your dad to start buying real estate. That's when we decided to have another child. Steven, I know you've already added up the years. They don't match. You are correct. I became pregnant with the child I never delivered. About three months into the pregnancy I had a miscarriage.

For over three years, I struggled greatly with that loss. I asked God a thousand times why my baby didn't survive. I never got an answer to my questions but God assured me that He had a plan. Steven, that plan was you. The doctor advised me not to have another child because of my age. I didn't listen to him. I wanted a boy. I prayed for a boy and God answered my prayers. When the doctor told me that I was pregnant, I quit working at the bag factory. In just a few weeks, we bought the grocery store and soon I had my little red-haired boy.

I was so proud of you. I still am. Sometimes when we went downtown to shop, Sarah would hold you or ride you in the stroller. People who didn't know us thought that you were her child. We would laugh and Sarah would smile and say, "No. That's my little red-haired brother."

One of the things I've never told you, Steven, is that when you were very young and did something wrong, Sarah would pick you up and run to hide you so you wouldn't get punished. She hid you in closets, out on the breezeway, anywhere she could find. She just couldn't stand to see you get a spanking. After a while, your dad and I just gave up. We decided that you would probably turn out okay with a few less spankings and you did.

Those years during and after the war were difficult times but they were also joyful times. That's just the way life is. We endure and we enjoy. Life is hard but life is good. That's how you have to see this time in your life. I'll talk with you more about that later. Now, I want to tell you about my family and how I discovered the truth about my parents.

23   *Two Roses Finally Meet*

Between the time we moved to New Orleans and our first ten years in Pine Hills, I had not thought much about my parents. Life had gotten busy. There were a few times when I wondered if they were still alive. But for the most part, I was focused on raising the two of you, taking care of the store, and being a good wife for your dad. At some point Jim was able to quit his job at the mill and work full time in real estate. That had been his dream all along.

Pine Hills was becoming a large small town. People were moving in every week. Businesses were doing so well that people started calling Pine Hills the Magic City. Your dad was selling and buying properties every month. At one point we added on to the store and we were making more money than we ever had. Life was good.

My family had spread out all across the South. Everyone except aunt Macy left Mississippi. Aunt Macy eventually moved to Pearl Valley and lived with Mrs. Ruth Stanfield who was a widow friend of hers. After the garment factory closed, Willie and Mack moved to Memphis. Mack got a job at a steel factory. Jennie married Cecil after the war and moved to Houston. He started working in the oil industry. Ellie and Gene moved to central Louisiana. Gene started the vending business that he still has today.

At the store, I was meeting new people every week. Most of them worked out at the mill. A few had started small businesses like ours. Slowly but surely many of the new customers became good friends. Most of them went to church and were good Christian people. For some reason, when the women came to the store, they wanted to talk about their lives. I became a counselor of sorts for many of them. I don't really know why. I didn't think of myself as a counselor. I just listened to them and shared my own experiences. Sometimes we even prayed together right there in the store.

In those early days, every once in a while I delivered groceries to some of our elderly customers when they were ill. They would talk about their ailments, the grandchildren, and the news around town. In other words, they gossiped a little bit about their neighbors. I had to be careful of my time but the visits seemed to cheer them up a bit and that made the effort worthwhile.

Now, I need to tell you about the day that changed my life forever. This is something that I have kept from you all. I was too ashamed to talk with you about it. I know now that I should not have felt that way but I did. I apologize for not telling you before. Once I share this with you, you may not be happy with me because, well, it is too late to change things.

Two years ago, a lady came in the store about eleven o'clock. I had never seen her before. She introduced herself as Mrs. Kennedy. She was a short, slender woman. Well dressed. In her mid-sixties. She wasn't actually shopping.

She just stood across the counter from me with a faint, almost reluctant smile. I asked if I could help her with anything. She said, "No, not really." Then she asked, "Are you Anne?" I said, "Yes." "Do you think that we could talk for just a moment?"

I had no idea what she wanted. She didn't look like a salesperson. I couldn't think of any problems we were having at the store. I agreed to talk with her and we went back to the office. When she sat down, she reached into her purse and pulled out an old photo. It was a picture of a baby and a young teenaged girl. They were sitting on the porch of a southern style farmhouse. The house seemed familiar to me. It must have been spring because the porch was surrounded on both sides by beautiful, beautiful roses.

She asked, "Anne, have you ever seen this picture?" I said, "No mam. I don't believe that I have." She said, "Anne, that's you on the porch of your grandparent's home." She was right. I remembered the porch. I asked how she had a photo of me. I thought that she was a relative I had never met. That's when she said, "Anne, I'm the young woman holding you. Anne, I'm your mother."

I don't think that I can put into words exactly how I felt at that moment. So many different emotions. Relieved that she was still alive. Confused about why she left me. Angry that she left me. Questions with no answers. Soon my emotions got the best of me and I started weeping. She reached across the desk and touched my hand. I looked up at her. She was struggling to hold back the tears. That's when she stood up and walked over to the window.

I just kept looking at her, wondering what she would say next. As she continued to look out the window, she said, "I know that you have a lot of questions. I'll try to be honest with you and tell you the truth. But the truth isn't pretty. I'm not a good woman. I wasn't a mother to you. I abandoned you. I'll try to explain it all but I doubt that you will ever forgive me. I'm sorry that I ruined your life.

That's when I finally spoke up. "You didn't ruin my life, mother. I've had a good life. God has taken care of me." That's when she turned, looked at me, and said, "I was supposed to take care of you." I didn't know how to respond. She continued. "I couldn't stand the ridicule and all the whispering, especially from the fine folks up at the church. My parents had to face the same thing. I hurt them. I ruined their lives too." Again, I just listened as I had done with so many of my friends at the store. It was almost as if I was her counselor or her pastor. She was confessing her sins.

After several minutes, she finally sat down. I could tell that she was emotionally drained. I got her some water and just waited. She continued. "I decided that the only way out of the situation was for me to leave. I didn't want to leave you, Anne but I just couldn't see any other way. I felt that the community wouldn't treat you the way it had treated me if I left. So that's what I chose to do.

The night I left, one of my friends drove me to the train station. She had an aunt who agreed to let me live with her in Memphis. I was only seventeen. The first few weeks were more than difficult. I cried myself to sleep most nights. I missed you and my family so much but I just couldn't go back. I wrote letter after letter to you all but I always tore them up before I mailed them. I was not well. At one point I even considered taking my own life. I tried going to church but I felt that God was so angry with me that He was like

everyone else. He probably didn't want me in His house.

After the first month, my friend's aunt told me that I would have to pay rent for my room. I had no money. I considered returning home but, again, I chose to stay in Memphis. I got a job at the local movie theater selling tickets. It barely paid for my rent. Back then the theaters didn't open until three o'clock in the afternoon. I got an early morning job at a little café around the corner from the house.

As the months passed by, I thought less and less about going back home. My friend never told anyone where I was and they never came looking for me. I know that they must have wondered whether or not I was alive. But I guess that I just didn't care enough to let them know that I was okay."

Again, I didn't know what to say. She had made so many poor decisions. It was hard for me to understand how you could leave your child and not even stay in touch to find out how she was doing. At that point I guess I was feeling a little angry. But she had decided to come to me. I didn't know what the future held at that point, but I was willing to listen.

"I had been in Memphis about three years when I met my husband. He was a friend of the family I was staying with. He worked at a local car dealership as a salesman. When he asked me to marry him, I had to make a decision. Was I going to tell him about my marriage to Arthur and, of course, about you? Again, I chose to hide my past. I never told him."

It was then that she said, "I guess the more I tell you about me the less sympathy you have. You are probably feeling that I was ashamed of you. I was not. I was ashamed of me and I wasn't ready to face myself." She was correct about my feelings at that point. I am human. More than angry, though, I was disappointed in her. She had a problem with honesty and integrity. But, again, she was there. Standing in front of me. Confessing. That's the only thing that kept me from expressing my disappointment.

After about an hour, I asked if she would like to go to lunch. I needed to get out of the store. She agreed. I told Jackie that I would be back around two o'clock. We went to Main Street Diner and sat in the corner booth. I asked her about my father. "After you left, did you ever hear from my father?" "No I didn't. I wasn't sure whether or not he ever told his family about me and you. His younger sister, Florence was my age but she has never contacted me.

"Do you know anything about my father?" "No. He left town so quickly. For a few years I hoped that he might come back for me and for you. He never did. I assume that he remarried and has children. I never filed for a divorce because the marriage wasn't actually legal. I've come to the conclusion that he never really loved me.

I made a terrible decision, Anne, one that I have regretted all these years. Please understand. I don't regret having you. I regret what I have put everyone through. I came today to ask for your forgiveness. I am truly sorry for what I have done to you. I can't imagine what you've had to endure. I'm sorry."

For a moment our eyes were fixed on each other. No words. Emotions, yes. But no words. Then she lowered her head and stared at the table. I had a decision to make. I wasn't even sure that she was being sincere but that didn't matter. I had to decide whether or not I was going to give her the gift of forgiveness.

That's the way true forgiveness works Sarah, Steven. It isn't based on whether someone asks for it or not. It doesn't

even matter if they have no remorse for what they've done. Forgiveness is a matter of our hearts. I thought about Jesus when He was on the cross. He asked God to forgive those who were killing Him. Forgiveness is not based on whether people deserve it or not. It's a decision for us and a gift for the other.

I decided to give my mother that gift. I placed my hand on hers and said those words. "Mother, I forgive you." At first, she didn't look up. For some reason I sensed that she was feeling unworthy of my forgiveness. I had experienced that a time or two myself. We have not all sinned alike but we all alike have sinned and when forgiveness comes we know that it is undeserved.

But then she looked up at me and through her tears she said, "Thank you. I love you, Anne." What my mother didn't know was that those were the words I had longed to hear. All those years, because of what she had done, I didn't think that she really loved me. If she did, she would not have left me. But I was beginning to realize that, perhaps, she left because she did love me and wanted the best for me.

We talked a bit longer. I asked mother about her family in Memphis. Her husband had died of a heart attack two years earlier. They had two boys. One lived in Memphis and the other in Knoxville. Her husband's parents were deceased. His brother still lived in Memphis and sister lived in Virginia.

When we got back to the store, I was wondering what was next. I asked mother if she was staying for the night. I told her that we could have the family over and everyone could meet her. She said that she wasn't ready to meet you all yet. She wanted to go back home and tell her family first. She said that she would call to let me know when she was coming back. We hugged and then she left. I was thankful that she had come.

I didn't tell you all that I had met her because I wanted to honor her wishes. You can guess now that she didn't call back. I never saw her again. There were so many times when I wanted to go to Memphis and talk with her but I didn't. It was her choice. I have lived with the pain of that for the past two years. All the while, I was hoping to see her again.

About three months ago, I received an envelope in the mail. There was no return address. It was postmarked, Nashville. Inside was the obituary of Emma Hill Kennedy, my mother. You can image what I looked for first, my name. It was there. The obituary showed that she was survived by her two sons and one daughter, Anne Hill Carpenter. I had not told mother that I changed my name to Gray.

Even though she still had problems with her past, in the end, mother was not ashamed to tell the world that I was her daughter. I would have loved to have spent those two years with her as a part of our family but it didn't happen. Perhaps mother even had regrets about that. But that's how life is at times. The endings are not always as happy as we want them to be. But life is still good.

24 *My Field Of Roses*

There are so many other thoughts and feelings that I would like to share with you. But time is short. So let me bring it all together by telling you about the roses.

I have taught you a lot about caring for roses over the years. How to plant them, how to nourish them, and how to protect them. But I have never told you why they are so special to me.

The roses are actually about everything I have shared with you in these pages. Maybe you will want to read the stories again once you understand. If it were not for the truth of the roses, I would have probably given up on life years ago. I pray that they will help you find love, strength and peace to carry on after I am gone.

My grandmother Eliza actually started the tradition of the roses. I don't remember her very well. I was young when she died. I believe that the picture of me with her, my grandfather, and my mother is in the box of photos. The picture was taken in front of their house. You should see the roses on both sides of the porch. I believe that I was only a few days old when the photo was taken.

Aunt Macy told me about Eliza and the roses. When an immediate family member died, grandmother would plant a rose bush in their memory. All the roses you see in that photo are memorial roses. Four of them were for grandmother and grandfather's parents. A couple were for their siblings who had passed on. One was for the child aunt Macy lost.

For years, I didn't know that when grandmother died, aunt Macy moved all those roses to aunt Mabel's house. The average rose plant lives for about thirty-five years. Some of those roses were over forty years old when I was a little girl. Aunt Macy loved the roses and cared for the roses just like grandmother did. That's probably why some of them are still alive today.

When the roses were in bloom, grandmother would cut them, place them in a vase, and put them by the graves of the family members. For her, it was a way to remember her loved ones. Aunt Macy told me that the tradition of the roses was picked up by other families in the area. Soon the cemeteries became places of beauty and peace instead of sorrow and loss. Imagine seeing a cemetery that looked like a field of roses.

After grandmother died, aunt Macy maintained the rose tradition. She continued to plant memorial roses and she placed roses at the cemetery just like grandmother Eliza had done. She did that until the day she moved to the nursing home. Often when we visited, we saw roses in her room and wondered if someone had gotten them from aunt Mabel's house. I asked her one day where the roses were from and she told me that they just showed up from time to time. I found out later that one of the single gentlemen who lived

there liked aunt Macy and brought her roses from the nursing home garden. She just didn't want us to know that she had a boyfriend.

That's how the rose tradition began and that is a part of the meaning of the roses. All the roses in our field were placed there in memory of a loved one who had passed on. Mrs. Wascom's roses are in memory of her husband. The roses that Mrs. Overstreet has are in memory of her mother.

The oldest rose in the field is mine. I don't know if you have ever seen it. It is a beautiful miniature rose with light pink petals. It is near the old oak tree in the far east corner of the field. I planted that rose in memory of a child that your father and I lost about twenty years ago. Please take special care of the little rose by the oak tree.

Just like grandmother Eliza, some of our ladies take their roses to the cemetery where their loved ones are buried. Sometimes they take roses to the nursing home and to shutins. Some make bouquets for special occasions. Others take roses to their churches for Sunday services.

In a very real way, the roses are a symbol of the loved one we remember. They help to keep that person alive in our hearts. They help us remember the good times we shared with that person. They remind us of their love and their care. The roses help us feel close to the one we loved. This may sound a bit strange, but the roses help us look forward to the day when we will see our loved ones again in Heaven.

You have probably noticed that some of our ladies just sit out in the field sometimes by their roses. Maybe you have even heard one or two of them talk to their roses like aunt Macy did. I'll tell you about one of our ladies if you promise not to tell anyone. Promise? Okay. You know Mrs. Doris

Willingham. Well, Mrs. Willingham's rose is in memory of her mother who died six years ago. When she takes her roses to friends in the hospital or to the shutins, she always says, "Mother wants to tell you hi and spend a little time with you." When she says that, it sounds as if she thinks that the roses are her mother. Hopefully, you're laughing right now because Mrs. Willingham is just joking. She's not crazy.

So the roses help us remember our loved ones who have gone on before us. The roses are a way to brighten up the days of those in need. But, for me, the roses mean so much more. God has used them to teach me an incredible truth. The real roses in our lives are the people who love us and help us and bless us through life. They are a gift from God.

In Second Corinthians, the second chapter, there is a beautiful description of Christians that reminds me of roses. The passage says that we are the aroma of Christ in this world. Isn't that beautiful? It is as if the people helping us are Christ Himself. They are His hands and His voice telling us that He is near and that we are safe. He uses them to share His love for us. God loves us. He loves us and He uses people to let us know of His great love.

In this past year, many of the ladies who have helped me through my illness have been the aroma of Christ for me. They have been my roses. Richard has taken me to all my treatments. He is one of my roses. Brother and Mrs. Owens have prayed with me and supported me. They are my roses. They are the aroma of Christ to me. Nurses and doctors have been my roses. Other patients who have shared their journeys have been my roses. God has sent so many people to help me through this valley.

I also believe that in a different way and for a different

purpose, God gave me my mother. I've had some time to consider what she did, why she came to see me, and what she shared with me. God used her to teach me about forgiveness. Mother was also one of my roses.

God gave me aunt Mabel, uncle Robert, and aunt Macy. I was so loved by those precious people. God gave me Ellie, Willie, and Jennie. They are my sisters and they always will be. Then God gave me you. I could not have wished for anything better than the family we have. We have love. We have the Lord and together we have the hope of Heaven. Thank you for giving me such a blessed life. Thank you for loving me. You have brought so much joy to my life.

In the weeks and months ahead, God is going to provide some roses to help you through. Friends, family, and others are going to be there for you. They are going to surround you with support and love. Let them help you. Remember, God has sent them your way.

Hopefully, by now, you have received a rose bush from Legacy Roses in Fremont, California. I had it made especially for the three of you. The name of the rose is Anne's Love. It is not a memorial rose for me. It is an honor rose for you. You are my loves. I pray that the rose will be a constant reminder of how much you are loved.

Just as I wished that things could have been different with my mother, I wish that I could have had more time with you. But the time we had was more than special to me. I enjoyed every day with you all and thanked God every day for the joy He placed in my life through you.

As I write these final words, I want you to know that God has given me an incredible peace about leaving. I know that might sound odd, but He has given me the assurance that

Heaven is real and that we will be with each other again. Hold on to that truth. Live your lives in joy. Jim, enjoy the grandchildren for me. Sarah, enjoy your marriage with Richard. Steven, I know that one day God will give you a wife who loves you. If you have children, tell them that their grandmother loves them from Heaven.

Please feel my love for you every day. More importantly, feel the presence and love of God. Remember that He never sleeps. He is always there to help, to guide, to comfort, and more. He will meet all your needs. He can calm all your fears. He can give you a peace that passes all understanding. Lean on Him. Trust Him. The Lord has been my strength. He can be yours too.

It is time to say goodbye, not forever but for now. I love you Jim. I love you Sarah. I love you Steven. You have been and will always be the most special part of my field of roses."

Steven had come to the end of his mother's journal. For several moments he just kept staring at that last page and those four words, words that his mother had shared with him every day of his life. "I love you Steven." He began to weep. He loved her too. She was his counselor, his anchor, his best friend, and so much more. He had no idea how he was going to live without her in his life.

As he began to reflect on his mother's story, Steven realized that all the questions about his mother had been answered. The mystery about her name had been solved. He learned the truth about her parents. He now knew about her childhood. It was all there and he was so grateful that his mother chose to share it with him.

But Steven now knew that the answers to his questions were not near as important as the life lessons his mother had

shared. He learned that the people in our lives are gifts, roses if you will, from God. They are the instruments God uses to bless us through life. We have to cherish each other and love each other. Life is too short and too precious to let petty disagreements or arguments hurt our relationships.

Steven also learned that we can't let the big things consume us either. His mother had faced great trials all her life. But through it all she overcame by her faith in God and the support she was given by friends and family. Steven knew that his great trial, losing his mother, was going to be a challenge. But he trusted his mother's words that God would see him through.

Steven had also learned a lot about God through his mother. God knows us and loves us. God is always close by and always ready to listen. God answers our prayers in His way and in His time. God doesn't always remove the storms of life but He will always see us through the storms.

Steven also learned a lot about himself and what he needed to do with his life. He learned that God has a plan and purpose for his life. In essence, that plan is to love God and love people, to be a servant like Jesus.

After Anne's death, Sarah and Richard reopened the grocery store. Sarah was just like her mother. She loved people. She loved talking with customers and helping those in need. Jim sold all of his real estate holdings, retired, and helped everyone with their roses. Every morning he went out to the field and sat down on a bench he had put next to Anne's rose. When the roses were in bloom he always had a few of them at the house. Their sweet aroma reminded him of the love of his life.

Steven graduated from high school and went on to

college. He became a minister and pastored churches for several years. He finally answered the call to lead a ministry for abused and abandoned children. Today, if you visit the campus of that ministry you will see beautiful, beautiful roses everywhere.

Anne was a remarkable person. In her lifetime she faced great challenges that could have broken her spirit and left her with a heart of sadness and defeat. But Anne was blessed by God with family and friends who loved her and cared for her. She, in turn, loved and cared for others. May we all follow in her footsteps and become a field of roses, the aroma of Christ for those in need.

CPSIA information can be obtained
at www.ICGtesting.com
Printed in the USA
FSHW010613191219
65261FS